# Readers love the Unfinished Business series by KEELAN ELLIS

## *I'll Still Be There*

"…a quick read, one I liked for its heartfelt message of taking risks and going for broke in the name of love."

—The Novel Approach

"…it contains two beautifully bittersweet romances, a touching ghost story, and two absolutely fascinating comparative socio-biographic pictures. Not to mention lovely characters and some unexpected yet all the more delicious sparks of humor."

—Prism Book Alliance

"If you read only one romance novel this summer, you'd be hard pressed to do better than *I'll Still Be There*."

—*Divine Magazine*

## *Anywhere You Go*

"It was a great read that I thoroughly enjoyed."

—MM Good Book Reviews

"I really enjoyed this unusual story… It was sensual, loving, kinky, and very hot."

—Rainbow Book Reviews

By KEELAN ELLIS

Misinformation

UNFINISHED BUSINESS
I'll Still Be There
Anywhere You Go

Published by DREAMSPINNER PRESS
www.dreamspinnerpress.com

# MISINFORMATION

## KEELAN ELLIS

Published by
DREAMSPINNER PRESS

5032 Capital Circle SW, Suite 2, PMB# 279, Tallahassee, FL 32305-7886 USA
www.dreamspinnerpress.com

Misinformation
© 2016 Keelan Ellis.

Cover Art
© 2016 Aaron Anderson.
aaronbydesign55@gmail.com
Cover content is for illustrative purposes only and any person depicted on the cover is a model.

ISBN: 978-1-63477-339-3
Digital ISBN: 978-1-63477-340-9
Library of Congress Control Number: 2016902329
Published June 2016
v. 1.1

Printed in the United States of America
∞
This paper meets the requirements of
ANSI/NISO Z39.48-1992 (Permanence of Paper).

# Chapter One

"COME ON, kid, time to get up." Ethan Daniels was back in his daughter's bedroom for the third time that morning. Each time the six-year-old would sit up and promise she'd get dressed, only to fall back to sleep the second he'd left the room. "Fiona, I'm not leaving until you're out of bed this time. It's the first day of school. Aren't you excited?"

"Uh-huh," Fiona mumbled. She didn't move, and all Ethan could see were a few wiry curls of copper hair peeking out from under the covers. He sat down on the edge of her bed and pulled the comforter down so he could see her face.

"What's up, Bitsy?" he asked, using the pet name she'd had almost since birth. "You nervous about the new school?"

"No," she replied.

"Then what is it?"

"Nothing," she said, finally sitting up and swinging her legs out of bed. "You'll say it's dumb."

"Come on," Ethan said. "Nothing's dumb. Is it because I'm taking you and not your mom? She'll be picking you up this afternoon and taking you home with her."

Fiona shook her head. "That's not why." She heaved a dramatic sigh. "I have a boy teacher this year."

"A boy teacher?" Ethan asked. "Is that like a boy wizard?"

"Daddy," Fiona said, clearly not amused.

"Sorry. What's wrong with a boy teacher?"

"It's weird," she replied, as if that much should have been obvious. "My old school didn't have any boy teachers."

"But now you're in big-kid school," Ethan said. "It's not weird to have boy teachers at big-kid school. Come on now. You have to get up or you'll be late, and then your boy teacher will be mad at me."

"Okay, Daddy." Fiona sighed again as if she were doing him a big favor and got up.

Although the school was close enough they could walk, they piled into a sedan that waited for them outside the building. Ethan would need to go straight from dropping Fiona off at her midtown elementary school to the ECHO News building in downtown Manhattan. For the past three years, he'd been hosting the seven o'clock show on the famously conservative cable news network. He was making more money than he ever had in his life. This allowed him to stay in the city where his ex-wife and little girl lived, which was the most important factor in all of his decisions. There were times when the positions pushed by the network made him uncomfortable— even angry—but he thought of his daughter whenever his conscience started nagging him too much. And anyway, he always reminded himself, it was basically a straight news show. That way, he was allowed to remain neutral and even sometimes play devil's advocate to the often rabid and sometimes frankly deranged so-called experts the network required him to interview.

Fiona balked at getting out of the car but reluctantly took Ethan's hand and allowed him to lead her through the front doors of the school. When they'd located her classroom, he stood outside the doorway with her and knelt down to her level. "You're going to have a great time at this school," he said. "Will you call me tonight and let me know how it went? You can tell me all about your boy teacher, okay?"

"Yes, Daddy," she said. She looked nervous. "Will you walk in with me?"

"Sure." Ethan hugged her and stood up. "I should say hello to your teacher anyway, since I wasn't able to make it to the orientation." He'd promised to go but had begged off for a work emergency at the last minute. His ex, Deirdre, was still pissed at him and claimed it showed his lack of investment in their child's life. That was easy for her to say, in Ethan's opinion—as a successful author, she didn't have work emergencies or bosses or producers constantly needing things from her.

The door was open, and there were several children at the back of the room near the coatrack and cubbies. Fiona perked up suddenly. "I see Lysette!" she squealed and ran off to find her friend without a glance back at Ethan.

At the front of the room stood a tall, lanky, bearded man of about thirty, holding an iPad. He was dressed in slim pants, a V-neck sweater, and ankle boots Ethan could tell from halfway across the room must have cost at least a week of a teacher's salary. *Gay*, Ethan thought. Also, before he could stop himself, his mind whispered, *cute*. He shook it off immediately. Since the divorce, he'd been thinking about men much more than he ever did before or during his marriage. He had no idea what that was about. It wasn't anything new—he'd always found himself attracted to certain men—but he'd never given it much thought. These days he was noticing men all the time. He'd be walking down the street and suddenly realize he'd been checking out every guy who passed by for the past five blocks. Whatever weird phase this was, Ethan's plan was to ignore it until it was over. He could have his idle fantasies, but acting on them was out of the question. The rumors had finally died down after that stupid story back in the spring, and the last thing he needed was to add more fuel to them.

The teacher watched the kids with a look of amused affection as they hung up their things and found their seats. Each chair had a nametag on it. As each kid sat down, the teacher poked at his iPad. Ethan cleared his throat, and the man looked up with an expectant smile. He had very warm-looking brown eyes behind a pair of tortoiseshell frames.

"Oh, Mr. Daniels!" he said, walking over with his hand extended. Ethan shook it. "I'm Fiona's teacher, Charles Woods." Now that he was standing closer, Ethan could see the beginning of a tattoo poking out beyond the edge of the man's V-neck. He couldn't tell what it was.

"Hi," Ethan said, pulling his eyes away from the guy's collarbone. "I just wanted to stop in and say a quick hello since I wasn't able to make it to orientation. My ex-wife filled everything out, and I hope she put my number on the forms too, but, uh...." He fished in his pocket for a business card. "Here. Could you put this with her file? In case you need to call me." *Oh God*, Ethan thought, *did that sound like I was flirting? On a television show, that would be flirting.* "We share custody of Fiona," he explained.

"Of course. Thank you. Will you be able to make it to Back to School Night? It's two weeks from now. We'll be able to show you some of the stuff the class is working on, and there will be sign-ups for conferences."

"I'll definitely see you then," Ethan said. *Goddamn it. Stop doing that.* "Nice to meet you, Mr. Woods."

"Oh, call me Charlie," he said. "Nice to meet you too."

Ethan looked around for Fiona and saw her already at her desk, chatting busily with the girl next to her. He hurried out of the classroom, telling himself he needed to get to work as early as possible. There was a lot of news to cover.

Once at work, Ethan sat on the sofa in his office, looking over what they were supposed to cover that evening. Most of them seemed to be the same recycled stories they'd been covering for weeks—in some cases, even months. There were the nonscandal scandals—these were stories most people who were not viewers of this network might not even be aware of. People who were viewers, however, thought they were the most important things in the news today. Then there were the nonstory stories. These were dug up from wherever his producers could find them, and the only thing that mattered about them was that they reinforced the narrative the network was pushing. Ethan found it disgusting, but he was a pragmatic person. As long as they kept paying him the same obscene salary, he could mouth the words they wanted him to say, and they could put his face out there to make them seem likeable. His priorities were elsewhere.

Deirdre had been so horrified when he'd taken this job she hadn't spoken to him for two weeks. She had sent him texts when she needed to communicate about their daughter. At pickups and drop-offs, she had constrained herself to hello and good-bye. It wasn't like they'd ever had a close friendship or anything. Their divorce a year earlier had been a mutual and mostly civil decision, but there had been several years of resentment and anger leading up to it. The baggage from those years still remained. Nevertheless, up until Ethan took the news job with ECHO, they'd gotten along pretty well. The silent treatment was an uncomfortable reminder of the last years of their marriage, and it hadn't taken long before he'd blown up at her about it.

She was the one who'd decided to move to New York. He'd been perfectly happy at his previous job with the evening news in Philadelphia, and it had been simple to make the hour drive west of the city where Deirdre was living to pick up Fiona. He was already being courted by ECHO News at that point, but was planning to decline their offer. When the rights to one of her early books was purchased for a major film adaptation and she'd called him and said she was finally going to realize her dream of living in Manhattan, Ethan made his decision. He didn't want to be so far away from Fiona, and he certainly didn't want to get into some long, drawn-out battle with Deirdre about where she was allowed to live.

It wasn't like he'd ever been a particularly politically minded person. He thought of himself as reasonable and generally resisted getting drawn into conversations about those topics. He was a journalist and believed in being impartial. Being at ECHO had made him uncomfortable for that reason more than any disagreements—and there were many—with the positions espoused by ECHO. Regardless of ideology, he felt news organizations should avoid trying to push the country in one political direction over the other.

He sighed and closed his laptop. There was no point in dredging all that up again. Deirdre had resumed verbal communication with him after they had a big fight over it. She understood he was doing it for Fiona. Ethan thought she probably respected that, although it didn't stop her from needling him about it every chance she got. He wondered if the next person he dated would have to be a conservative, since anyone to the left of Dick Cheney was bound to have some pretty serious issues with how he made his living. For some reason the image of Fiona's teacher—*Charlie*—floated to the front of his mind. He most definitely was not in the ECHO News demographic. Not that he was going to be the next person Ethan would be dating. He needed to find a girlfriend. If he didn't do it soon, the rumors would start churning up again. He'd only signed on for a one-year deal with ECHO and the year was almost up. Contract negotiations would go a hell of a lot better if there weren't whispers about his sexuality.

There was a knock at the door, and his assistant, Abigail, walked in. At twenty-three, she was exceptionally competent and energetic.

Ethan assumed she must be ambitious, but she'd never spoken to him about her goals. Then again, he'd never thought to ask. If he were to be honest, he didn't care. All he wanted to know was if she could keep his appointments straight, remember his coffee order, and run interference for him with his boss, when necessary.

"Hi, Ethan," she said, looking down at her tablet. "At eleven you have a meeting with the producers. Kevin, in particular, has a series of segments he wants to pitch to you. It's about Christian business owners and their struggles with being forced to serve Muslims and sexual minorities." She was looking at him with a completely neutral and professionally detached expression. Ethan wasn't fooled. He could see how badly she wanted to roll her eyes.

Ethan rolled his in sympathy and said, "That's not news. What else do I have today?"

"Um...."

"What, Abby?" he asked.

"Mr. Martin asked me to set up a meeting with you for this afternoon." Vincent Martin was the president of ECHO News, but he wasn't some distant figure in a top-floor office. He took a hands-on approach to his job and was a frequent visitor to the offices of all his on-air personalities. Ethan hated him.

"So? Did you set it up?" Ethan asked.

"Yeah...." She averted her eyes and pressed her lips together.

"What? For Christ's sake, just spit it out."

"He...." She sighed and pinched the bridge of her nose for a second before continuing. "He gave me a couple of inappropriate compliments. Borderline actionable, frankly, not that I'd screw my career over it. Then he asked me if you and I... if I felt like there was any chemistry between us. At first I was just weirded out, and I didn't know why the hell he'd be asking me about stuff like that, but then...."

"Then you figured it out," Ethan said grimly. "He thinks I need a beard."

"Ethan, I'm sorry. He's such an asshole. I told him I have a lot of respect for you and you'd never behave in an unprofessional way."

6

"It's only been a year since my divorce," Ethan said, realizing at the same time how weak that sounded. A year was a pretty long time. He should have at least gone out and tried to get laid by then.

"Sure," Abigail said, smiling at him with too much sympathy. "Well anyway, I decided I'd leave it up to you. I mean, if you want to have dinner out with me once in a while, or take me to a function, it would be okay with me. Not that I think you need a fake girlfriend. I'm sure you can get a real girlfriend if you want to. Or if you *don't* want a girlfriend, that's obviously fine too. You know that, right?"

"Abigail," Ethan said wearily, "what time am I supposed to go up there?"

"In twenty minutes," she said apologetically. "I didn't want to give you too much time to stew about it."

"Right." He put his feet onto the sofa and reclined, closing his eyes. "You can go now, Abby," he said.

She left without another word, closing the door very softly behind her. Ethan pressed the heels of his hands to his forehead in an attempt to ward off the ache he felt building behind his eyes. That fucking article was going to haunt him forever. He had been completely blindsided by it. Goddamn Becca Jacobs and her big mouth. Becca was a blogger now, and a well-known one in the world of leftist journalism. Their paths rarely crossed, but they'd ended up at the same party about two weeks before the stupid article—no more than a two-paragraph blurb on Page Six—ran. It wasn't too hard to do the math, but what he didn't understand was why she'd done it. He knew she had a hate-on for ECHO News, but he hadn't done anything to her personally. He'd said hello to her and made small talk for a couple of minutes that night, but that was it. The story was complete bullshit. According to the so-called source, it had been a threesome, and Ethan was the only one named, but he wasn't sure the real story would be any better for his reputation.

It was during his sophomore year, and he'd been seeing Becca for a little over a month. He could already tell it wasn't going to get serious, but he liked her well enough. She was great in bed and smart enough to carry on a conversation with, so he was in no hurry to move on. Another good thing was she liked to smoke weed, but that had never been a particular weakness of Ethan's. He was a drinker, and was aware of his own tendency to overdo it when he was around people who did the same. Now that he was hanging out with Becca, he was drinking less. Since he wasn't crazy about the way he felt when he smoked, he rarely indulged. His grades had already improved.

One night he'd gone to her dorm room to find her hanging out with a guy who lived on her floor. His name was Jared, and Ethan had seen him before around the campus. It was hard not to notice a guy like that. He was about six feet tall, with long, shiny dark hair and blue eyes. He always wore some kind of tie-dyed shirt, so Ethan had assumed he must be a Deadhead or some kind of hippie.

"Jared brought us some treats," she said, rubbing Ethan's arm.

"I don't really feel like smoking up tonight," Ethan said.

"Me neither." She pulled out a small baggie with some tiny pills in it. "It's Ecstasy," she said, grinning wildly. "Have you ever done it?"

Ethan hadn't, but he'd heard about it. He knew it was supposed to make you feel like you loved everyone around you, make you want to touch other people. He glanced over at Jared, his long legs stretched out across Becca's bed. Ethan would never be able to think about touching him under normal circumstances. He had long had the habit of directing his mind away from those kinds of thoughts. *If you're fucked up, you'll have an excuse*, his mind prodded.

They swallowed the pills and left the building, walking around the dark campus. After a while Ethan began to wonder if the drugs had been fake. He wasn't feeling anything. They found a dark spot behind the dorm that was hidden from most people who might be walking by. They stretched out on the grass. It was late May and had been warm all day but was now starting to cool down. The grass was damp, and Ethan could feel each individual blade pressing against the palm of his hand.

"The stars look like they're magic," Jared said softly. Objectively Ethan knew that was an inane thing to say. On the other hand, when he looked up at the stars, they did seem impossibly beautiful to him.

"Yeah," Ethan said. "I know what you mean."

Becca, lying between them, began to giggle. "You guys are so fucked up," she said. Ethan and Jared both laughed. Becca rolled over and kissed Ethan, running her hands up and down his body. When she finished she said, "Is it okay if I kiss Jared too?"

Ethan touched her face. "You can do whatever you want to do," he said, and to his amazement, he meant it. He didn't care what she did. And he couldn't blame her for wanting to kiss Jared.

She rolled over and kissed Jared, but pulled back after a second and frowned in confusion. "Don't you want to kiss me?" she asked.

"Sure," he said, "in a minute." He crawled over her and onto Ethan, straddling his waist and bracing himself on his hands. Ethan stared up at him, unable to move or speak. "First I want to try something," Jared said and leaned down to kiss him. His soft hair brushed against Ethan's face. He smelled like patchouli and pot, but his mouth was minty, as if he'd recently brushed his teeth. Ethan was turned on—at least, he was pretty sure that's what he was experiencing—but all he wanted was to feel Jared's skin. He pushed his hands up under the ratty T-shirt and ran his fingertips over the boy's smooth stomach.

"Wow," Becca whispered. Ethan and Jared both looked over at her. She was staring at them with wide eyes and her mouth hanging open.

Jared laughed and reached a hand out to her. The three of them rolled around in the wet grass, taking turns with each other. Ethan couldn't get enough contact, enough skin against his. He felt frustrated and yet completely satisfied at the same time. They shed some of their clothing, but not all because they were outside. At one point one of them mentioned going back upstairs, but they never did anything about it.

Ethan didn't remember how the night ended, but he knew he'd woken up in his own bed the next morning. He and Becca saw each other a few more times, but neither of them ever spoke about anything from that night. He never talked to Jared again either, and when they passed each other on the campus, they always looked away. Thinking back, Ethan felt sort of bad for both of them. They'd obviously made much more of it in their minds than it had actually been. They'd been fucked up, after all. One person he didn't feel a bit of sympathy for was Becca because this was all her fault. Not the actual night in question— Ethan took responsibility for his own decisions. The lies that had spread all over the Internet—that was all her.

Abigail knocked again, startling him out of the memory. She poked her head in and said, "You should go up now. You know how he is about lateness."

"Yeah," Ethan sighed. "Thanks." He sat up and took a deep breath. He needed to play this off as casually as possible. He knew the last thing Martin wanted was to have to ask him about anything directly. This was good, because the last thing Ethan wanted was to have to give a direct answer. He didn't want to be forced into a situation where he had to tell an outright lie. He had a sense of how terrible that would feel, but he also knew that if cornered, he would do exactly that.

When he got to Martin's suite of offices, the secretary told him to have a seat. Vince Martin might have hated lateness, but he certainly didn't mind making others wait. It was such a transparent power move that it would have been funny if it weren't so effective. By the time he was ushered into Martin's inner office, Ethan was both more nervous and angrier than he'd been when he arrived.

Martin was sitting behind his giant desk and waited for Ethan to close the door before standing. He was in his late fifties, fit and overly tan. Whenever he looked at Martin, Ethan half expected a golf caddy to be lurking ten steps away. Martin walked out from behind the desk and held out a hand to Ethan.

"Ethan!" he boomed. "Thanks for coming in."

"No problem, Vince. Good to see you," Ethan lied.

Martin gestured to a leather armchair near the desk and sat down in the one next to it. He crossed his legs and leaned back casually as if this were a friendly visit. "So how have you been, son?"

"I've been fine. My daughter started school today. First grade. Very exciting," Ethan said with a self-deprecating chuckle.

"Your ex has certainly been making the rounds, eh?"

"Her book is doing very well," Ethan replied, nodding. Deirdre's latest novel had been referred to by one critic as "the thinking woman's *Bridget Jones*," and she was currently in talks with a major studio about doing an adaptation. She was hoping for Jennifer Lawrence to play the lead role, which Ethan found amusing because he knew she'd based the book on her own experiences in her twenties.

"I watched a few minutes of her appearance on ECHO and Company this morning, as a matter of fact. She mentioned she'd started seeing someone. Met him yet?"

That brought Ethan up short. Deirdre hadn't mentioned anything to him about a boyfriend. He hoped she wasn't bringing him around Fiona yet. "Uh, no. Nope. Must be pretty new," he said.

"Well, it's been what, a year since your divorce? Makes sense. How about you? Seeing anyone?"

"Vince, was there something in particular you wanted to talk to me about? I've got a lot of work to do and not much time to gossip about my ex-wife's love life. Or mine."

Martin leaned forward with a grin on his face that didn't quite reach his eyes. "Listen, son. Those rumors last year—that was nothing. It was obviously bullshit. I had your back then and I have it now. But you need to start moving on. People look at you and they see a good-looking, successful guy, and some might start wondering why you can't find yourself a woman. Hell, I wonder myself sometimes."

Ethan opened his mouth to start talking about how his divorce had been difficult, about how he'd been focused on a new job and new city, all the while trying to keep his shit together for his daughter—all true. But then something in his head clicked, and all he felt was anger. He was pissed at Martin, sure, but also at himself. He wasn't about to defend himself to this asshole. "Vince, I don't give a shit what people wonder," he said. "My private life is my own business. I'll date when I'm ready to date. I'm not discussing this with you any further."

"Wanting to keep your personal life private is totally understandable. You know what else it is? It's what people say who have something to hide."

"Whatever you say," Ethan shot back. He stood to leave. "Oh, and please leave my assistant alone. I like her. She's good at her job and doesn't get on my nerves. Do you know how rare that is? I don't want to lose her when she brings a sexual harassment suit against this network."

Martin laughed as if they'd been engaging in some friendly banter and clapped Ethan on the shoulder. "Your contract is up for renewal in a couple of months," he said. "So don't forget who your audience is, Ethan."

Ethan shook his head and walked out of the office.

That evening he made three mistakes while reading from the prompter. His mind was all over the place, and he was having a very hard time concentrating. He'd been interviewing the network's pet psychologist during a segment about the negative effects of receiving government assistance, and at one point found himself staring at the woman, unable to form a coherent response to what she was saying. He had the task, at times, of framing statements made by his guests in order to make them sound reasonable, even obvious. It wasn't always easy because sometimes they said some crazy shit, but he was good at it. He didn't like it, precisely, and it always made him feel a little bit dirty. But it was a skill like any other, and he took pride in his mastery of it. That night, though, he paused a bit too long, and he was pretty sure he had a stunned expression on his face. He'd even stammered a bit when he finally found a way to respond to a statement that, frankly, sounded like something from Nazi Germany. It would no doubt be up on YouTube in the next hour with a title like "Even Ethan Daniels Can't Believe What This Crazy Bitch is Saying." He left as soon as possible after it was over, brushing off Abigail's concerned questions. There was a bar two blocks from his building, and he told his driver to drop him off there. He needed a drink.

# Chapter Two

CHARLIE TOOK his time cleaning after his students had left for the day. He'd always enjoyed the slightly spooky feeling of an empty classroom and the way his footsteps echoed in the abandoned halls as he walked out of school. There were still a few people around—other teachers and some administrative staff—but mostly he had the building to himself. By the time he left, the main lights had already been shut off on his floor, and he entertained himself by imagining he was the last person in Manhattan left untouched by the zombie epidemic. Each time he turned a corner, he mentally prepared himself to ward off the undead. When he reached the dimly lit stairwell at the end of the hall, he'd psyched himself into almost being afraid to use it, so when his phone rang the second he took the first step, he almost tumbled headfirst to the next floor.

Grasping the rail, he checked the screen and found that his friend Josh, a teacher who had started at Fuller Academy the same year he had, was calling. "Jesus Christ," Charlie said, "I just literally died of fright."

"I know I'm only an art teacher, but I'm pretty sure you're not using that word correctly," Josh shouted. Charlie could hear a lot of noise in the background, and his friend was speaking very loudly. "I'm drinking," he said. "At McShea's."

"That stupid fake Irish pub? Why on earth?"

"Because it's close, and they have good cheap apps at happy hour. You should come meet us!"

"Who is us?" Charlie asked warily.

"Me and Janice," Josh replied. "Please come. You know I love her, but she's crushing my spirit right now. I need reinforcements."

"I guess," Charlie said. "But you owe me a blow job."

"Don't tease. You know if I really thought you were into it, I'd be all over that."

Charlie ignored that comment and said, "I'll be there in ten minutes." He hated when Josh said stuff like that. Josh had sort of hit on him the first time they hung out, but when Charlie turned him down, he'd shrugged and said, "I had to try." That was five years ago, and they'd been friends ever since, but he still made those comments from time to time. There was nothing wrong with him. He was a big, sweet, friendly guy, scruffy and good-looking in a way that made Charlie think of fishing boats and wool sweaters. He was undoubtedly someone's ideal—just not Charlie's.

The bar was crowded but not as bad as he'd feared based on the noise on the phone. Josh and Janice were sitting at a table near the window and had a cocktail waiting for him when he arrived. He slid onto the bench next to Janice and gave her a side hug. "How was your first day back?" he asked, winking at Josh, who was glaring at him.

"Well, let's see. There's the kid on the spectrum who can't muster the impulse control to stop speaking his thoughts out loud whenever he disagrees with me. Which is often. One time he was even right, and it probably won't be the last. There's the kid who forgot his lunch and his school supplies, which isn't a big deal on the first day, but it doesn't bode well. There's the kid who can barely read. There's the kid who's reading on a high-school level—what the hell am I supposed to do with her? But all of that is okay. I'm a professional, and it's my job to deal with those issues. What gets me is it took me all of twenty minutes to identify the clique of bitches who are definitely going to make life hell for some poor little girl. In *second grade* this bullshit is already in full swing. Oh, and one little asshole told me my outfit was 'basic.' Whatever the fuck that means."

"Oh, what does she know? You look cute."

"She? Oh no, this was one of the boys. So I can only assume he knows what he's talking about." She took a deep breath and let it out. "Fuck it. All I can do is teach the entitled little shits. I can't make them decent."

"You see?" Josh asked, gesturing at Janice. "She makes me want to go back to school and become an investment banker. Whatever that means."

"Then you'd still be dealing with the same people, but grown up," Charlie said. "You'll muddle through. I mean, think about it—Janice complains a lot, but she has been doing this for almost twenty years. How terrible could it have been?"

Janice patted Josh's hand. "It starts to wear pretty thin around year fourteen, in my experience. So you've got a little time to formulate an escape plan."

"My escape plan is to meet and marry a wealthy man so I can spend my days painting and drinking."

"This is probably not the place to find your sugar daddy," Charlie said. He finished off his drink and looked around. "Do we have a server?"

"Ever the optimist," Janice said. "You can buy the next round while you're up there."

Charlie walked toward the bar, pushing past midlevel managers and administrative assistants who were starting to get loud. One more drink and then he was out of there. He ordered a double scotch for Josh and a dirty martini for Janice, which almost made him gag. He thought about telling her it was basic so she'd stop drinking them. For himself he got some kind of complicated but delicious sounding whiskey and ginger cocktail from their list of specials. He looked around the room while he waited and noticed a guy sitting way down at the end of the bar. The guy sat by himself, drinking something brown with ice in it. He wore a shirt opened at the collar with a tie hanging loose around his neck. He looked pretty cute, at least in profile, but weirdly familiar. Charlie stared at him, trying to figure out if he knew him, until the man looked over. As soon as he did, Charlie realized why he looked so familiar. It was Ethan Daniels, that news anchor guy whose daughter was in his class. Charlie gave him a lame wave and a smile. He couldn't tell if Daniels recognized him because all he got was a squint and then a nod before the guy turned back to his drink.

Charlie collected the drinks the bartender had set in front of him and made a beeline back to the table.

"Ethan Daniels is here," he said.

"Where?" Josh asked, craning around to get a better view of the bar. "Oh yeah! Damn, he's even hotter in person."

"Well of course he is," Janice said, "because when you see him on TV, he's busy being a mouthpiece for right-wing bigots."

"Oh, he's not that bad," Josh replied, still staring at him. "He seems almost reasonable compared to everyone else on that channel."

"That's worse. That way he gives them cover."

"I met him this morning," Charlie said. "His daughter is in my class."

Janice raised her eyebrows. "Really? He actually walked her in himself? What was he like in person?"

"Actually, it was weird. He almost seemed like he was flirting with me."

"You've heard the rumors, right?" Josh asked.

"What, the story about a threesome in college or something like that? So what? Straight guys have threesomes. They like… take turns or something. Or I don't know exactly how that works, but it's a thing."

"That's not the way the story made it sound," Josh said.

Charlie shrugged. "It was college. And anyway, it's probably wishful thinking. If he was ugly, no one would give a shit." But he had been flirting, Charlie was pretty sure—very awkwardly, but still. He glanced over at the bar again. Daniels was holding up an empty glass to the bartender and gesturing for another.

"Maybe you should go hit on him and see what happens," Josh said.

Janice swatted Josh on the forearm. "Gross! Don't even joke about it. The last thing Charlie needs is to get involved with some right-wing closet case. Jesus, Josh."

"Who said anything about getting involved?" Josh asked. "And no hitting," he added, smacking her lightly on the shoulder.

"He needs to stop screwing people he knows he doesn't want anything to do with," Janice said, looking straight at Charlie now. "When was the last time you saw someone more than three times?"

"Okay, Mom," Charlie said. "You can set me up with that nice doctor."

Janice ignored his comment and said, "That guy Devon was hot and seemed really sweet. What was your problem with him?"

"Too young."

"You're only twenty-nine. How young is too young for you?"

"When I told him I taught first grade he said, 'Oh man. I remember my first grade teacher crying on the morning of 9/11.'"

Janice snorted. "Okay, fine. But come on. It's like you're not even trying."

"Because I'm not," Charlie said. "I don't need a boyfriend. I'm fine with things the way they are. I don't want to give up my freedom so I have someone to go antiquing with on the weekends or whatever it is old queens do with their free time. That's not for me."

"Internalized homophobia, huh? Maybe you *should* go blow that guy at the bar, then."

Josh burst out laughing. "Ooh, burn!" he said. "Seriously, though, Jan, let him be. Someday his prince will come. You can't rush these things."

"It doesn't work that way," she said, shaking her head. "But I can't stay here and explain relationships to you children any longer. I need to get home."

"Me too," Josh said. "Want to split an Uber?" Josh and Janice lived in the same Queens neighborhood. Charlie had been considering moving out there too in the last year or so. His Lower East Side apartment was expensive and small compared to his friends' places. As a teenager in New Jersey, Charlie had romanticized living in The City, but the older he got the more it seemed like a pointless struggle.

"I can't waste money on that," Janice said. "I have a kid in college. Let's go get the train."

"Fine," Josh said, sighing dramatically. "Can you get home on your own, dear?" he asked Charlie.

"I can manage, thanks. I think I'll have another drink before I go."

Josh frowned at him. "You know I was joking about hitting on that guy, right?"

Charlie laughed at him. "Don't be ridiculous," he said. "See you tomorrow."

Josh kissed him on the cheek, and they left. Charlie looked down at the ice in the bottom of his glass and then over at the bar. Ethan Daniels was nowhere to be found. Charlie felt unaccountably disappointed. He hadn't really been considering saying anything to him anyway, but part of him had hoped Daniels would strike up a conversation. The whole thing was stupid anyway because what if they did chat for a minute or two? What was he hoping would happen then?

Charlie felt wired and not at all ready to go home or to be alone. As he got up to leave, he took out his phone and opened Grindr. This was probably not what Janice had in mind, but he didn't understand why she was pressuring him to find someone to settle down with anyway. She'd gotten married in her twenties, and now she was divorced with a kid in college. Her last boyfriend had been an alcoholic pharmaceutical rep who lived in Hoboken and couldn't stop talking about the band he'd played with back in the nineties. Why would anyone want to rush toward an outcome like that?

It didn't take him long to find a guy who looked hot enough, was online and on the closest subway line. He sent a message that read *Hey, you're cute. What are you into?* He left the bar and leaned up against the building while he waited for a response. It came in pretty quickly: *Guys my own age? Sorry.* Lovely. He sighed, and as he started to look through the other possibilities, a message from a beefy older guy came in. *You looking to get pounded by a giant cock?* Charlie snorted. He didn't know why he ever bothered to try to be tactful. *Not really*, he responded. Definitely not his type and besides, he never fucked on a first hookup.

Cigarette smoke drifted in front of his face. He waved it away and looked up to find Ethan Daniels standing right next to him. He must have been there the whole time. Charlie smiled at him and Daniels flicked the butt into the gutter.

"Sorry," he said. "I don't even smoke anymore, really. It's only when I've had too much to drink. I bummed that one."

"Oh," Charlie said, "no problem. Bad day?"

"You could say that. I don't really want to talk about it, though. How about you? Looking for company, huh?" At Charlie's stare, Daniels laughed and said, "On your phone. Sorry. I wasn't trying to be nosy; I just happened to see."

Charlie felt his face turn red, but at least the sun had begun to go down, and it might not be too obvious. "Just looking, really," he said. "Anyway, nice to see you, Mr. Daniels. I should get home." He lifted a hand in farewell and quickly turned to walk to the subway station.

"Hey, wait," Daniels said, striding over to catch Charlie's elbow. "I'm sorry. I told you I was drunk. Totally inappropriate." He slurred at the end of the last word. "Are you drunk too by any chance?"

"I only had one," Charlie said.

"Let me buy you another to make up for being such an asshole."

Charlie shook his head. "If you buy me another one, then you'll have another one, and that seems like a really bad idea. I think you should go home."

Daniels nodded slowly and leaned in close to Charlie. "I think I should too. And I think you should come with me. You can have a drink there."

"I'm not sure that's a great idea," Charlie said. Now that this was happening, he was starting to feel weird about it.

"I think it's the best idea I've had all day," Daniels said. He reached out and tugged lightly on the end of Charlie's scarf. "My building is only six blocks away from here. We can walk."

"Mr. Daniels...."

"It's Ethan. My name is Ethan. Okay?"

Charlie met his eyes and held them for a few seconds before saying, "Yeah, okay. Ethan. Let's walk."

Ethan grinned and stuck his hands in his pockets. He really was hotter in person, but a little unusual-looking for a television news guy. His eyes were slightly wide set and a very warm brown. He had a square jaw and a lean face. He was almost conventionally handsome, but there was an almost wolfish quality to his toothy smile. It was hard to tell how old he was. "Just so you know, I would have worked a little harder for it if you'd made me." He started walking and Charlie fell in step beside him.

"I wasn't trying to make you work for it," Charlie said. "I really don't think it's a good idea."

"Why are you doing it, then?"

Charlie looked at him in amusement. "Fishing for compliments?"

Ethan shook his head and laughed softly. "I'm being a child. Don't mind me."

They walked for another block in silence, but it didn't feel uncomfortable. The evening had turned cool but not cold.

"So...." Charlie cast around for something to talk about. There were so many things that seemed off-limits. It seemed weird to talk about the way they'd met—invoking the man's child seemed like a surefire way to spook him. What Charlie really wanted to know about were those rumors, but it somehow seemed like too personal a question, despite the fact they were apparently about to have sex. Ethan had already said he didn't want to talk about his day. "How long have you lived around here?" Charlie finally asked.

"About a year," Ethan said. "Moved up from Philly when I got the job with ECHO." He stopped suddenly and took Charlie's arm. "I'm not in the mood for small talk, okay? I'm just... I'm tired."

"Oh." Charlie frowned, not sure how to take that. "I get it. Maybe I should head home."

"No," Ethan said, shaking his head. "That's not what I meant. I—" He glanced around and then pulled Charlie into a small alley between two buildings. He pushed him up against a stone wall—not roughly, but insistently—and kissed him. Somehow the combination of scotch and that cigarette was a turn-on, even though it was also disgusting. Ethan grasped his hip as he pressed himself into him, and Charlie felt his cock, hard beneath his pants. Charlie ran his hands under Ethan's jacket and over the smooth fabric of an obviously expensive shirt. When the kiss broke, they were both breathing harder. Ethan pulled away, blinking as if he was coming back from a daze. "I'm sorry. That was presumptuous, wasn't it?"

Charlie took hold of his tie and pulled gently so he was close enough to be kissed. "Not so much," he said softly, leaning forward until their lips met again. "But we should probably get inside, huh?"

Ethan nodded, and they took off walking, much faster now. They didn't speak again until Ethan said, "I'm over there," gesturing across the street at a beautiful old apartment building with a doorman standing outside.

"Hey," Charlie said. "Are you sure about this?" he asked. He hadn't really wanted to ask, but he'd felt like he should.

"What do you mean?" Ethan said. He pushed the button for the crosswalk.

"Um... the doorman? Aren't you worried about people seeing us?"

Ethan waved the question away and began to cross the street, even though the lights hadn't changed yet. A car horn blared as Charlie grabbed him and pulled him back to the sidewalk. Ethan didn't seem to be worried about anything at all.

"How much did you drink, anyway?" Charlie asked.

"I'm fine," Ethan replied. "I wasn't paying attention." He looked at Charlie and smiled. "I'm a little distracted."

They crossed safely after another thirty seconds. Ethan greeted the doorman by his name—Roland—with an expansive drunken grace. Roland, who was tall, black, and incredibly attractive, gave him a big smile and said, "Good evening, Mr. Daniels." Charlie walked inside as quickly as he could in hopes that Ethan wouldn't decide to introduce him. He might not care now, but Charlie knew he would if he weren't so wasted. Maybe he shouldn't be helping him stay in the closet, but he didn't want to explode the guy's career over some impulsive hook-up.

The elevator was empty, and Ethan kissed him for the entire ride to the tenth floor. He was maybe two inches shorter than Charlie's six feet, but he had a way of making himself seem bigger and more powerful. Charlie wondered if that was one of the things you got when you sold your soul to the devil. Suddenly, what he really wanted was to see Ethan on his knees for him. He wanted to stick his dick into the mouthpiece of ECHO News. He wanted to get hard every time he saw a clip of that horrible program.

Ethan's apartment was at the end of the hall. When they got inside, Ethan tossed his keys into a bowl on a table by the door and turned on the lights. Charlie took a second to note how amazing the apartment was before turning to Ethan again. He started to reach for him, but Ethan cleared his throat.

"You want that drink?" he asked.

"Nope," Charlie replied. "Maybe later." He walked up to Ethan and kissed him, reaching up to pull his loosened tie over his head. The first button was already undone, and Charlie began to work on the rest. Ethan was breathing faster again, but when Charlie pulled back to look at him, he seemed less lustful than nervous. "Relax," Charlie said. "I don't want to do anything too intense tonight. No expectations.

I know you're pretty drunk anyway." He gave him a reassuring smile and slid his hand between Ethan's legs. At least that part of him wasn't experiencing second thoughts. "I really want your mouth on my cock, though."

Ethan groaned and put his hand on top of Charlie's to make him press harder as he kissed him some more. Charlie walked backward to the couch, pulling Ethan along with him. He sat down, but Ethan stood in front of him awkwardly. Charlie held out his hand and tried to pull him onto his lap, but Ethan frowned and shook his head. Instead, he dropped to his knees and started to fumble with the button of Charlie's pants.

"Hold on," Charlie said, "let me help you out there. Hand-eye coordination not at its peak tonight, eh?"

Ethan shrugged and gave him a crooked smile. He sat back and licked his lips as he watched Charlie unzip his fly. When Charlie pulled his cock out of his pants, he heard Ethan suck in a breath, which was flattering but kind of funny. Charlie knew he didn't have anything to be ashamed of in the size department, but he wasn't some kind of porn star by any stretch. He stroked himself while Ethan watched and rubbed himself through his pants.

Charlie scooted forward to the edge of the sofa cushion and put his hand on the side of Ethan's head, stretching his fingers around to the back. He continued to run his fist up and down his shaft. "Come on," he said, "suck me, Ethan."

Ethan seemed to startle at the sound of his own name, but he nodded and took a breath. He wrapped his right hand around Charlie's cock and leaned forward. He was tentative at first, licking him from base to tip and then taking only about half into his mouth before backing off. Charlie groaned and grabbed a handful of Ethan's hair. Ethan kept it up like that for a couple minutes—sucking him lightly before pulling back to lick it some more. Obviously it was some kind of teasing maneuver, but it started to get boring after a while.

"More," Charlie growled. "I want to fuck your throat." Ethan let out a small moan and unzipped his own pants. He let more of Charlie's cock into his mouth, but it still wasn't enough. His hand still in Ethan's hair, he pushed him farther down. Ethan promptly gagged and backed off. "Sorry," Charlie muttered, taking his hand away.

Ethan pulled off and shook his head. "No," he gasped, wiping his mouth. "That was good, do that again."

*Well, okay, then.* Charlie threaded his fingers into Ethan's hair again. It was soft and light brown with glints of gold and possibly a little gray. He shoved Ethan's head down, harder this time, and said, "That's better. Take it all." He might have laughed at his own cheesy porn dialogue, but he was too turned on. Ethan had his dick out and was touching himself as he gagged on Charlie's cock. Charlie leaned down and whispered, "Hold on. I want to come all over your face."

Ethan pulled off and stared at Charlie. He was breathing heavily with his mouth hanging open. Charlie grabbed his own cock and jerked himself quickly, finishing after a few seconds. His come spurted out and landed in droplets on Ethan's cheek and lips and a little bit in his hair.

"Oh shit," Ethan gasped, pulling up hard and fast on himself. He cried out as he came, his eyes focused on Charlie's face. After a few seconds, his body sagged and he sat back on his heels.

"Here," Charlie said. He knelt down next to Ethan and wiped his face clean with some tissues he'd found on the end table. He handed him a few more to clean up what was on his hand, kissed him and ran his fingers through the soft hair again. "I wouldn't mind that drink now," he said.

"Bar's over there," Ethan replied, gesturing wearily across the room. He got up and flopped down on the sofa where Charlie had been sitting. "Help yourself."

Charlie fixed a gin and tonic for himself and filled a glass with water for Ethan. He looked pretty out of it. He was leaning back on the couch and staring up at the ceiling. When Charlie got back to the couch, Ethan's eyes were closed.

"You should drink some water," Charlie said. "And go to bed." Ethan mumbled something unintelligible, so Charlie nudged him. "Hey. Here." When he opened his eyes he handed him the glass of water. "I'm going to take off so you can get some sleep."

Ethan took a sip and said, "Yeah, okay." He put the glass on the coffee table and let his head fall onto the arm of the sofa. "Night."

Charlie hesitated for a few seconds, unsure of what his ethical duty was here. Ethan was going to be miserable in the morning anyway, but if he slept like this it would be ten times worse. Then again, this was a grown man, plenty older than Charlie and capable of dealing with the consequences of his own mistakes. Whatever his reasons for getting so drunk, they weren't any of Charlie's business. He shrugged and drank his gin and tonic quickly. He rinsed the glass and left it on the bar.

# Chapter Three

ETHAN WOKE suddenly as if an alarm had gone off next to his ear, but the apartment was silent. He had no idea where he was or how he'd gotten there, and so he stayed perfectly still, keeping his eyes closed as his mind worked through things. After a moment he realized that opening them would most likely help him figure it out, and when he did, he saw he was in his living room. It was still dark outside, but there was enough light to see by coming in through the large window along the side of the room. His head was pounding, but the worst thing was the feeling of panic beginning to curdle in his stomach. He hadn't gotten so drunk in years, and he had a strong sense he'd really fucked up in some way, done something stupid or reckless and embarrassed himself. He stood up on shaky legs and tried to stretch the tendons in his neck, which ached from sleeping upright on the sofa. His pants slid down his hips, and he saw they were unzipped.

He suddenly felt heavy, and the room began to spin. He sank back onto the sofa and closed his eyes as memories of the night before slowly came back to him. He could only access fragments. Drinking alone, bumming a cigarette from the bartender—he still remembered how amazing that had felt, and he knew he must never do it again if he didn't want to start back up—and then talking to someone outside the bar. Fiona's teacher. *Charlie. Oh no.* Had he really done that? He couldn't remember walking home at all, but he remembered they'd been here together. He reached up to touch his lips, and he had a clear sense memory of the rough beard against his face.

Before any more of the night could come back to him, Ethan stood up again and walked to the kitchen for something to drink. Other than a highball glass in the dish drainer, there was no evidence anyone else had been in the apartment. He poured orange juice into the glass and chugged it down. It was a relief for a second, but then his stomach rebelled. He rushed to the bathroom and puked until he felt like there was nothing left in his body. When he was finished, he swallowed three painkillers and stared at himself in the mirror. Aside from looking a little rough, he was the same person he'd been the day before. There was nothing different anyone could see from the outside, but he felt different. He'd crossed a line he never intended to cross, and all it took were a few too many drinks. That was a pretty lame excuse by anyone's measure. He couldn't blame the alcohol. He'd wanted something like that to happen ever since his divorce and probably before—maybe even before his marriage. That desire had been with him for as long as he could remember, but he'd never acted on it. He'd been content enough with things the way they were. So why now?

The clock on the microwave told him it was not quite five o'clock. If he thought he would be able to fall back asleep, he'd try to get another hour in, but he knew there was no way his mind would let him be still long enough for that. He showered and dressed, trying to keep his mind on the day ahead. It was exhausting to think about, but it was better than dwelling on the events of the night before. It was still early by the time he was ready, so he lay down on the couch with a cool cloth across his eyes. That might reduce the puffiness a little bit. Forty-five minutes later, he was jolted out of sleep by the sound of a text coming in on his phone. It was from Deirdre, asking if they could get lunch. He was immediately suspicious. He and his ex didn't have that sort of friendly relationship. They were cordial, but they didn't hang out. He texted back.

*Something you need to talk about?*

*Nothing bad. Can you meet me or not?*

Ethan sighed. He was pretty sure she'd said "nothing bad" when she'd wanted to tell him she was moving to Manhattan. Just because it wasn't bad didn't mean it wouldn't screw with his life. He said he'd meet her and to text him the place.

The day had dawned gray and windy with a light rain that hit the windows in gusts. The daytime doorman, Diego, held an umbrella over him as he got into the sedan waiting out front. As he thanked Diego, he was hit unexpectedly with another memory from the night before.

Roland had been at the door when he brought Charlie home with him. Roland was his favorite doorman. He was always on duty when Ethan got home from work, and he always gave him that great smile. He was funny too. He'd always made jokes about ECHO but in a way that didn't make Ethan feel like he was being attacked personally—as if Roland didn't include him in that entity, somehow. Still, even though they were friendly, Ethan still felt exposed. Roland was probably being nice because that was his job.

He avoided people all morning, as much as possible. He told Abigail he needed time to prepare for that evening's interview with someone from the natural gas lobby, which was true, but when he sat down with the prep materials, he found himself unable to look at it for long. He couldn't think of much besides the previous night. Instead he spent some time looking up Charlie Woods on social media. He was on Facebook and Instagram, and of course Grindr—not that Ethan was going to go on that site to look. His Instagram had all the usual business—pictures of food, selfies in various places, some pretentious close-up shots of architectural details from around the city. There was a picture of Charlie with his arm around a tall, sort of burly guy with a sweet smile and a blond beard. He reminded Ethan of some kind of big friendly dog, like a golden retriever or something. They looked good together, actually, and he wondered if the guy was an ex-boyfriend. Or a current one, for that matter. How would he know?

Finally, it was time to go to lunch. He made it to the restaurant first and ordered a club soda, hoping it would help to settle his stomach. It was about ten past noon when his ex-wife arrived, looking as gorgeous and dynamic as ever. Her hair, a little darker than their daughter's copper strands, but just as curly, flowed over her shoulder like lava. She was wearing a royal blue dress and, as always, heels to compensate for her height, which was just over five feet. Ethan stood when she approached the table and gave her a half hug and a kiss on the cheek before sitting back down.

"How are you, Deirdre?" he asked.

"Couldn't be better," Deirdre said as she settled herself in her chair. "I did three morning shows last week." She spoke with a lilting Irish accent that had faded considerably in the years since he'd known her. Her family had moved to Pennsylvania when she was in high school when her father got a job with a pharmaceutical company there. When Ethan met her, she had just finished her MBA at Wharton, but her working-class Dublin accent was still in evidence. During her first and only year working as a financial analyst, she began to make an obvious effort to refine her speech, which Ethan found disappointing. He'd loved the way she sounded when he met her. She'd published her first book while working for a big firm in Philadelphia, and when it hit big, she quit and never looked back. Sometimes in interviews she would self-consciously play up her accent for effect, but in her personal life she sounded like a news broadcaster. He could relate, of course—he'd worked hard to scrub the Philly out of his own speech—but it was still a loss.

"Well, ain't you a bigwig down the cracker factory," he said, putting on an accent like the Lucky Charms leprechaun. When they were together, he would sometimes look up Irish slang and use it to annoy her. Early on, she'd found it amusing and would join in. In the last few years of their marriage, both his motives and her reaction had changed quite a bit.

Deirdre smiled at him with something like fondness. The anger and resentment between them had dissipated after their divorce and had been replaced with a slightly sad nostalgia. "Sucking diesel, so I am," she said, winking at him. "And you?"

*Sucking cock*, he thought, pushing down a slightly hysterical laugh, which threatened to escape. "I'm all right," he said out loud. "Already stressing about the contract negotiation bullshit."

Deirdre rolled her eyes. "Surely you have other options. Somewhere else you could go."

"They're not exactly beating down my door with offers. I'm making good money at ECHO. They treat me well. I don't see any reason to look elsewhere."

"Really, no reason at all," Deirdre said. She looked like she was gearing up for a fight but was interrupted by the waiter coming to their table. She ordered a glass of wine and a salad. Ethan asked for a cheeseburger and fries. He knew he might regret it later, but now he needed something substantial in his stomach.

"So," he said, "I heard you were seeing someone." He could hear the negativity in his voice, and he knew she must have as well.

Deirdre cleared her throat and readjusted the napkin on her lap. "As a matter of fact, I have been, yes," she said, looking him straight in the eye. "Do you have some sort of problem with that?"

"No," Ethan began carefully, "but it might have been nice if you'd mentioned it to me."

"It's not exactly a secret. I talked about it on ECHO and Company."

"That's kind of my point. You could have said something to me first. As it was, I had to find out from Vince fucking Martin who used it to blindside me before asking when I was going to get on the stick and find a girlfriend."

"Oh for fuck's sake," Deirdre muttered, sounding much more like herself than she had in a while, at least around him. "Because of that stupid rumor, I suppose. Honestly, Ethan. This is what I'm talking about. He has no business interfering in your—"

"Stop," Ethan said, holding up his hands. "I am well aware of your opinions about this. That wasn't my main concern anyway. Has Fiona met him?"

"Of course not," Deirdre said, frowning at him now. "She doesn't even know I go on dates. Do you honestly think I'm not keeping our daughter's well-being in mind?"

The waiter stopped by to drop off her wine. When he'd gone, Ethan said, "I guess not. I got taken by surprise, somehow. Probably I shouldn't have been."

Deirdre sipped her wine and then sighed as she set it down. "Probably not. Haven't you gone out with anyone since we split?"

"I didn't feel ready," Ethan said, which was partly true. He hadn't been at all prepared for what had happened in his apartment the night before.

"It's been long enough," Deirdre said, patting his hand. "Which brings me to the reason I asked you to lunch."

Ethan raised his eyebrows and tried to keep his face composed while he waited for her to speak. He did not like the sound of this at all. "Okay…," he said warily.

"I was talking with a friend of mine—well, honestly, not exactly a friend. An acquaintance. Actually, she's my hairdresser. She's a successful hairdresser, quite sought after. She's lovely, in her early thirties and single."

"A hairdresser."

"Don't be a dickhead, Ethan. She's quite intelligent and a great conversationalist."

"Why are you doing this?" Ethan asked.

"I realize it's not exactly traditional for the ex-wife to be playing matchmaker. I wouldn't have thought of it except she reminds me of you in some ways. You'll like her sense of humor. And let's face it—it's time."

"I don't know. It makes me a little uncomfortable. Actually, it makes me a lot uncomfortable. If it doesn't work—"

"If it doesn't work out and things get weird, I'll find a new salon. Give it a go, would you?"

This seemed like a bad idea on the face of it, but it might be a good thing to do. He wasn't too excited about it, but perhaps once he met her, he'd feel different. It was possible, he thought, the reason he'd been so obsessed with men since the divorce was because it was hard for him to think about women other than Deirdre, but perhaps diving in would change the way he was feeling.

"All right. Text me her number."

"Really?" Deirdre's face lit up with a surprised smile. She picked up her phone. "Her name is Willa."

Ethan shrugged and smiled back at her. It felt nice to be able to make her happy again after years of making each other miserable.

Ethan felt better after lunch and was able to get his work done. He didn't do any more Internet stalking, and he ended up feeling okay about the interview with the fracking guy. By the time he left work, he was in a pretty decent mood. He'd go home, call Willa, and then maybe hit the gym.

Roland was working the door when Ethan's car service dropped him in front of his building. "Good evening, Mr. Daniels," he said. "How was your day?"

"Excellent," Ethan said. "Very successful dissemination of lies and half-truths today if I do say so myself."

Roland grinned at him. "Congratulations, sir."

"Also I had lunch with my ex-wife and she wants to set me up on a date with her hairdresser," Ethan said. "Probably a terrible idea, but I said I'd try."

"Is he as cute as that guy you were with last night?"

"What?" Ethan said and then laughed uncomfortably. "No—I mean, her hairdresser is a woman. And that guy was just a friend I ran into at the bar."

"Oh, okay," Roland said, nodding in understanding. "Well, good luck with that." He opened the door to let Ethan in. "Your friend was really hot, though."

"I'll pass it along," Ethan said as he walked into the lobby. He got into the elevator and sagged against the wall. That was incredibly embarrassing but probably for the best. Roland gave him the opportunity to deny what had happened, which was good because if Ethan brought it up out of the blue, it would have seemed a little defensive.

He stared at his fridge and realized there was nothing in there he wanted to eat for dinner. He pulled some take-out menus from a drawer and started rifling through them as he dialed the number Deirdre had given him. He doubted the idea was going to seem better with age, so he figured he might as well move things along. Willa picked up on the second ring.

"Hi," Ethan said as he looked through the menu of the Thai restaurant, "this is Ethan Daniels. I believe my insane ex-wife might have mentioned I'd be calling you."

Willa laughed and said, "She might have mentioned it, but I didn't really think you'd do it. It is a little weird, right?"

"A little?" Ethan asked. "But for some reason I decided to give it a shot anyway. Would you like to get drinks with me this week?"

"This week is actually really bad for me. I'm sorry—I know that sounds like an excuse, but it's for real. I have a friend visiting from out of town. Would next week sometime be okay for you?"

"Sure. Next Friday, eight o'clock? You pick the place."

"That works," she replied. "I'll text you when I decide where we should go."

Deirdre dropped Fiona off on Friday for her weekend with Ethan. Fiona gave Ethan a big hug, and he swung her up into his arms.

"Oof," he said, pretending he could barely lift her. "You're huge!"

"No, I'm tiny," she replied. "You should eat more vegetables to get stronger."

"Yuck, vegetables," Ethan said. He threw her over his shoulder. "See? I don't need vegetables. I have super strength." She giggled and kicked until he put her down. "Now go put your stuff in your room, and we can go get dinner."

When she'd run off, Deirdre immediately said, "I heard you called Willa."

"I see you're keeping abreast of the situation."

"She called to tell me."

"I'm not seeing her until next week," Ethan said, "and I'd really appreciate it if you'd try not to gossip with her about me. It's weird enough as it is, okay?"

Deirdre rolled her eyes. "I don't gossip."

"Right."

"So you're dropping her off at school on Monday, yes?"

"Uh, yeah," Ethan said. His heart inexplicably sped up at the prospect.

"Something wrong?" Deirdre said, frowning at him.

"Of course not." It was a ridiculous reaction. He didn't have to walk her into the classroom this time anyway. He probably wouldn't have to run into Charlie.

"Well, anyway. So I won't see you until Tuesday, then." Ethan tried to look like he knew what she was talking about as he wracked his brain. Finally, she huffed and reminded him. "Back To School Night? We're supposed to go in and listen to some spiel from the administration and speak with her teachers, remember?"

"Oh yeah," Ethan said, his stomach giving a lurch. "Do we both really have to be there? It might be tough for me to leave early enough to get there on time."

"We absolutely do, Ethan. We're both her parents. Just because I have her during the week doesn't mean you don't have to be involved in her education. It's really important that you're familiar with her teachers." Her frown deepened as she looked at him. "What's the matter with you?"

"Nothing, nothing," he replied. "Just stressed. Work stuff. I'll be at the thing on Tuesday."

"See that you are," she said.

Ethan took Fiona out to eat. On Saturday they went to the Natural History Museum, which—despite it being a nightmare of crowds—she seemed to really enjoy. On Sunday he made blueberry pancakes, and they sat at the kitchen island eating them as she told him about school. She was an outgoing girl who called everyone her friend and seemed to have absorbed personal details about all of them. She also talked a great deal about Mr. Woods and how he made the class laugh all the time with silly jokes.

"So you're not worried about being taught by a boy wizard anymore?" Ethan asked, winking at her.

"Daddy," Fiona said, rolling her eyes in the perfect image of her mother. "I never said he was a wizard."

"I must have misunderstood," he said. Despite the unsettled feeling in his stomach whenever the topic of Mr. Woods came up, he couldn't resist pumping her for more information. "So what kind of silly jokes does he tell?"

"Like, um… how do you put a giraffe in the fridgerator?"

"How?"

"First, you open the door," she began, drawing it out slowly, "then you put the giraffe in. Then you close the door!"

Ethan smiled. "Good one."

"How do you put an elephant in the fridgerator?"

"Open the door, put the elephant in, close the door?"

"No!" she shouted gleefully. "First you open the door. Then you take the giraffe out…." She dissolved into giggles. When they'd tapered off, she said, "Also he has a tattoo." Her voice lowered in something like awe. "I could only see a little bit of it. The class tried to get him to show us, but he said it was private, and we should all respect other people's privacy."

"Well, that's definitely true," Ethan said. He got up to put away the syrup and tried not to think of the ink he'd seen under Charlie's

V-neck sweater. They hadn't gotten far enough that night for him to get a look at it and now his curiosity was piqued again. Too bad he'd never get a chance to find out now.

On Monday morning he dropped Fiona off in the hallway outside of her classroom. Mostly he was dreading the possibility of being spotted by Charlie, but he couldn't deny there was a small part of him that hoped he would be. To what end, Ethan had no idea. It wasn't as if they'd have a chance to talk about anything there in the classroom, nor would he want to even if there were. The problem was, everything felt so strangely unfinished. He'd woken up in his empty apartment and—other than his pants being unzipped and an empty glass in the drainer—it was as if nothing had happened. In any case, as far as he could tell, Charlie didn't see him. Ethan caught a glimpse of him, though. He was sitting in his chair with a tablet device, his legs propped up on the desk. He looked entirely comfortable and in his element, which was amazing to Ethan. Being a first-grade teacher was the last thing he could imagine doing.

At work on Tuesday morning, he was barraged by a million tiny crises. A guest had canceled. They hadn't been able to get confirmation from a source about a story they were planning to run. Ethan had been skewered by *The Daily Show*—as if anyone cared now that Jon Stewart was gone. When things finally quieted down, Abby knocked and came into his office. Ethan was at his desk, but he put his phone down and sighed. "What is it now?" he asked her.

"I wanted to ask if you'd like a sandwich. We're ordering lunch."

"Oh," he said, rubbing at his eyes. "Sure. Something with turkey."

"That's specific," Abby said, rolling her eyes.

"Take care of it, okay?" Ethan hadn't meant to snap at her, but that was definitely how it came out.

"Sure," she said warily. "Are you okay, Ethan? You look stressed out."

"I'm fine. I have this fucking back-to-school thing at my daughter's school tonight."

"That's it? Seriously? What's so stressful about that?"

Ethan wanted so badly to tell her. He realized he hadn't truly stopped thinking of that night with Charlie for the past week. He'd been doing his best to occupy his mind, but it played on a constant loop in his subconscious, as if he'd fallen asleep with the television on and it had influenced his dreams. Maybe if he talked about it, he'd be able to get some perspective. It was a huge risk, but just then he felt the same sort of recklessness come over him that he'd felt at the bar before inviting Charlie home with him. He'd heard people with addictions describe their relapses in this way—it was a loss of self-control, in a way, but what it really amounted to was a loss of desire for self-control.

"I slept with Fiona's teacher," he said. "Well, not slept, of course. We just—anyway. It never should have happened."

"Well, why not?" Abby asked. "Maybe she wasn't the best choice to get back in the saddle with, but what's the big deal?"

Ethan dropped his face into his hands and groaned, shaking his head slowly back and forth. "His name is Charlie," he said.

Abby didn't speak for a full second and then she said, "Oh. Well, okay." She walked around behind his desk and patted him on the back. "Okay, Ethan. Look, it's fine. I promise you don't have to worry about me saying anything until you're ready."

"It's not fine, and I'm not going to say anything to anyone else about this, ever. I want to get past it and pretend it never happened, but before I do that I have to see him tonight. I have to sit there next to Deirdre and talk to him and act like this is not completely fucked up."

"Jesus, Ethan," Abby sighed. "You do realize this is 2016, right?"

"Not here it isn't," Ethan said, almost growling at her. "You might recall my contract is up in two months."

"They can't—"

"Yes, they certainly can. They're under no obligation to re-sign me. They don't have to give me a reason, even though I'd know exactly what the reason is."

"Right," Abby said, "okay. So you're gay, but instead of ever having a decent relationship, you're going to keep working for this company and pretending everything is fine?"

"I'm not gay. I'm perfectly happy being with women. I always have been, and there's no reason I need to change it at this late date."

"And that's why you hooked up with a dude the other night. Because it's not important to you at all. More of a nuisance? Like a fly you can brush off, something like that?"

"I was drunk and I was in a low mood. It just happened. It won't happen again."

"Sure," Abby said, "so what's your problem, then? Do you think he'll blab to someone? Or did someone else see you?"

"Well… the doorman at my building saw me go in with him. He's—I don't think he'd say anything. Probably. Actually, I don't know. He asked me about it the next day, but I told him it was a friend I'd run into. I don't think he believed me, though."

"Yeah, probably not," Abby laughed. "But I think if he was going to tell anyone, he'd have done it already. It would have already turned up somewhere. Try not to worry about it too much. But Ethan—"

"Don't," Ethan said, holding up his hand. "I know what you're going to say, and I don't need to hear it."

"I don't think you know what I'm going to say."

"You were going to say I'm never going to be happy if I'm not making decisions from an honest place. That I'm lying to myself about what I want. That continuing to work here saying the shit on air that I have to say is eventually going to wear me down until I'm physically ill. That I'm making a big fucking deal out of nothing because I'm scared. That about cover it?"

Abby stared at him and for a second she looked like she might cry. "Shit, Ethan," she said. "I was just going to say everything will work out for the best eventually. Or some kind of meaningless crap. Do—would you like a hug?"

Ethan laughed somewhat miserably and shook his head. "I'm good. I just need to get through tonight. Then I'll be golden."

Abby looked skeptical, but she said, "Do you want me to text you halfway through and pretend we have a journalistic crisis?"

"I knew there was a reason I hired you."

Ethan left work as early as he was able to, but he still came very close to being late to the school. Traffic was a nightmare, as always. The network paid for his car service, but he often wondered if it wouldn't be better just to take public transportation. It wasn't like there hadn't been plenty of traffic in Philadelphia, but it seemed somehow more manageable. He hated sitting in traffic for many reasons but most of all because it gave him too much time to think about things he didn't want to dwell on. Just then it was the fact that he didn't like living and working in Manhattan as much as he'd hoped he would. He'd never been one to romanticize the city, but he'd hoped when he got settled in it would grow on him. Of course there were a lot of benefits to it—great cultural opportunities, amazing restaurants—but he wasn't sure it would ever feel like home to him. He rarely took advantage of those things anyway because his job was so demanding, and in his free time he had Fiona with him.

The driver dropped him off at the door of the school, and he rushed in to find a crowd of parents milling about in the lobby, waiting to be told where to go. He spotted Deirdre across the room and made a beeline for her.

"Cutting it a bit close, eh?" she asked.

"I got here on time," he said. "I left as early as I could. I told you it might be difficult."

"Fine," she sighed, casting her eyes around the room. Ethan looked at the other parents as well. It was quite a homogenous group of well-dressed, mostly white people.

"I feel like maybe we should have found a more diverse school for her," he said.

Deirdre laughed sharply. "Don't let anyone from your adoring public hear you say that," she said. "Diversity is like a curse word to them."

"I wouldn't worry too much. There's no one over the age of seventy here as far as I can see."

She shook her head at him in wonder and opened her mouth in order, presumably, to give him more grief about his job, but was interrupted by one of the teachers instructing them to proceed to their child's homeroom. Ethan stuck close to Deirdre as they climbed the stairs to the first-grade hallway. As long as they were together, there was no chance he'd have to have a conversation with Charlie about anything other than his daughter.

When they entered the room, Ethan immediately spotted Charlie chatting with one of the parents—a fairly well-known actress—and busied himself with finding Fiona's desk. There were folders on each desk with some work from the first two weeks of school. When all of the parents had filed into the room, Charlie walked to the front of the classroom and introduced himself.

"Good evening! I'm Mr. Woods, and I'm your child's first-grade teacher. I'm going to give you an idea of what we do during a typical day and what we hope to accomplish by the end of the year. Afterward I'll be happy to answer any questions you might have and to chat briefly with you, but I can't go into specifics about any individual child tonight. There's a sign-up sheet for conferences that will be held next month, and I hope you'll all reserve a slot."

He spoke for about twenty minutes and didn't look in Ethan's direction even once. In a strange way, it made Ethan feel a little better. At least he wasn't the only one who was uncomfortable with the situation, which meant he probably wouldn't be in any hurry to bring up anything that happened. When he was finished with his speech, Charlie took several questions from parents, all involving their particular child. Ethan wasn't surprised, but he still managed to feel annoyed about it. Maybe if half the group hadn't been trying to covertly look at their phones when Charlie was speaking, they would have gotten the message.

There were refreshments provided for the parents at the back of the classroom. Ethan would have just as soon left right away, but they had to wait another ten minutes before their appointment with the art and music teachers. He followed Deirdre to the table and poured himself a cup of bad coffee. If only he still had the excuse of needing to step outside for a smoke, but she'd just yell at him.

Deirdre grabbed his forearm and said, "Oh look—it looks like Mr. Woods is free for the moment, let's go and say hello."

"Why? We've signed up for the conference. We'll talk to him then."

"Because it would be rude not to. What's wrong with you? Come along now." She started to walk toward the front of the room, and Ethan followed her because that's the way Deirdre was and had always been. She had a way about her that was hard to resist. When they were in the process of separating, Ethan had started to believe that everything that had ever happened in their relationship was because of that quality in her.

After a while he'd been able to see more clearly the part he had played in all of these decisions—getting married, having a child, separating, and eventually his choice to follow her to New York—and stopped holding her entirely responsible for them. He didn't exactly regret any of them anyway. Their marriage had been a happy one for several years, and he would never regret Fiona. The move to New York was harder to swallow, though. He hadn't felt like he even had a choice to make. She hadn't convinced him to do that, the way she normally did. She'd forced his hand, and he still resented her for it.

"Mr. Woods," Deirdre said as she approached him, blocking out another couple who looked like they were about to pounce on him. "I'm not sure if you remember me, but—"

"Ms. McNaughton, of course I do. It's great to see you." He shook Deirdre's hand and then looked at Ethan. And Mr. Daniels, I'm glad you could make it tonight." He smiled politely and held out his hand to Ethan. Ethan shook it and was extremely conscious of how clammy his palm was. He was suddenly not at all sure he was going to get through this.

"Fiona is a wonderful kid," Charlie said. "She's already reading well, and she gets along great with her classmates. She's a pleasure to have in class. Oh, and she's also pretty funny, but I'm sure you know that."

"You mean she's a smart aleck," Deirdre said.

"Well, yes, that's exactly what I mean," Charlie said, grinning at her. "Which I have no objections to at all, though she does need to work on knowing when it's appropriate. I'm sure she'll figure it out, though."

"I'm sure we can talk about all it at the conference next month," Ethan said. "We don't want to monopolize your time."

"Oh, I have a few minutes if you wanted to chat about Fiona. I'm not a stickler." He looked directly at Ethan in an almost challenging way.

Deirdre touched Ethan's arm and said, "Emilie Huang is over there—you know, Lysette's mom? I wanted to catch her and see about a playdate. Fiona's been asking." She looked at Charlie. "Will you excuse me?"

"Go right ahead," Charlie said. "Those two are great friends."

Ethan started to walk away too, but Charlie said, "Mr. Daniels? Can you hang on another minute?"

Ethan closed his eyes briefly and nearly groaned but said, "Sure. What's up?"

Charlie walked away from a group of parents and lowered his voice. "Look, I should have called you to do this, but I feel like I owe you an apology."

Ethan frowned and shook his head. "I can't imagine why. Whatever it is, don't worry about it."

"Ethan," Charlie said, speaking even more quietly. "I'm serious. I didn't realize how drunk you were until we were back at your place, but when I did I should have stopped the whole thing. I'm really sorry."

"Jesus Christ," Ethan said. He was getting pissed off now but he kept his tone even and very quiet. "First of all, this is not the time or place for this. Second, it's ridiculous—no, that's not even the word. It's insulting. I'm a grown man, not some Sarah Lawrence sophomore. I'm not going to cry remorse rape, okay? I made my own choices, and I can live with the regrets."

Charlie's eyes popped open wide and his mouth made a thin line. "You sound exactly like some of those people you interview on your show. I guess when you're surrounded by that kind of garbage all day you can't help absorbing some of it. So I guess I'll see you at the conference. Or you could ask your wife to come by herself. Maybe that would be best."

"Maybe so," Ethan said.

"Have fun with your regrets." Charlie turned around and smiled at some parents waiting to speak with him.

His heart beating with a combination of anger and nervous energy, Ethan leaned on a desk for a second before he found Deirdre near the classroom door. His phone buzzed with a call just as he got close to her.

"It's my assistant," Ethan said. "I need to take this." He went out into the hallway. "Hey, Abby," he said, picking up the phone. "What's up?"

"Blah blah blah, crisis, emergency. You need to come deal with this, Ethan. Or not. Depending on how your evening is going."

"Oh shit," Ethan said. "Are you serious? Why do you need me to come? This thing is still going on. I can't just leave."

"So, did you see the guy yet?"

"Yes, I handled that already," Ethan said, glancing over to see if Deirdre was buying his act.

"Well? Are you okay?"

"I'll come down there if I absolutely have to, but—uh-huh—yeah. Fine." He disconnected and looked at Deirdre. "They're having a crisis about this story we're supposed to do tomorrow. They wanted to get my input. I can absolutely stay if you need me to."

Deirdre narrowed her eyes at him and then sighed. "You do what you have to do, Ethan. I guess I'll see you Friday when I drop Fiona off."

"Thanks. Oh! Wait. I'm supposed to see your friend. The hairdresser. On Friday. Would it be okay if I pick her up Saturday morning instead?"

"Seeing as how it was my idea, I don't know how I could refuse. Right, then." She kissed his cheek. "Off with you."

"Night."

Ethan left the building quickly, feeling guilty about lying but incredibly relieved to be out of there. The anger that had come up in him so suddenly and fiercely during the conversation with Charlie had mostly faded. Now he felt like shit. He started to walk in the direction of his building, but when he reached it, he kept moving. He walked several more blocks, not giving any thought to where he was headed because his mind was preoccupied with other things. Why had he gotten so angry? Charlie hadn't actually insulted him, so why had he chosen to take it as one? Charlie was a kind person. He treated others with respect. That was clear from the way he'd spoken about Fiona, and from the few interactions Ethan had observed with the kids in his charge. Fiona was obviously taken with him. He hadn't deserved what Ethan said to him. It occurred to Ethan that maybe he was the one who owed an apology—not only for what he'd said but also for the way he'd behaved that night. He hadn't seen Charlie as a person at all but as a way to fulfill some stupid fantasy—to scratch an itch he'd had for as long as he could remember.

He turned right at the next corner and again at the next one. He glanced at his phone to check the time and thought maybe if he walked fast he could get there before the event was over. He had nothing in his mind except apologizing. He'd been in the wrong in all kinds of ways.

When Ethan reached the block where the school was located, he could see people streaming out of the front doors. He ducked into a nearby alley to wait—the last thing he needed was for Deirdre to catch him slinking back. How the hell would he explain that? He waited until the crowd had dispersed and hoped his assumption was correct that the teachers would be the last ones to leave. When he thought it was safe, he approached the building. Some of the interior lights went out just as he pulled at the door, and Ethan cursed. Probably only the cleaning staff was still there by then. Still, he went into the quiet, dimly lit lobby and looked around. It was an old building with worn marble floors in the entranceway. He wondered if it had once been a bank. Just as he started up the stairway to the second floor, someone rounded the corner and nearly collided with him. In his surprise, Ethan was only able to register a striped scarf and some trailing earbud wires at first. As Ethan looked up and realized who it was, Charlie reached out and grabbed his arm to steady him.

"Sorry," Charlie said. "I wasn't paying attention." He didn't move his hand, and he was smiling at Ethan as if nothing had happened, or maybe as if he knew exactly why Ethan had come back.

"Me neither," Ethan said. "I came back to say I'm sorry. What I said—it was wrong." He locked eyes with Charlie. "And for being so drunk and stupid that night. That's probably why I got so pissy about it tonight, you know? Because it should have been me apologizing, not you."

Charlie shook his head and didn't break eye contact. "No need. I had a good time. I think you did too, but maybe you can't remember."

"I remember enough," Ethan said. He felt like someone had stopped time and they were completely alone in the world. Neither of them spoke for a few seconds. When another set of lights went off and plunged them into nearly complete darkness, Ethan climbed one step so he and Charlie were on the same level and pressed a kiss to his closed mouth. Charlie responded by grabbing his hips and pulling him in roughly, deepening the contact and swiping his tongue across Ethan's lips. Ethan opened to him and used his body to push Charlie against the bannister.

Panting, Charlie broke the kiss and said, "Ethan, are you—"

"Yeah," Ethan whispered. "Whatever you're asking, yes. I want—" He gave his head a brief shake and kissed him again. "You. I want you. Come home with me."

Charlie looked at him like he was trying to figure something out but quickly shrugged. "Sure. Let's get out of here."

They walked the six blocks to Ethan's place quickly. The night had turned cool and a light mist was falling, but Ethan felt warm everywhere. He had an urge—immediately suppressed—to grab Charlie's hand. Instead he swayed slightly to let their shoulders brush together.

Roland was working the door and Ethan wasn't sure if he should be relieved or worried. This was only going to confirm his earlier assumptions. He figured the only thing he could do was to play it as brazenly as possible and act like nothing unusual was happening.

"Evening, Mr. Woods," Roland said, smiling at him with slightly raised brows as he opened the door.

"Hey, Roland," Ethan said. He went into the building but not in time to miss the look that passed between the doorman and Charlie. Great—now he had to deal with jealousy in addition to stress about being exposed.

This time they weren't lucky enough to have the elevator to themselves. An older couple got on at the same time they did and their stop was three floors below Ethan's, but as soon as they stepped off, Charlie put his hand on Ethan's back. Ethan looked around nervously but didn't say anything. He had a feeling if he did it would break the mood, and that was the last thing he wanted to do.

They entered the apartment, and he noticed Charlie looking around the living room.

"I didn't get a chance to mention it last time, but this is an amazing place," Charlie said.

"Thanks," Ethan said. "Want to see the rest of it?"

Charlie grinned. "That would be a nice change."

Ethan led him down the hallway to the master bedroom at the end. Charlie whistled when he opened the door. "This room is bigger than my whole apartment."

"You need a better job. I could put in a word for you at ECHO News," Ethan said, winking at him as he loosened his tie and toed his shoes off.

"Ha," Charlie replied. He took off his scarf and tossed it on a chair by the bed.

Ethan pulled off his tie and walked over to him. He kissed him and moved his hands to Charlie's fly, unbuttoning his pants and lowering the zipper.

"Hey," Charlie said, "since you're a little more conscious this time, maybe we should talk about what we're doing here." He put his hands over Ethan's and stopped him. "I don't know what you like. Just so you know, I'm versatile. So if you have a preference…?"

Ethan looked confused for a second and then said, "Oh," when his words had sunk in. "Uh, well I don't—I mean, I'm not, uh—"

"Or we can, you know, whatever," Charlie said quickly. "We don't have to fuck. That's cool."

"It's not that I—I just—" He let out a sigh. "It's just that I don't know." He sat down on the bed. "I'm sorry. I should have said this before, but I didn't get a chance. I've never actually… been with anyone. A man, I mean. Obviously." He laughed awkwardly. "I mean, I thought about it. I wanted to. But I got married before I ever tried it. So… I realize that might make it bad for you. Or weird. Or something."

Charlie sat down next to him. "I'm glad you told me. I promise it won't make it bad for me. I don't want you to feel like I'm being, I don't know, insulting or condescending or anything. But I feel like I have to make sure you're okay with it. The worst thing would be for us to do… whatever, and then you don't feel good about it. I mean, I'm being selfish here. It would make me feel like shit if that's the way it went, and I don't want to deal with that. I'm going to have to see you again. I like you and I want to stay, but it's not like I don't have options, you know?"

Ethan snorted. "Sure. You could probably go downstairs right now and get a hand job from the doorman."

"Probably," Charlie agreed. He put his hand on Ethan's leg and rubbed it up and down slowly. "I'd rather see what you can do for me."

"I'd prefer that too. I don't know if I can promise how I'll feel about it, though. I can promise I won't take it out on you."

"I guess that's good enough." Charlie pulled Ethan down onto the mattress and slid his hand up to Ethan's chest. While they kissed he unbuttoned Ethan's dress shirt with one hand. He teased his right nipple, circling it until it was a hard nub and then brushed his thumb across it. Ethan grunted into the kiss as his cock jerked in response. "So I guess I'll have to be in charge, if that works for you," Charlie said, pulling back from the kiss.

"I think it's clear that's the best way forward," Ethan said. He pulled Charlie's hand back to his chest. "We're off to a good start."

Charlie smiled and lowered his head to lick the nipple instead, earning a groan from Ethan. He rubbed it with his thumb again as he sucked on the other one. Ethan grabbed Charlie's free hand and moved it between his legs. His cock was aching. He'd never been with a woman who'd paid much attention to that part of his body. He hadn't realized they were so sensitive.

"I'm making an executive decision," Charlie said, pulling his hand free and sitting up. "We have too many clothes on."

"Agreed," Ethan replied and got up to remedy the situation.

Ethan tried not to be obvious about watching Charlie undress, but apparently it didn't work, because Charlie caught his eye and laughed at him. "It's okay to look," he said. "I don't go to the gym for nothing."

"I go so I don't look fat on television," Ethan said.

"If you're trying to get me to admit there's an upside to you working at that place, don't hold your breath," Charlie said.

Ethan had undressed down to his boxer briefs. Charlie walked over to him, completely naked. Ethan stared, unable to help it. Charlie was so beautiful. His tall, lanky frame was perfectly proportioned, with a broad chest and long, ropey muscles in his arms. He wasn't overly hairy, but it didn't look like he waxed either. He looked natural and comfortable with himself and that put Ethan a little more at ease as well. Ethan rubbed his thumb over the tattoo on his chest and smiled. "A lightbulb, a dollar sign, a badge, and a... what do you call the one with the staff and the snakes?"

"It's a caduceus. I'll tell you about those later. We're doing other stuff now." Charlie lightly trailed his fingernails over the bulge in Ethan's shorts. "Can't do much with these on," he said.

"What are we going to do?" Ethan asked, suddenly nervous.

Charlie kissed him. "Nothing you don't want to do," he answered. "Don't you want me to touch you? I didn't get to do that the last time. You beat me to the punch."

Ethan's face heated up. "I was drunk," he said.

"I know. And you definitely liked sucking my dick. Like, a lot."

Ethan licked his dry lips. "Yeah," he said, glancing down involuntarily. "I want to now."

"I want that too, but don't touch yourself. Wait. Let me do it."

Ethan nodded. He hesitated for a second before peeling off his briefs, hissing as the waistband scraped against his cock, and then he dropped to his knees. Charlie was only half-hard so Ethan stroked him loosely a few times and licked all along his length. Charlie let out a satisfied sigh as he stiffened up, thrusting forward slightly so his cock rubbed against Ethan's cheek. Ethan let him do that a few times before he opened his mouth and guided him in. Ethan's cock throbbed when he felt the head of Charlie's hit the back of his throat. All thoughts and willpower left him, and he grabbed his own shaft, pumping up and down a few times. It felt so good. All he wanted to do was let go. He hadn't felt like this since he was a kid.

Charlie pulled out of Ethan's mouth. "I'm thrilled that you like sucking me off that much, but you have to slow it down."

"Sorry," Ethan said. He put a hand on Charlie's thigh and tried to calm his body.

"Listen. I'm not a dom. I'm not issuing commands to be obeyed. I just don't want the fun to be over so quick, and if you do that, it's going to turn me on too much and it'll be a repeat of the last time." He reached a hand down and said, "Let's go to bed."

"Yeah," Ethan said, "all right." He got up and pulled the covers back. They climbed in, and Charlie came up behind Ethan, pushing him gently onto his hands and knees. Ethan had no idea what exactly was going to happen, and he wasn't sure if he wanted to know ahead of time or not. The little pinpricks of fear that kept poking him were keeping him aroused almost to the point of pain. Charlie's large, warm hands rubbed across his back and around to his chest. He kissed the small of Ethan's back and kept kissing until he reached the crack of his ass. Ethan should have expected what happened next—it wasn't like he'd never watched gay porn—but he was taken by surprise anyway. When Charlie's tongue dipped into the crack of his ass, Ethan started almost violently and grasped at the sheets.

"Relax, you'll like it," Charlie said.

"Okay," Ethan said. "I just wasn't expecting it somehow. No one's ever done that to me."

"Well, that's the hottest thing I've heard in a while." He massaged Ethan's ass with his hands for a bit and then gradually started with his mouth, pressing kisses to the cheeks and then going deeper, his warm mouth heating up everything it touched. He let his right hand wander, sometimes stroking Ethan's cock or fondling his balls, other times stretching up to play with his nipples. Ethan's whole body felt like it was strung tight, and his mind was a blank. He let himself get lost in the physical sensations until it was nearly unbearable. He needed something else, something more. Just when he thought he might scream, Charlie took his mouth away and replaced it with his fingers, probing and rubbing against his hole.

Ethan let out a long moan and reached back to touch Charlie's knee, which was just within reach. It was a relief, somehow, to be doing something rather than passively having things done to him. Charlie might have understood what he was feeling, or something like it, because he reached up to pull at Ethan's shoulder. Ethan knelt up and turned around to kiss him as he reached for Charlie's cock. It stood up hard and straining like Ethan's.

"What should I do?" Ethan asked.

"Lie back," Charlie said and stretched out next to him. They kissed some more, not touching each other's cocks except incidentally. After a while Charlie said, "I don't suppose you have any lube here."

Ethan almost said no, but then he remembered picking some up on an impulse at the drugstore several months earlier. He'd told himself it would be good to have around—just in case—because sometimes women needed that. Not that he'd had any candidates in mind at the time. "Bottom drawer," he said, gesturing at the night stand. "Condoms too."

Charlie got both out, opened the condom packet and tossed it on the bed. He crawled around to face Ethan and pushed his knees back before squirting lube into his hand. He rubbed it around Ethan's hole and slowly pushed one of his fingers in, stretching him in a way that felt strange and not nearly as nice as his tongue. The longer he stayed in, the better it began to feel, especially when he wrapped his now-slick hand around Ethan's cock and pumped him slowly and steadily. More fingers were added, but Ethan barely noticed. All he felt was heat and pleasure. He had no concept of time by then. This could have been going on for ten minutes or two hours, for all he knew, when Charlie withdrew his hand and moved between Ethan's legs. He slid his cock into Ethan's ass crack and moved it back and forth across the hole, which made Ethan want to scream. He wanted nothing more than for Charlie to be inside of him. It seemed strange to him to want something so badly that he'd never even felt before.

"Please," he finally gasped.

Charlie was panting, his mouth hanging open as he stared down at Ethan. "Please what?"

"Do you want to know what I want you to do or are you trying to get me to call you sir?" Ethan said in an attempt to maintain his composure.

"Ha," Charlie said. "What do you want me to do? You have to tell me, or I won't do it."

"Fuck me," Ethan whispered. "Can you fuck me now?"

"Can I or will I?" Charlie asked, and Ethan stared at him. He could not be serious. "Kidding," Charlie said. "I'm going to fuck you now." He put the condom on and positioned himself to enter Ethan. "Don't forget to breathe," he said, and then he began to push in slowly. He stopped at intervals to let Ethan get used to the feeling, but each time he did, Ethan had the urge to push forward. All he wanted was for him to move, to really do it, but Charlie held him back every time. When he was all the way in, he asked, "Doing okay?"

"It feels so weird," Ethan said. "Not bad but...."

Charlie nodded and shifted so Ethan's hips were more elevated and the angle of penetration changed.

"Oh God," Ethan said. "Oh...."

Charlie began to move then, carefully but steadily. Every time he pushed back in, Ethan felt it again. He closed his eyes and gave himself over to it, and soon Charlie began to thrust harder, faster, until Ethan couldn't hold back a shout. Charlie paused and touched his stomach. "Good or bad?" he asked.

"Good," Ethan croaked, "So good." Charlie picked up the pace again, and Ethan couldn't keep quiet anymore. He uttered more inarticulate cries as the feeling built up. "Oh fuck, oh fuck," he yelled. He felt Charlie's hand come around him but before he could do anything, Ethan was coming harder than he ever remembered coming. It shot halfway up his stomach, flowing out of him, and it seemed to go on forever.

Charlie gave a few more thrusts and then pulled out, whipped the condom off and jacked himself off on Ethan's abs, pooling their fluids together. He collapsed at Ethan's side, breathing heavily.

Ethan felt strange, sort of hollow now. He noticed, almost absently, that he was trembling a little bit. Charlie rubbed his arm and said, "One sec." He heaved himself out of the bed and walked to the big master bathroom, coming out with a damp washcloth. He lay down again and brushed his fingers through Ethan's hair as he cleaned him up. When he'd tossed it aside, he pulled the covers up over both of them.

They lay quietly for a few minutes. Ethan was too wrung out to try to form words for a conversation. Finally, Charlie said, "Well, we learned something new about you tonight, I guess."

"Yeah. Does that mean I'm a bottom?" Ethan asked.

"Let's not jump to conclusions," Charlie said, grinning up at the ceiling.

"Are you hungry?" It was a non sequitur, but Ethan suddenly realized he was starving.

"I could eat."

"If you go get the menus from the kitchen, I'll order whatever you want, my treat," Ethan said. He was definitely not ready to get up yet. Charlie sprang out of bed and headed for the door. "Cupboard above the microwave!" Ethan called after him.

They ordered food from a Thai place and sat in bed eating it in their underwear. Ethan handed Charlie the remote control, and he started flipping through the stations, eventually landing on MSNBC. *All In With Chris Hayes* was on, and they watched for a few minutes without comment from either of them. He had a panel of three guests—Michael Steele, Sam Seder, and a woman Ethan didn't immediately recognize. He was paying more attention to his food than the television. It wasn't until she spoke that he jerked his head up and stared at the screen.

She looked a lot different than he remembered—more polished, her mass of dark curls corralled into a bun. She wore stylish glasses, which seemed to be part of that network's uniform. But now that he was paying attention, he knew it was Becca Jacobs, his college girlfriend and the architect of his current work stress. She was talking about the presidential race.

Charlie cleared his throat. "You want me to change this?"

Ethan sighed. "You know who she is?"

He shrugged. "I've read her blog from time to time. She's smart. Pretty insightful about politics."

Ethan narrowed his eyes at him. "And?"

Charlie looked down at his food and started picking through it with his fork. "I heard she might be the source of that story about you. I mean, I know about the rumor." He glanced up quickly. "That totally untrue, unfounded rumor that you like guys."

Ethan opened his mouth to protest but closed it immediately. He ate a few more bites of his food and said, "Fair enough. But the story is actually pretty much bullshit. I never had any threesome in college. It was stupid. We were on Ecstasy, if you want to know. It was dumb college shit. All we did was roll around on the grass."

"Really?"

"Why would I lie to you about it now?" Ethan asked. "But forget about that. It's almost a distinction without a difference if I'm being totally honest. I was attracted to that guy. I did want to kiss him, the drugs notwithstanding, so whatever. She still didn't have the right to tell anyone. It was a shitty thing to do, and I still can't understand why she did it."

"Did the relationship end badly?"

Ethan shook his head. "We both did the fade away if I recall correctly. It was fifteen years ago, and it wasn't anything serious anyway."

"I'm sorry. You're right. She shouldn't have done that." He moved closer to lean up against Ethan. "She's quite striking," he said.

"She looks better now than she did back then. I went out with her mainly because I thought she was cooler than me."

"Clearly," Charlie said.

He stayed another hour or so, and they each had a glass of the ridiculously expensive—and admittedly delicious—scotch he'd gotten from Vince Martin for his first Christmas at ECHO. They switched from cable news to some British detective show neither of them was particularly interested in, but Charlie put his arm around him, and they sat together watching it. Ethan nodded off by the end, and Charlie had to nudge him awake.

"I have to go," he said.

Ethan yawned and grabbed his phone from the nightstand. "I'll get you an Uber."

"You don't need to do that. I always take the subway home."

Ethan shook his head. "It's late."

"Ethan, I'm a big boy. I can handle my own transportation."

"Yeah, I know. Could you let me do this, though? I'd really like to. Tonight was… well, it was great. And this is no big deal." He shrugged. "I make a lot of money doing something I feel sort of conflicted about, okay? Let me spend it on something that makes me happy."

"Well, when you put it that way." Charlie pulled him by the shoulder and kissed him lightly on the lips. "Thanks."

# Chapter Four

CHARLIE COULD think of little other than Ethan for the entire next day. It was distracting, and he kept losing his train of thought while talking to his students. Ethan was so different from what Charlie might have expected from a closeted conservative news host. For one thing, he was willing to be led and didn't insist on being "the man." His honesty about his lack of experience had been disarming. For another thing, thankfully, the ideology seemed to be irrelevant to him. Not that Charlie thought it was okay to work at a place like that when you didn't agree with the things you had to say. It struck him as cynical and irresponsible at best, soul-damaging at worst, but at least politics shouldn't be too much of an issue between them.

He pulled himself up short when he realized what he was envisioning was an actual relationship. His brain had conjured an image of the two of them lounging on a cream-colored sofa in a loft somewhere with brick walls and floor to ceiling windows, newspapers spread across a coffee table. It was most likely something he'd seen in a print ad for a laptop or something and internalized as a romantic ideal. Newspapers? Honestly.

But he did plan to see Ethan again, that was for certain. It was the best sex he'd had in a long time, part of which was definitely Ethan's responsiveness. He wasn't jaded yet and didn't feel the need—or possibly have the ability—to act bored by the whole thing. It had also been a while since he'd been with someone who really loved bottoming. Lately he'd run across a string of guys who were strict tops and wanted to boss him around. That wasn't Charlie's thing, regardless of his role.

Ethan was funny too, in a subtle way Charlie enjoyed. He wasn't constantly trying to get in good lines, but he found his spots. He was self-deprecating in a way that conveyed modesty rather than self-loathing, and it was disarmingly attractive. And holy fuck was he gorgeous. He was beautiful in a slightly off-kilter way that translated best in motion. The still pictures Charlie had seen of him on buses and billboards never did him justice, but on television he was golden. In person, Charlie found him astonishingly hot.

Charlie realized he was doing it again. He was picturing them walking around at some kind of outdoor festival, fall leaves glowing in the October sunshine. What the hell was he thinking? Cozy sofas and apple picking? Next it would be an evening meal with a crowd of friends in the backyard of a brownstone, lanterns strung up above the long, beautifully set wooden picnic table. He was having some sort of monogamous gay fever dream.

He decided if he wanted to stop obsessing over this stuff, he needed to unburden himself to someone. He wouldn't tell anyone who it was—not yet—but he could at least explain the situation. During his planning period, he went down to the first floor to the art classroom. The class was busy working on what looked like pointillism projects, and Josh sat at his desk looking at his phone. Charlie waved at him to get his attention, but he was absorbed. Eventually Charlie was flailing his arm frantically with no success until finally one of the students said, "Mr. Carpenter? I think maybe Mr. Woods wants to talk to you." The entire classroom burst into laughter.

Josh looked up, startled, and grinned at Charlie. "Get back to work, you brats," he said as he hurried over to the door. He came out into the hallway and closed the door behind him. "What's up?"

"I need to talk to you. Can you get drinks after work?"

"Sure," Josh replied. "Why didn't you text me, though?"

"Oh," Charlie said, shrugging. "I just wanted to make sure you could do it."

Josh got a smile on his face like he knew something. "You wanted to tell me whatever this is right now, didn't you? Something good happened, huh?"

Charlie did his best to keep himself from smiling helplessly but was not successful at all. "Okay, yeah. But I can't get into it here. I need to tell you about someone I met."

"Wow," Josh said. "Seriously? I can't remember the last time you wanted to tell me about someone."

"Yeah. I know. I'm kind of freaking out about it."

Josh raised his eyebrows at him and said, "Meet you down here as soon as you can get out. Don't fuck around up there like you normally do."

They ended up going back to McShea's, which ordinarily might have bothered Charlie. He found places like that sort of depressing, but today he didn't care at all. He bought a round of drinks for them and sat down across from Josh.

"So? Who is this guy?" Josh asked.

Charlie opened his mouth to answer but all at once realized he wasn't sure what he could say. Technically, of course, he had a right to say whatever he wanted to. It was his life too. Ethan hadn't asked, and Charlie hadn't agreed to keep any secrets, but he still got the feeling Ethan wouldn't want his name being used.

"He's… well, I don't want to tell you yet," Charlie said.

"What the hell are you talking about? You're the one who said you wanted to tell me all about this dude. Why are you keeping secrets?" His face darkened. "It's not Brady, is it?" he asked. Brady was Josh's ex. They were together for two years, but it ended badly.

"No! Jesus. It's no one you know. I want to wait a little while to tell you his name, all right?"

"I guess, weirdo. You are so squirrelly about relationships. So can you tell me what he does?"

"He's…." Charlie sighed and shook his head. He couldn't tell him that either.

Josh looked at him quietly for a few moments. "Right," he said softly, "so what can you tell me? What is it you like so much about him?"

"We've hooked up twice. Once when he was way too drunk, but the other time he wasn't at all. He… he's not very experienced with men." Charlie glanced at Josh to gauge his reaction. He could hear the way it must be sounding to him. Josh didn't say a word, so Charlie went on. "He's funny and so hot and I just… I just like him," he finished lamely. Meeting Josh's eyes now, he said, "Go on. I can tell you have something to say."

"Charlie…." Josh sighed and rubbed his forehead. "It's obvious this guy, whoever he is, is in the closet. Right?"

"For right now," Charlie said, "he's in a difficult position." He could hear how weak that sounded, but he pressed on. "He's going to come out eventually." As he said it, he realized he had no idea if that were true. But it had to be—if they were going to see more of each other, there was no way he could keep it secret for long.

"Oh he is? For you, you mean? Do you hear yourself? You know what you sound like? A mistress. 'He'll leave his wife for me because he loves me oh so much.'" His eyes widened and he said, "Shit—is he married?"

Charlie looked away and took a sip of his drink. "Not currently," he muttered.

"You can't even tell your best friend the name of the person you're seeing. When was the last time that happened? High school? You know what this is, right? What it means for you?"

Charlie looked down and nodded. "It's Ethan," he said quietly. "His name is Ethan." He looked back up at Josh. "It's Ethan Daniels."

Josh's mouth fell open. "No fucking way," he breathed.

"I know," Charlie said, "and I hear you. I understand why you're saying it. I'd say the exact same thing to you. I want to give this a little time. I want to see what happens. He's—God, he's just…."

Josh rolled his eyes. "I know what he's just. He's just gorgeous. He's just sexy. If that's it, then I get it. But it kind of seems like you think it's more than that."

Charlie shook his head. "I don't think it's anything. Not yet."

"Not until he's ready to be honest," Josh said. "Promise me."

"Yeah, of course. I promise."

Josh reached across the table and smacked him in the head. "You can't promise that, idiot. The fact that you think you can, makes it clear you're not going to be able to handle this." He looked at his glass, which was empty, and said, "I'm getting us more drinks."

He came back with two shots and two beers. "We're doing these shots, and then you're going to give me all the gory details."

Charlie stared at him. "You're the one who was being all disapproving of it. You're seriously going to get all high and mighty and then ask for a play-by-play?"

"Shut up and drink your whiskey. Go on." Josh picked up his shot glass and tossed it back.

Charlie shrugged and drank his too, chasing it with a long drink of beer. He never much liked doing shots and felt slightly nauseated from it. "Look, I don't feel right about telling you all that shit. We hooked up twice. The first time he blew me. The second time I fucked him. And that's it. That's all you're getting."

"He's a bottom?" Josh asked, leaning forward. "Nice."

"I feel weird even telling you that much. I probably shouldn't have. Josh… I know this is going to bother you, and I hate even asking but—"

"But don't tell anyone about your secret gay boyfriend? I'm not going to out someone, Charlie. Even that asshole. But you need to take a good look at what's happening here."

"He's really not an asshole," Charlie said. "He just plays one on TV."

They finished their beers and headed off on their separate ways home. Charlie couldn't stop thinking about what Josh had said. There was no way to argue with any of it. But maybe he'd been making assumptions. Maybe Ethan would decide to come out, sooner rather than later. Maybe they wouldn't have to hide. As he walked to the subway, Charlie pulled out his phone and sent Ethan a text asking him if he wanted to go out Friday night. If they could actually go out for drinks and be seen together in public, it would make Charlie feel a lot better.

A minute later a response came in.

*Wish I could, but I have Fiona on the weekends.*

Charlie felt horribly disappointed—way more than he'd expected—but after another minute he heard the text ping again.

*How about tonight? Don't want to wait longer than I have to.*

Grinning like an idiot, Charlie stopped in the middle of the sidewalk to text him back.

*This time my neighborhood. Meet me at seven.*

He added the address and sent it off. He stood there for another few seconds rereading the message until some guy bumped into him and muttered, "Good place to hang out, asshole," as he walked ahead.

Charlie had a shower as soon as he got home and started thinking of places he could take Ethan. He probably wouldn't want to go anywhere too busy where there would be a higher chance of being recognized. Then again, a more intimate place might make it obvious they were on a date. Eventually he decided on a bar about two blocks from his place. It was a trendy place that made good cocktails and served pretentious food, but it wasn't romantic.

Charlie changed out of his school clothes into jeans and a black T-shirt that he threw a button-up checked shirt over. Looking at himself in the mirror, he thought maybe it looked like he was trying too hard to look like he didn't care. He exchanged the shirt for a slim jacket and then was pretty sure he looked stupid. He then scrapped the whole thing and wore the checked shirt from the first outfit. As if Ethan cared what he was wearing anyway. He'd probably still be in his suit from work.

A text came in at about quarter to seven. It was Ethan saying he was going to be half an hour late. When he finally showed up—almost forty-five minutes late, in fact—he was dressed in jeans and a black sweater. His hair was even a little mussed from the wind. Charlie just blinked at him at first because he looked almost like a different person. He looked a lot younger, for one thing, and less imposing.

"Sorry I'm so late," he said. "I wanted to change so I went home first, but then I wasn't sure what to wear. I don't know where we're going." He smiled and said, "Can I come in or what?"

"Yeah," Charlie said, finally smiling at him. He stood aside to let him through the door. "You look nice."

"So do you," Ethan said. He came up fast on Charlie, held him by the waist and leaned in to kiss him as soon as the door was closed.

Charlie's response was immediate. His dick hardened as Ethan pressed himself against Charlie's body. Ethan didn't let up for some time. He slipped his hands under Charlie's shirt and rubbed his thumbs across the nipples, lowering his head to suck on Charlie's neck. When Ethan fell to his knees, Charlie decided they could go out later. He wasn't hungry anyway.

Ethan unzipped Charlie's pants and pulled out his cock. He licked it and rubbed it across his mouth before sinking lower to mouth his balls. He stroked the shaft as he did that and raised his eyes to meet Charlie's.

"Steep learning curve," Charlie murmured down to him.

Ethan smiled and raised up to take his cock in. He let Charlie press against the back of his throat, this time managing to keep the gagging to a minimum. Maybe being sober was helpful. Like before, Ethan reached into his own pants and began to touch himself, but he seemed to be in much better control this time.

Charlie leaned against the wall and looked down at him. He stroked his fingers through Ethan's hair and watched him pump his hard cock up and down. When Charlie let his hand slide down to caress the side of his face, Ethan let out a soft moan and leaned into the touch. It was a sweet gesture Charlie hadn't expected at all.

"Hey," Charlie said, tightening his fingers slightly in Ethan's hair. Ethan raised his eyes. "Stop for a minute."

Ethan pulled off, panting, and sat back on his heels. "What's up?"

"Let's go into the bedroom. Take our time."

"Don't you want to go out?" Ethan asked.

"Later," Charlie said.

They walked to Charlie's room and took off their clothes without speaking. They knelt on the bed, and Charlie took Ethan's face in his hands. He kissed him and pulled him down, hooking a knee over Ethan's legs and pulling him in close. Ethan wrapped an arm around him and pressed his hand to the small of Charlie's back. His eyes fixed on Charlie's, holding him in a steady gaze until Charlie felt the need to close his. This was so intimate.

Charlie didn't do this—ever. Not since his first and only real boyfriend. That had been in college and when it ended in a storm of drama and betrayal, he'd decided to take a break from relationships. He hadn't intended for it to turn into a permanent break, but he'd found he liked it. He hurt no one and no one hurt him and he got all the sex he wanted. Anything more than that, he figured, was what friends were for. Of course that wasn't entirely true, and sometimes a little voice would pipe up and remind him. Coffee and sofas and the *Times* and all—that was couple stuff. But he knew none of it was real, so he was always able to silence the voice. What was happening right now with

Ethan, was something else. This feeling was some other thing he'd been missing without even realizing. He wasn't entirely sure he could handle it.

He felt Ethan's hand come around his cock and begin to move, so Charlie did the same to him. They lay side by side, lazily kissing and touching each other, for a long time. Charlie would have been happy to stay right there and come that way, but after some time, Ethan asked, "Will you suck me?" and Charlie realized he hadn't actually done that yet. He'd intended to on the first night, but Ethan had jumped the gun.

"Of course," Charlie said. He started to move down, but Ethan grabbed him and kissed him hard first.

"I like you a lot," Ethan said.

Charlie stared at him for a second and then smiled and nodded. "Me too," he said. That was okay. He could say he liked him. It was pretty obvious anyway, and it didn't have to mean anything more. He sat up and leaned over, draping himself across Ethan's stomach to get at his cock. He hadn't looked too carefully at it before, but he took a moment now. It wasn't huge, but it was pretty—well proportioned and rock hard, maybe slightly longer than average. He cupped Ethan's balls and stroked his fingers behind them as he slid his mouth over the head. Ethan grunted and strained upward. Charlie didn't mind. He sucked him slowly, getting into a nice rhythm as Ethan stroked his back, sometimes moaning or saying, "Yes," and "That's good." Then he let his fingers trail down into the crack of his ass, rubbing and pressing into his hole. Ethan suddenly jerked and grabbed his hair roughly.

"Stop," Ethan said, becoming rigidly still, and then, "shit." He pushed Charlie's head down and bucked up hard several times. Charlie felt the come hit the back of his throat and heard Ethan's long, guttural groan.

Ethan touched his shoulder. "What do you want me to do?" he asked, after a moment.

Charlie stared at him for a second and then said, "You tell me."

Ethan sat up against the headboard. "Come here. Lie back on me."

Charlie smiled and said, "That sounds nice." He turned around and let Ethan pull him in and encircle him with his arms. Ethan's body felt hard and strong against his back and his mouth was warm and wet on Charlie's neck. The hand that came around his cock was sure and steady, confident of his abilities at least in this area. Ethan's other hand roamed across his chest, brushing against his nipples. "That's good," Charlie said softly, "feels so good."

Ethan picked up his speed, and Charlie pressed his body back into Ethan's as he felt himself nearing the finish. He wanted to get closer, as close as he could, and Ethan responded by holding him tighter. Charlie turned his head to catch Ethan's mouth in a sloppy kiss. "Gonna come," he said, not to warn him but just because he wanted to hear himself say it. He cried out and rocked into Ethan's fist, the whole time holding on to the arm wrapped around his waist. When he'd finished, his entire body went limp against Ethan.

Ethan's arms slackened but stayed around him. They stayed where they were for what felt like a long time. Charlie had no desire to move from the warm, relaxed embrace and had begun to doze off when Ethan spoke into his ear, saying, "Should we get dressed and go out?"

Charlie grunted softly and snuggled in closer. "We can if you want to. Are you hungry?"

"Not really," Ethan said. He began to absently rub his fingers in Charlie's hair. "Maybe in a little while."

"I should get cleaned up," Charlie said. "I'll be right back."

He got up and went to the bathroom for a washcloth, then into the kitchen to grab two beers. When he got back to the bedroom, Ethan had put on his shorts but was still sitting in the bed. Charlie handed him the beer and sat next to him.

"So…," Ethan began. He sounded almost nervous, like he was about to say something unpleasant. Charlie thought he might know what it was. "We've had sex three times now, and I feel like I should—"

"Ethan, it's fine," Charlie interrupted. "I don't expect anything from you. This can just be sex; it's okay."

Ethan went silent, staring at him for a few seconds before looking away and taking a sip from his bottle. "That's not what I was going to say."

"Oh. I'm sorry. What were you going to say?"

Ethan shook his head. "Doesn't matter."

It looked like it mattered, though. Charlie thought about the sex they'd had, and he knew it hadn't felt like nothing, at least to him. It had felt like there could be something more there, but it had been so long since that had happened for him, it was difficult to process. Maybe Ethan had felt the same thing. "Please don't do that," he said. "I want to hear what you were going to say. I shouldn't have assumed."

Ethan gave a short laugh and said, "I was thinking we should get to know each other a little bit. Because, you know, I was hoping we could keep doing this for a while. I can have sex that's just sex. If that's what you want. But I'm not sure how long I can keep it up. Eventually I'm going to start feeling stuff. Or at least—at least I want to be friends. Otherwise, it's just...." He sighed. "I haven't really done that. Maybe because it's a lot harder to do when you date women. A one-night stand is one thing, but if you keep going back, they expect something more. But I guess I sort of feel that way too."

"Huh," Charlie said, thinking of his own experiences. "It's funny, but I think I do too. That's probably why I hardly ever see anyone more than two or three times. I never thought about it like that."

Ethan nodded. "So do you want to stop this?"

"No," Charlie replied immediately and without any thought. "I like you."

"Okay." Ethan drank some more beer and then asked, "Do you have any siblings?"

Charlie laughed and looked at him. "Changing the subject?"

"I want to know something about you."

"Oh, I see." Charlie put his beer on the nightstand and slid down onto his pillow. "Yeah. I have a sister and three older brothers. I'm the baby."

"Wow, five kids. That seems crazy."

"My parents were religious. Catholics. I mean, they're not dead or anything. They're just not religious anymore. I think it was my mom who was so into it, but then she had some kind of crisis of faith when I was little and gave it up. Stopped going to church, stopped the older kids' religious education, everything."

"Seems like a lucky break for you, if you think about it," Ethan said.

"Oh, I've thought about it, believe me. The thing is, it was a little more complicated than that. After she dropped the church stuff, my parents got divorced. And then she came out about a year later."

Ethan's eyebrows shot up. He moved down to lie on his side, propped up on his elbow. "Before you did?"

"Yeah, this was when I was like five. It was probably pretty weird for my brothers and sister, but I wasn't fully aware of what was happening. By the time I understood, everything had settled down. My dad's remarried, and my mom has been with the same woman for about ten years. We do holidays together." He shrugged. "What about you?"

"Jeez, pretty boring compared to your story. I'm an only child. My parents are still together. Not sure they particularly like each other, but they're hanging in there. I wasn't raised in any religion. My mom was raised Methodist, and my dad is Jewish, but neither of them seemed to care about any of it, so I don't know much about either of those traditions. The only Jewish thing we did was eat Chinese food on Christmas."

Charlie smiled at that rather cute detail. "Where did you grow up?"

"In Philadelphia. You?"

"South Jersey," Charlie said. "Actually, I used to see you on the local news when I'd go home and visit my family. I had a little crush on you back then."

"I guess my move to ECHO destroyed it, huh?"

"Temporarily," Charlie said. He rolled onto his side and reached for Ethan. Ethan responded by moving closer and kissing him. "I used to hate-watch you sometimes on ECHO. Not that you're the worst one or anything, but I hated you the most because I had liked you before."

"I'm sorry," Ethan said.

"I don't do it anymore. I don't want to get mad at you for that. It wouldn't be fair. It's not like I went into this not knowing who you are."

Ethan winced and flopped onto his back. "I don't like it, you know. I don't believe that stuff. I do my best to be responsible about how I report things. But I'm already operating within a set narrative, so everything I say is coming from that perspective."

"Why did you go to work for them, then?" Charlie honestly couldn't understand it. He knew it paid well, but he couldn't imagine working for those people for any amount of money.

"I was happy doing what I was doing on local news. I never had big ambitions. I'd had offers before, but I never wanted to disrupt my life that much. Then Deirdre moved here," Ethan said. "She had custody of Fiona, so she took her along. I could have stayed where I was and seen my daughter on weekends, but it would have been hard, and I wouldn't have been as involved in her life, and that's not how I wanted it to be. The offer from ECHO came at exactly the right time, and I didn't feel like I had much of a choice."

Charlie was quiet for a while as he digested this information. It seemed like a justification, but it wasn't a terrible one. He believed him about it not being about the money, although undoubtedly the money was a plus. "I guess that makes sense," he said finally, because it did. He still didn't like it, but at least he could understand it.

"What about you?" Ethan asked. "Was it always your goal to teach privileged six-year-olds to read?"

"Oh please, they already know how to read. Parents like the ones we get are competitive. They all have to have the cutest, smartest, most talented kid of all."

"You're talking like I'm not one of them."

Charlie shrugged. "It's not a bad thing, really. They take an interest and there's nothing wrong with that. They just go overboard sometimes. But you and—you guys seem to be relatively normal. It's refreshing."

Ethan tilted his head. "Does it bother you to talk about her?"

"No, but I don't know how to refer to her. I call her Ms. McNaughton at the school. You call her Deirdre."

"You called her my wife back at the school," Ethan said.

"Well, I was mad at you." Charlie surged up suddenly and straddled Ethan's hips. "Now I'm not." Charlie leaned down to kiss him and began to lightly move back and forth against Ethan's boxer-clad groin. Charlie hadn't bothered to put any clothes back on. He began to get hard as he felt Ethan respond to the friction.

"Are you going to fuck me this time?" Ethan asked.

"Do you want me to?"

"God, yes."

Charlie grinned and kept kissing him and grinding against him. "I could do that. I want to tell you what I'm going do to you. Do you like that?"

Ethan's cock pulsed. "I think I would, yeah."

"First, I'll lick your asshole. Remember when I did it to you the first time?"

"Yeah…." Ethan panted. "I loved that. Do it."

"Be patient," Charlie said. He sat back and palmed the bulge in Ethan's shorts, dragging his hand up and down. "After I eat your ass, I'm going to suck your dick while I put my fingers inside you."

"Oh God, please."

Charlie peeled down Ethan's boxer briefs and tossed them aside. "And then what?" he asked.

"Then you'll fuck me."

"You want me inside you?"

"Yes," Ethan groaned.

Charlie leaned over and kissed him. He wrapped his long fingers around both of their cocks and began to stroke them together. He could feel that Ethan was on the verge. It seemed unlikely he'd last much longer. "I could do all that," Charlie said, "or I could make you come right now."

Ethan closed his eyes, and Charlie felt him swell in his hand. He let himself go too, and they went over the edge together as Ethan grabbed his head and crushed their mouths together.

"Jesus Christ," Ethan muttered. "I don't know what's wrong with me. I'm not usually so quick on the draw. I wanted to last a lot longer."

Charlie rubbed his chest. "No problem. I was actually kind of tired from before. I did that on purpose."

"It's still weird. It's like I've never had sex before."

"Well, how long has it been since you last had sex?"

"Jesus," Ethan said. "You have a point there. It's been well over a year."

Charlie nodded. "Besides, it makes a certain kind of sense, doesn't it? It's a new kind of sex for you, which in a way might be like you've never had sex." He reached over the side of the bed and grabbed his own underwear to mop up the come, then settled his head on Ethan's shoulder. "I'm sure it will resolve itself, so let's not worry about it."

"All right." He turned his head so his nose was buried in Charlie's hair. "Hey, I'm actually kind of hungry now."

"Me too, but I don't feel much like getting dressed. Should we just raid my cabinets?"

Ethan snorted. "Is that a euphemism? Because I think that's what I wanted you to do to me before you tricked me."

"I tricked you into blowing your load like a teenager?" Charlie said. "What a jerk."

Ethan sat up, dumping Charlie onto the bed. "I'll find something. You wait here." He walked out into the kitchen naked.

Charlie tossed his underpants into the hamper and put on a clean pair along with a T-shirt. He sat down on the bed and picked up his phone to find he had three texts from Josh. The first one said, *I'm sorry I rained on your parade. I was worried.*

About forty-five minutes later, one came in that read, *OMG. Did you end up seeing him tonight?*

The last one, twenty minutes later, was, *Text me when he leaves so I know you're okay.*

That seemed overly dramatic even for Josh. Ethan was a closeted bisexual news personality, not a serial killer. He texted back.

*Everything's fine. He's in the kitchen finding food for us.*

*Don't let him stay over. It's a bad idea.*

Charlie turned off his phone. Josh didn't understand the whole situation. Of course it looked bad from his perspective, but he didn't know Ethan. Josh couldn't see the way his face looked when he was about to come. He didn't feel the way Ethan kissed him or the way his voice changed when they were talking in bed afterward.

He could hear Ethan banging around in his kitchen, but he decided against investigating. Whatever he brought, Charlie would eat. He liked having Ethan there, in his space and using his stuff. He very much wanted him to stay over, and he couldn't even remember the last time he'd even come close to wanting that. Usually he couldn't wait to get a guy out of his apartment.

Ethan brought in grilled cheese sandwiches and the half bottle of white wine from the fridge, along with two glasses. "I'm not an accomplished chef, I admit," he said.

Charlie smiled up at him. "I love grilled cheese. Plus I know the only cheese I had in there was that expensive taleggio, so they have to be good."

"I'll buy you more cheese if you want," Ethan said. He poured wine into the glasses and handed one to Charlie.

"Ooh, you'll be my cheese daddy?"

"All the cheeses for you, baby," Ethan said. He took a bite of his sandwich and said, "Mmm. Damn, this is great cheese."

"Only the best. What else would I do with my extravagant salary?"

"Speaking of that, I think you avoided answering one of my questions earlier, about becoming a teacher. Was that intentional?"

Charlie sipped his wine. "I don't know. Maybe. I'm a little conflicted about it, to be honest. I started out as an acting major. I was in a few plays and I don't think I was bad, but I guess I didn't have the all-consuming fire about it some people have. Plus… you know, my family is all pretty practical. I grew up working class. My brothers are, respectively, a cop, an accountant, and an electrical contractor. My sister is a nurse. It felt wrong to me to not have something to count on, so I got a degree in education. I figured it would be a fallback, but what I didn't understand was that when you have a fallback, you usually end up falling back on it. It's less terrifying. But then something weird happened, and I realized I actually loved it."

"So you're happy? Not secretly longing for the boards?"

"I'm happier than a lot of people. Maybe most people. I like my job and I have friends. I always wanted to live in New York, and now I do."

"I never got that," Ethan said, "wanting so much to live here. You could get a much bigger place somewhere else on whatever it is you make."

Charlie nodded. "I've started to come around to that idea in the last couple years. I might not be here forever. Then again, I don't have any other ideas at the moment."

They finished eating, and Charlie took the dishes out to the kitchen. When he got back to the room he found Ethan putting his shirt on. He looked up when Charlie walked in. "Hey," he said. "I thought I should get going."

"Oh. You—okay. But you could stay. I mean, if you want to. I wouldn't mind."

Ethan stopped buttoning his shirt halfway up. "You wouldn't mind? Or you want me to?"

"I guess I really want you to."

Ethan smiled and started unbuttoning. "I'll have to leave pretty early," he said.

"If it's too much trouble—"

"That's not what I said," Ethan interrupted. "All I meant was I should get some sleep if I'm staying."

"The wine made me sleepy anyway," Charlie said. He pushed back the covers and got under. Ethan followed and lay down next to him.

"Good night," Ethan said.

"Night." Charlie turned out the lights and turned onto his side to sleep. After a restless few minutes, he reached back to touch Ethan's hand with the tips of his fingers. That was apparently all the encouragement Ethan needed to roll over and press himself up against Charlie's back. Charlie wasn't sure if he could sleep like that, but then Ethan kissed him on the shoulder, and he knew there was no way he was going to move.

"Your tattoo," Ethan mumbled, just as he was drifting off. "I get it. For your family."

"Yeah," Charlie whispered.

"That's nice," he said and then fell silent. As Ethan's breath evened out with sleep and the space between them warmed up, he found himself lulled by the comfort. He let his mind shut off, and he drifted into sleep.

# Chapter Five

ETHAN'S MORNING had started even earlier than he'd planned, but for a good cause. Charlie had woken him up and done all the things he'd promised to do the night before. He'd already fallen back to sleep by the time Ethan was dressed and ready to leave. Ethan had never felt so torn. Part of him wanted to crawl back into the bed with Charlie, call in sick, and convince him to do the same so they could spend the whole day together. The other part wished he'd left the night before so he could keep thinking of this as simply something crazy he'd decided to do for a while, but which would shortly be coming to an end.

He took a cab back to his building and went upstairs to shower and get ready. He went through his morning routine on autopilot while he thought about what was happening with this relationship.

Staying over might have been a mistake. He'd been taken by surprise when Charlie asked him to stay, because he'd gotten the idea that he wasn't the type to get involved. He'd been expecting to be kept at arm's length for however long this thing lasted. For some reason Charlie had decided—or felt compelled—to let him get close, and the truth was that Ethan liked it. He'd solicited it and encouraged it. Even though he knew it was a bad idea, he wanted to get closer to this person he'd felt so drawn to from the first moment he'd looked at him.

The intense physical pleasure they'd shared had also taken him by surprise. He hadn't expected the sex to be so intimate. He certainly hadn't expected to like being fucked in the ass as much as he apparently did. Having someone inside you was a strange combination of power and utter vulnerability. It was hard to describe, but he wondered if that was how women felt about it. Of course, there was no one he could ask about such a thing.

He hadn't even been sure he'd ever want to try it, but now he thought he wouldn't mind it every time. He'd think about it randomly during the day and feel his dick start to get hard like some twelve-year-old kid. It was embarrassing but also amazing that something—someone—could make him feel this way. He'd gotten the feeling Charlie might like it sometime too, but it was intimidating. He didn't want to do it wrong and hurt him or have him not enjoy it. Although the thought of sticking his face in Charlie's ass was kind of a turn-on.

He shifted his half-hard cock in his pants before returning to his shaving. *Ridiculous*, he thought. *I am ridiculous.*

He spent the day feeling detached from everything and everyone around him. He did his job and answered people when they asked him things, but the whole time he was acutely aware of his body and the lingering sensations from that morning. He wanted to text Charlie and ask him to do something that same evening, but he knew that was the wrong move. Nobody likes desperate. Then again, it was his turn because Charlie had asked him out last. He figured that was probably the rule—he had no way of knowing for sure since the last time he'd dated, there wasn't much in the way of texting. But he'd wait until the following day, at least. Maybe they could make plans for Sunday night.

Abby came in with lunch—she hadn't asked this time, just brought him a turkey sandwich—and paused at the door when she was leaving. "Did something happen to you, Ethan?" she asked. "You're acting a little spacey today."

"I'm fine," he said. "I've got a lot on my mind."

She closed the door and walked over to sit in the chair nearest him. "Have you seen that guy again?"

It was fairly presumptuous of her to ask, but then again he had blurted it out to her before and she'd been nice about it. It was good to have someone to talk to. Maybe it would keep him from turning it into a disaster.

"Yes," he said. "Two more times."

"And you want to see him again?"

Ethan nodded as he unwrapped his lunch. "Honestly, I kind of want to see him all the time. It's like that, you know? That stage. But it seems way too soon. I don't want to freak him out, for one thing. And also…." Ethan sighed and shook his head. "Also, I don't have much to offer someone like him."

Abby frowned at him. "What are you talking about? Ethan, I'm going to be honest with you now, and you probably already knew this, but you are one of the most attractive men I've ever seen in person. You're also smart, rich, and a pretty decent guy despite what you do for a living. You have a lot to offer. How do you not see that?"

"What I do for a living is the problem. I can't come out. I can't be with him in the way I'm sure he'd want me to—need me to. You can't conduct a real relationship like this. It's probably unfair of me to even keep seeing him at all. If I were decent, I'd tell him that, but…."

"But you like him a lot. Obviously. Are you seriously going to let Vince Martin dictate the way you conduct your personal life? It's not worth it. This place. Even if it weren't for this guy, it might be some other guy. You can't live like that—for yourself, not anyone else."

Ethan shook his head. "I can't right now. I can't do what I'd need to do. It would fuck up everything in my life."

"Not everything," she said. "Some things might get a lot better."

"Yeah," Ethan said, "but not my relationship with my kid. I took this job so I could be close to her. I can't throw it in the trash because I feel like screwing someone who's inconvenient."

Her expression changed. Her eyebrows drew down, and she pressed her lips together. "That sounds like self-serving bullshit to me, Ethan. I said before, I thought you were a decent guy, but you're not doing the decent thing here. You're trying to have your cake and eat it too, and you're going to hurt someone in the process—someone you're clearly getting attached to already. If you feel that way, don't you think it's possible he's having similar feelings?"

"I don't know," Ethan said. "I think he sleeps around a lot. This is a big deal for me for all kinds of reasons, but it might not be the same for him."

"I don't believe you," Abby said. "I don't think you believe yourself either." She stood up. "You do what you need to do. I can't listen to this anymore. It's making me think less of you. Let me know if you need anything." She walked out, closing the door a little harder than necessary.

Every day, Ethan would think about texting Charlie, and each time he'd remember what Abby had said to him. She'd been acting differently with him since their conversation. She was extremely competent and professional as always, but not friendly. She didn't ask him how he was or joke with him about how he was going to approach certain guests. That absence made him acutely aware of how few friends he had.

He'd been on good terms with his colleagues in Philadelphia and would go out for drinks or meals with them. They weren't close confidants, but they were good company. The culture at this network was nothing like that. It was highly competitive and socializing wasn't something that happened often. His producers had made a few overtures in the beginning to invite him out for drinks, but he always declined. Now he regretted that because he ended up spending a lot of evenings alone.

He was spending Thursday evening in just that way—binge-watching *House of Cards* and eating an entire bag of purple grapes—when he heard a text come in. When he saw it was Charlie, he got a jolt of excitement followed by a sick feeling of guilt. He should have been the one to text.

The text said, *Hey, how are you?*

Ethan texted back. *Okay. Sorry I haven't texted. Been really busy.*

The reply didn't come in for a few minutes. It read, *Sure. I was wondering if you felt like making plans to do something.*

Ethan wanted nothing more than to text back and say *Just come over right now. I miss you.* He didn't.

What he did say was, *Monday night okay? Drinks after work?*

The response said, *Sure. I can stay after school to get some work done. You can meet me there when you're finished.*

The next night was his date with Willa, which he'd been half dreading since agreeing to it. She had texted him the name of a bar that struck him as a weird-sounding place for some fashionable, youngish hairdresser to be taking him. It was called the Hunt Club. It wasn't until the night of the date that he looked it up for directions and saw it was, rather than the stuffy, old-money place suggested by the name, a trendy new gay bar in the West Village.

Ethan's first reaction was to laugh. It wasn't often that irony presented itself in such a blatant way. Then he felt panic and considered canceling the date. The last thing he needed was to be seen or even photographed walking into a bar like that. Why the fuck was she taking him to a gay bar anyway? What kind of weird first date was that?

In the end he decided to go. If he was going to back out, he should have done it at least a day in advance and not two hours before they were supposed to meet. He put on jeans and an understated black shirt, ran his fingers through his hair so it wasn't too tidy and chose a brown suede jacket. Before he walked out the door, as an afterthought, he grabbed a scarf and wrapped it around his neck the way he'd seen Charlie wear them. He hoped no one would recognize him if he looked like some kind of hipster.

He was relieved to find it wasn't a loud or outrageous kind of bar. It was surprisingly nice inside—warm colors and lots of natural wood—and not crowded yet, as it was only eight o'clock. He got a few lingering looks and one from someone who seemed to recognize him before spotting the gorgeous black woman waving to him from a high-top table along the wall toward the back of the room. She had a glass of red wine sitting in front of her. Deirdre hadn't mentioned she was so beautiful. In fact, he recalled her saying "intelligent and a great conversationalist," which from some people (men, mostly) would have been code for unattractive.

She stood up when he approached the table, flashing him a dazzling smile. He shook her hand and they said hello. "I was wondering if you'd come," she said as they sat back down.

"You mean because of the venue?" Ethan asked, gesturing at the room. "Were you trying to get me not to come? Or was it a test?"

"Well, no. Not a test, exactly." She ran her finger around the rim of her glass and looked up at him from under her lashes. "I figured it would be a good vetting process for both of us. If you have a problem hanging around with gay men, you shouldn't be with me. I'm a hairdresser. I have a lot of gay colleagues and friends. If you asked to go somewhere else or didn't show up, then I'd know."

"That sounds a lot like a test," Ethan said, smiling at her.

"Which it seems you've passed," she said. "I'm pleased but a little bit surprised. Deirdre told me you weren't like you seem on TV, but it's kind of hard to imagine."

Ethan nodded. "That's fair enough, I suppose." He glanced up at the bar. "I'm going to get myself a drink. Can I get you anything?"

"Not yet. I have a tab going. I'd like to buy you a drink since you were such a good sport about meeting me here."

Ethan hesitated, wondering if this was yet another test. Was he supposed to accept or refuse? He decided to roll the dice and said, "I have no objections to a beautiful woman buying me a drink, but I don't need to be rewarded for being a reasonable human being."

"Well, then, I'll buy you one because you're so cute." She rested her chin on her hands and smiled at him.

Ethan grinned back at her and went up to order a drink. The young, incredibly hot bartender came over to lean on the bar. "What can I get you, sweetie?" he asked.

"Lagavulin on the rocks, please," he said.

The bartender poured the drink without comment, but as he slid it across the bar he leaned forward and smiled at Ethan. "Get lost on your way over from the studio?"

Ethan gave his best attempt at a good-natured smile, despite his anxiety over being spotted. "Just meeting a friend," he said, gesturing at the table.

"I know. She said she was getting your first drink if you actually showed up." Ethan thanked him and started to turn away, but the bartender said, "By the way…." Ethan turned around. "You don't look nearly as out of place here as you might think."

Ethan looked directly at him. "You seem pretty sure you know what I think," he said, before walking back to the table. His heart was beating fast after that conversation, but he tried to keep it from being obvious.

"Looked like the bartender was flirting with you," Willa said.

Ethan snorted. "More like trying to piss me off. He didn't." He needed to start talking about something else. Maybe if they were having a decent conversation he'd stop feeling so self-conscious. "Deirdre tells me you're a highly sought after hair stylist."

She smiled at him like she knew what he was trying to do but said, "I've worked hard at it. I started doing my friends' and my sister's hair when I was eight. By the time I went to school for it, I had ten years of experience under my belt. I had the advantage of being comfortable with all different kinds of hair. But mostly, it's because I love doing it. The right hairstyle can transform a woman."

"And the wrong one can make her cry," Ethan said.

Willa laughed ruefully. "Don't I know it. It's been a while since I've made anyone cry, though." She suddenly got a big smile on her face, but it wasn't directed at him. "Some friends of mine are here," she said. "We don't have to hang out with them, but I'd like to say hi if you don't mind."

"Sure. Of course." It wasn't like he could say no, though he wished he could. The last thing he wanted was to have any attention drawn to him.

Willa waved at someone across the room. "They're coming over here," she said.

Two men came over to stand beside the table and one of them leaned in to kiss her cheek. "I didn't know you were going to be here!" he exclaimed unconvincingly. He looked over at Ethan. "And who's this?"

"This is Ethan, which I'm sure you know because I told you about my date, and you absolutely knew where I was going," she said, laughing. "Ethan, this is Trevor, and his boyfriend John."

John lifted a hand and said, "Hey."

Trevor clearly knew the score and seemed to be enjoying this. "Can we join you guys for a round? My treat."

Willa looked at Ethan, questioning and a bit apologetic. Ethan could see she was in a difficult position. He shrugged and said, "Why not?"

They all decided to move to one of the low tables in the front half of the bar. Trevor was a talker, and even though he was good about trying to include Ethan in the conversation, mostly Ethan was happy to sit back and listen. John was also pretty quiet and was on his phone a lot. Willa kept catching Ethan's eye and smiling at him, like she was checking on him but also like she was observing him. They ended up having two rounds instead of one before Willa insisted that they had to get going. She got up to pay her tab, and when she was away from the table Trevor said, "She was looking at you like she wanted to eat you up."

"You think?" Ethan asked.

"I think you're definitely in." He sat back and crossed his arms. "If that's what you want, of course."

Ethan rested his arms on the table and leaned forward. "Did you want to ask me something, or are you trying to make me uncomfortable?" He hoped the guy wouldn't ask him anything outright because he didn't want to have to lie. He would do it, but he knew it would bother him.

"None of my business," he said.

"That's true," Ethan replied.

Willa reappeared and stood next to Ethan's chair. "Ready to get going?" she asked.

"Sure." He looked at Trevor and John and said, "Nice to meet you both. Thanks for the drink."

When they were on the sidewalk she said, "I'm sorry about that. I didn't know they were going to show up. You were very patient."

"I didn't mind. First dates can be kind of awkward anyway. Maybe it's good to have other people around as buffers."

She turned her head to smile at him. "I live pretty close to here. Would you like to walk me home?"

"I'd be thrilled to," Ethan said. Maybe this was exactly what he needed. If she wanted to invite him up, he'd be crazy to turn her down. It wasn't like he met women like her all the time.

They walked along in silence for a minute or two, and then she linked her arm with his, leaning into him. It felt nice. It had been a long time since he'd been able to walk down the street with someone as a couple. He imagined they looked good together. Then it hit him—this was what he'd wanted to do with Charlie that night they'd walked back to his place together. He'd wanted to take Charlie's hand, but he hadn't. He hadn't felt like he could. It made him feel like shit; he felt guilty about enjoying this with Willa, and he felt awful about the way he'd been treating Charlie. He deserved someone who could hold his hand in public. He deserved to be treated with respect and not some kind of terrible secret.

They reached Willa's building, and she did, in fact, invite him up. Ethan wasn't in the mood anymore. He was attracted to her on some level, but she wasn't what he wanted. Not then. What he wanted, he probably couldn't have, but he wasn't going to go through the motions with her. That would just add another name to the list of people he was being unfair to. "Maybe another night," he said. "I really like you, and I had a good time, but right now isn't great for me."

"Maybe another night? Come on. Don't be a dick. Be honest."

Ethan sighed. "You're incredibly beautiful and sexy. Normally I'd be totally into it, but recently I've been seeing someone. Deirdre doesn't know about it, which is why she wanted to set us up. It's not a serious thing, and it hasn't been going on long, but it's been on my mind a lot. I don't feel like I could give you the kind of attention that you're clearly entitled to. At least not tonight."

She narrowed her eyes at him. "Well, that's honest. Thank you. Would you like me to refrain from mentioning the person you've been seeing to Deirdre?" She didn't emphasize the word "person," but Ethan was intensely aware of the word choice. So she was wondering too, like her friend Trevor. They'd probably discussed it ahead of time. Great.

"I'd appreciate it. I'd much rather tell her myself." That was a lie, of course. He didn't want anyone to tell her.

"All right. Well, good night." She held out her hand and Ethan took it.

"Good night."

He hailed a cab back to his place. His head started to ache about halfway through the drive, and it was getting worse. All he wanted was to get home and lie down in the dark. When he got to his building, Roland smiled at him sympathetically.

"Date didn't go so well, Mr. Daniels?" he asked.

"It went okay," Ethan said. "I was just tired. I need to head upstairs."

"Of course. But, uh… I need to show you something first. Before you go up."

Ethan frowned at him. "What could you possibly need to show me that can't wait until the morning?"

Roland pulled out his phone and opened Facebook. He clicked on a post and handed Ethan the phone. "This guy I know, John, he posted it."

It was a picture of Ethan that he was obviously unaware was being taken, along with a check-in at The Hunt Club. The caption said, "My friend's date tonight." Ethan groaned. Looking at the comments underneath, he saw John had clarified that his friend was Willa, and there was another photo of the two of them together, but he knew perfectly well no one would pay attention to that. He was already dreading the meeting he'd have to take with Martin on Monday. He handed the phone back to Roland. "Thanks for the heads-up," he said.

"Listen, Mr. Daniels, this is none of my business." Ethan hated when people started sentences that way. "I think you're a good guy. And it's not fair if people are saying something about you that's not true, even though it's not something anyone should see as a bad thing. I mean, I wouldn't want someone to think something about me that's not who I am." He looked at Ethan like he wanted it to be clear he was making a point.

Ethan leaned against the side of the building and closed his eyes. "I know who I am," he said, "and I'm fine with who I am. But right now who I am is a problem for me in a practical sense. Can you understand that?"

"I know where you work, sir," Roland said. He didn't seem too sympathetic, and Ethan couldn't really blame him.

"I'm tired," Ethan said. "I'm going up to bed."

Roland held the door open. "Good night, Mr. Daniels," he said.

Ethan pulled a twenty out of his pocket and handed to him. "Thanks," he said and went inside.

Ethan got undressed and climbed into bed but had a hard time falling asleep. He felt like he should have been able to enjoy himself. There was no good reason he was going to be able to give Deirdre about why it hadn't worked out. He thought about calling Willa the next day and asking her out for another date. Maybe if they went to dinner instead of a gay bar where people kept being so goddamn curious about him, he'd be able to focus on her more. The idea didn't hold much appeal for him, but at least it might get Vince Martin off his back. *Christ.* Monday was going to be a nightmare. First Martin and then after work he was going to see Charlie. He was going to have to be strong and do the right thing. He needed to be a decent person. That was how he'd always thought of himself, and he had to live up to that.

Deirdre dropped Fiona off early the next morning. When she asked him how the date had gone, Ethan said, "She seems great." Then he'd quickly told her he wanted to get moving because he had a lot of plans for Fiona that day. She looked like she wanted to ask more questions, but he didn't give her a chance.

The weekend went by fast. Ethan packed it with activities so he wouldn't have much downtime to worry about Monday. They saw the latest Pixar movie in the morning, had lunch, and then went to the Central Park Zoo. On Sunday, on a whim, he decided to get his little used car out of the garage and drive down to Philadelphia. Even though Fiona had only been living in New York for a year, there was a lot she didn't remember about the city. He took her to visit his parents and then they split a cheesesteak at Shank's. Actually, *split* was a generous term because Ethan ended up eating at least three quarters of it, and he had to brush the onions off of her portion. It was a beautiful day, and they walked around for a while before driving back. She fell asleep on the way home, unfortunately, which gave him time to dwell on his situation.

It was late when they got back to the apartment, and Ethan carried his sleeping daughter upstairs. Fiona opened her bleary eyes briefly when they got into the elevator but fell back to sleep when he said, "Shhh, we're home." He put her in bed, hoping she'd gone to the bathroom recently enough that she wouldn't have an accident. He was just sitting down on the sofa with a scotch when he heard a text come in. He couldn't imagine a text that he'd want to get at that moment.

The text was from Charlie and it read, *You didn't have to lie about having a date.*

Ethan sighed and tossed the phone onto the couch.

He finished his drink before picking it back up and typing, *You're right. I'm sorry. About everything.*

His finger hovered over the send button for a few seconds, but then he erased the last line. He didn't want to get into anything over text. He had to say it in person.

The response that came back was, *Why the hell were you at that bar anyway?*

Ethan replied, *I'll explain when I see you. It's been a long day, and I'm going to bed early.*

Ethan waited awhile, but Charlie didn't reply to that one. Eventually he got up and showered before going to bed, full of dread about the next day.

When he got to work, Abby was waiting for him in his office. "What the hell, Ethan?" she asked. "Pro tip for staying in the closet—don't go to gay bars and hang out with a bunch of gay guys."

"I was on a date with a woman," Ethan said, "as Vince more or less ordered me to do."

"Why did you go to the Hunt Club?"

Ethan shrugged. "I told her to pick the place. That's the place she picked."

"See? That's karma."

"I don't think that's how karma works," Ethan replied.

"Meeting with Vince at ten," Abby said. "I e-mailed you the segments for tonight." She got up to leave.

"Abby, wait," Ethan said. She turned around to look at him. "I thought about what you said. You were right. I wasn't being decent. I'm going to fix that."

"You're going to come out?" she asked with a big smile on her face.

"No," Ethan said. "I'm going to break it off with the guy. I haven't been honest—with myself or with him."

"Oh, Ethan," she sighed. "That's not what I wanted you to do."

"It's all I can do," he said.

Abby shook her head and then walked out.

Ten o'clock rolled around, and Ethan realized he wasn't worrying at all about the stupid meeting with Vince Martin. All he could think about was what he had to do after work, and in comparison this seemed like nothing.

For once he wasn't kept waiting. He was ushered in as soon as he got to the reception area. Martin was behind his desk, and he looked pissed off. Ethan was pretty sure he wasn't going to try to buddy up or offer him any expensive whiskey this time.

"What the fucking hell is going on?" Martin asked, not bothering with a greeting.

"Good morning, Vince," Ethan said. "I'm not sure what you mean. Nothing is going on that I'm aware of."

"You know perfectly well what I'm talking about. Your little bar jaunt on Friday night is all over the goddamn Internet."

"I really don't think many people are focused on my sex life," Ethan said. "And besides, the people who watch this network aren't exactly big social media types."

"They're all on fucking Facebook these days, Ethan. They want to see photos of their grandkids. And they're going to catch sight of your name somewhere and think, 'oh, I'd like to read whatever this is about that nice, handsome young fellow on ECHO News,' and then they're going to see that. And yeah—I know. You were out with a woman. Fantastic, except you kind of buried the lead there, son."

Ethan hated it when older men called him "son." He didn't know if that happened regularly to other adult men—it had never occurred to him to ask—but he felt like he got it more than other people. He did look young for his age, so maybe that was it. Whatever it was, it annoyed the shit out of him every time, and more so right now.

"You know, Vince," he said, his anger coming through clearly, "this is the last meeting I'm going to be taking regarding this matter. It's none of your business who I see or where I go. Obsess about it all you like, but if you say anything else about it, I'm going to sue you for sexual harassment." He got up and stormed out, slamming the door behind him. That perked his mood up slightly for the next few hours, but the closer he got to the time he was to meet Charlie, the worse he felt.

In the car on the way over, his mind kept trying to convince him he didn't need to end it. Or worse, that they should have sex one more time before he ended it. He'd sent a text to say he'd be there soon, so when the car service dropped him off in front of the school, Charlie was already waiting outside. He looked up from his phone and smiled at Ethan. "Hi," he said. He looked like he wanted to hug him or maybe give him a kiss, but he didn't. He said, "Did you want to just go back to your place?" he asked.

Ethan shook his head. "No, let's go get drinks," he said.

They found a small, unassuming bar across the street from McShea's. Ethan ordered drinks for them, and they slid into a booth. "I feel like it's been forever since I've seen you," Charlie said. "You know, I kind of missed you. I hope you don't think that's weird."

Ethan smiled at him, but he knew it probably looked sad. "It's not weird. I missed you too." He swallowed hard. This was going to be terrible, but the best thing was to get it over with. "That's why I have to do this, and why it's going to suck so much." He gripped his glass more tightly. He couldn't bear to look at Charlie's face, so he stared down at the table. "We can't see each other anymore."

"Because of that woman, right? Have you checked with your employer to make sure it's okay to date a black person?"

Ethan looked up then and met his eyes. "I guess I deserved that. But no, it's not her. That was nothing. Deirdre set it up. I didn't feel like I could say no, but nothing happened with her. I'm not planning to see her again."

"Then why?"

"I can't give you the kind of relationship you want and should have. If I'm being honest, I can't offer you any kind of relationship at all."

Charlie gave a disbelieving laugh. "Then what was all that shit about last week? You wanting to know me better, you wanting to be *friends,* staying over—was that some kind of mind fuck? Because you should know, Ethan, that I don't usually do that."

Ethan nodded and looked down again. "I got that feeling. I'm so sorry. I did it because I wanted to. Because I like you so much. It was selfish. And it was ultimately stupid and self-defeating because that's how I know we can't do it anymore. If this was just going to be about fucking, I wouldn't feel bad about keeping it a secret. But I don't think that's the way it is for you, and I know it's not for me."

Charlie smiled bitterly and leaned in again. "What the hell is wrong with you?" he asked. "You're creating this situation for yourself. How do you not see that? Forget me—that's nothing. We didn't get far into this thing. I'll be fine. But you? You'll end up hating yourself. If you don't already."

"This is harder than you think," Ethan said.

"What are you talking about? You think I don't know how hard it is to come out?"

"It's not the same thing. I'll lose my job—"

Charlie threw up his hands. "That is so weak. You could get another job. You know you could."

"Yes," Ethan said quietly. "But what I was going to say was, it's not only that. If I came out, my entire life would be open for scrutiny. I'm a public figure. Strangers would be making all kinds of wrong, shitty assumptions about my marriage. It's not just about me. It's about Deirdre and Fiona too."

"I think you're full of shit," Charlie said, pulling on his jacket. "You're scared and you're hiding behind them. Well, that's your choice. Good luck living with yourself." He walked out without looking back.

Ethan knew he had to get out of there right away. He'd already paid for the drinks and he left his half-full glass on the table. He walked back to his apartment as quickly as he could and didn't say a word to Roland as he held the door open. All he wanted was some privacy so he could be miserable without anyone seeing. He turned on the television for company, started drinking, and didn't stop until he passed out on the couch.

The next morning, he woke up with a pounding head and a mouth that tasted like ten different flavors of dog shit. He swallowed a most likely ill-advised number of ibuprofen tablets and stood in the shower for forty-five minutes. By the time he got out, he felt more or less human. He still felt sad, but lighter than he had the previous week. He'd done the right thing and now he felt like he'd be able to function properly again.

At work he brushed off Abby's questions and ignored her concerned looks. He paid more attention to his job than he had since the whole thing with Charlie had started, and was able to compartmentalize again. His personal feelings were not the point. This was something he'd decided when he took the job, and he'd been fine with it for a long time. Doubt had begun to creep in even before he met Charlie, but now he was refocused. He had a job to do, he understood what it was, and he was good at it.

Other than work, the only thing he thought about was seeing his daughter on Friday. She was the only thing he really cared about. He was going to rent movies and make popcorn and they could sit together on the couch under a blanket. It was so comforting to feel her leaning up against him, trusting him, depending on him. Why it should be comforting to be responsible for someone else, Ethan had no idea, but it was.

Deirdre called him as soon as he got home on Friday. "Listen, I have a question for you," she said.

"Okay...," Ethan said. He was afraid she was going to ask him about Willa.

"Fiona's been invited to sleep over at her friend's house tonight, at the last minute. I haven't said yes yet—it's your time with her, so it's your decision."

Ethan felt let down to a degree that was completely disproportionate with what was happening. He almost felt like he was going to cry. But he'd see Fiona the next day. They could rent movies and eat popcorn and whatever the fuck else he'd been planning on Saturday. He'd been holding out for this. He'd been able to keep his shit together in part because he had this to look forward to.

"Yeah," he said, "of course. She should have her sleepover. Just, uh, give them my number in case anything happens, okay? If someone needs to come get her, I'd like to do it. And text me the address and what time I should pick her up in the morning."

"I'll do that," Deirdre said. "Ethan, are you sure? You sound kind of down."

"I'm sure. She should go. That's the whole point of me living here, right? So she can have a more normal life. If we were still together, there would be no question of her not going, so there shouldn't be a question now."

He knew he didn't sound right. His voice was almost unrecognizable to himself, and there was no way Deirdre didn't notice.

"It's not my place to insist anymore," she said, "but you're worrying me a little bit. Would you like me to come over there?"

Something like relief washed over him and he said, "Would you?"

When he opened the door to her, she immediately frowned deeply at him and put her hand on his arm. "What's going on?" she asked, her voice softer than it had been in a long time, at least around him.

"You want a drink?" Ethan asked.

"I'll get it myself," she said. "You sit down." She mixed herself a large gin and tonic and brought it over to the sofa. "Now, what's all this? Why are you so sad?"

Ethan looked at her and tried to answer her in some way, but no words would come. His face crumpled, and he dropped his head into his hands. He felt Deirdre's hands on him, pulling him down so his head was resting on her lap. She stroked his hair as his body shook with silent, painful sobs. It was a long while before they stopped, but she didn't say a word the whole time. He stayed where he was after he finished crying, mainly because he didn't want her to see his face. Finally, his voice hollow and hoarse, he said, "I need to tell you something."

"Well, I'm listening," she said, but he could hear the slight edge of fear in her voice. He understood—starting a conversation that way rarely boded well.

"I was seeing someone for a little while. I didn't tell you about it because—well, for a lot of reasons, I guess. But mainly because I didn't know how to tell you this thing about myself. The person I was seeing, it was a man. I'd never been with a man before, but… it wasn't exactly news to me that I might want to. I always knew that."

Her hands had stopped moving through his hair. "I don't understand, Ethan," she said. "We were together for nine years. How could you not have told me something so important? What did I do to make you think you couldn't be honest with me?"

Ethan sat up and looked at her. She looked bewildered and hurt. "Nothing. You didn't do anything. I was scared. Terrified. I thought you wouldn't believe me."

She shook her head in confusion. "Believe you about what?"

"That I loved you," he said simply.

"Oh," she said. Her lips trembled, and there were tears standing in her eyes. She blinked, and they streaked down her face. "Oh, Ethan, I'm sorry," she whispered. She hugged him and they were both crying, but it was much less painful now and tapered off pretty quickly. They pulled away, wiping their faces. "Why aren't you seeing him anymore? The guy?"

"I can't do that," he said. "Can't date a guy publicly."

"Why on earth not?" she asked. "Oh—never mind. I guess I know why." She swatted him on the arm. "You bloody eejit. Is there some sort of clause in your godforsaken contract?"

"Vince Martin's made it pretty clear he wouldn't sign me again if anything like that were to be made public. He hasn't said it outright, but it's not particularly subtle either. But forget that for a minute. I want you to think for a minute how that would be for you. How do you think people will see our marriage? How do you think they'll see you? I know you, Deirdre. They'll be so goddamn sympathetic, you'll want to haul off and punch someone in the face."

"Can I tell you how many fucks I give about what people think? Take a guess."

Ethan smiled despite himself. "Like, ten? Ten fucks?"

She laughed. "Zero fucks, Ethan. Don't use me as an excuse."

"That's what he said."

"Well, he sounds brilliant. What's his name?"

Ethan swiped a hand over his face and laughed softly. "Jesus," he said, "that's another problem altogether. Who he is."

Her eyes widened. "Is he famous? Is it Rudy Giuliani?"

"Ack," Ethan said. "No, not famous." He closed his eyes and groaned. "Look, it's over, okay? There's no reason you need to know."

"Well, there is now, for Christ's sake. You can't build it up like that and not tell me."

"Fine. You asked for it. It's Charlie Woods."

"Who?" she asked. Ethan waited and after a few seconds recognition dawned in her face. "You mean Mr. Woods? Bitsy's teacher?"

Ethan nodded. "He's cute, right?"

"Yes," she said slowly, "but it seems like not the best choice you could have made. What if it had ended badly, and he took it out on her?"

"It did end badly, but he wouldn't do that. He's mad at me, not her. He's a good teacher. He's a good person."

She smiled at him and patted him on the leg. "Okay. I choose to trust you about that until I hear otherwise." She picked up her drink and downed half of it in one gulp. "I'm not going to tell you what to do, you know. That's not my job anymore. You'll get that sorted on your own, sooner or later. So… do you want me to hang around, or do you want me to go?"

"Want to watch a movie? I'll make popcorn."

"That sounds lovely," she said.

She fell asleep toward the end of the film—the three pint-sized gin and tonics might have contributed—and Ethan threw a blanket over her before he went to bed.

# Chapter Six

"I'M SO fucking pissed," Charlie told Janice and Josh. He'd gone straight across the street to McShea's. "I should have been the one to stop it. I knew he wasn't going to come out. I fucking knew it, but I let myself like him anyway, and then this shit happens. Goddamn it. I should never date anyone ever." This wasn't the first time he'd covered this ground since he'd arrived at the bar, but the more he drank the more incredulous he was about what had happened.

"I'm not sure that's the lesson you want to take from this, buddy," Josh said. "You should never date someone in the closet, maybe. That's not a bad life policy. It doesn't mean all relationships are bad." When Charlie waved him off dismissively, Josh's face changed. "You know, I think you picked someone like him because you knew it couldn't work. That way it didn't have to be your fault. He did your commitment-phobic ass a favor."

"Fuck," Charlie said. He put his face in his hands. "I'm too drunk. I need to go home."

They got him an Uber and sent him home after he promised he didn't need to throw up and could get into his apartment okay. He bumped into a few things on his way to the bathroom, but he made it just in time to puke in his own toilet. After that he felt better and went to pass out on the bed.

He called in sick the following day. After sleeping in until late morning and drinking two large cups of coffee, he spent the rest of the day cleaning his apartment. He'd been letting it go a little since the school year had started back up. It felt great, and he cleaned well into the evening.

The rest of the week was okay. He didn't think of Ethan too much, except to revive his practice of hate-watching his program on television.

Looking at him on the screen, he could hardly believe he knew the man. He seemed nothing like the person he'd spent time with. Charlie wanted to believe he could see desperation in his eyes, or grief, but they looked empty to him.

Josh and Janice kept stopping by his classroom after school to check on him. It was nice of them, but after a day or two, it got ridiculous. He couldn't imagine what they were so worried about. He was fine. He'd liked Ethan, sure, but it had only been a few dates—if you could even call them that. After a week of it, he told them to cut it out.

Seeing Fiona every day in class was difficult. Of course he didn't hold any of what happened against her, but it prevented him from being able to put Ethan out of his mind completely. She looked a lot like her mother, but her smile was so much like Ethan's that it hurt a little to see it.

On Saturday morning Charlie's mom's partner, Donna, called to ask if he wanted to come down for dinner and stay over. "You know how your mother is," she said, "she complains that she misses you, but it never occurs to her to call. When I tell her she should call, she says she doesn't want to bother you. We see your brothers and your sister all the time with them still being in the area, plus they like to bring the grandchildren, but she misses her baby."

Charlie sighed. "I'm sorry. I know I don't come as often as I should. It's kind of a pain to get down there without a car." It really wasn't such a big hassle, but for some reason he always built it up as one in his head. Once he was out of the city, he felt sort of naked without a car. He'd always had a car in high school and college—castoffs and hand-me-downs from his brothers and parents.

"Will you come today? I'll pay for your Amtrak ticket."

"There's no need, Donna," he said. "Despite how my mother sees me, I'm not an actual baby. I'll text you the arrival time so someone can come get me."

To his surprise it was his brother Bill who picked him up at the station. Bill was the closest to Charlie in age, but there was still a five-year gap. The rest of them were around two years apart. He sometimes wondered if his mom had been making plans to leave long before he was born, but his surprise existence had delayed her escape. She'd never said that or anything else to make him think he hadn't been wanted, but when you looked at it objectively it made sense.

"Hey, Billy," Charlie said as his brother nearly suffocated him in a hug. Bill was a police officer in Camden, and his main hobby was lifting weights. He wasn't bulked up to the point of looking weird, but he was a huge guy. Charlie had seen him in his uniform, and he looked intimidating, but he was a sweet guy. Maybe when you were that big you could afford to be, even as a cop. "Donna didn't say you were going to be at the house. Are Kelly and the boys there too?" Bill had three-year-old twin sons.

"Yep. Mark, too, and Dan and his family. Tess has to work, but she'll be there in time for dinner. Oh, and Dad said he might stop by too."

"Is there some kind of anniversary I've forgotten about? What's the occasion?"

"No occasion, bro," Bill said, "but we never get to see you. Donna said you were coming down, so we all invited ourselves over."

Charlie grinned. "Cool," he said. "It'll be nice to see everyone." He loved the chaos of family. His family anyway. They were loud, and there was a ton of them. When he was a kid, Charlie would sometimes stand still in the middle of the room and imagine they were a tornado swirling around him, and he was at the eye of the storm. Now that he thought about it, that was pretty much classic youngest child thinking.

They arrived at the house and hugged a bunch of people. He hadn't seen any of the kids since the summer, and the twins already looked way different. He sat down and played with them, making them laugh by pretending they were parking garages and driving one of their trucks on their arms and legs. When they seemed to be getting bored with him, he wandered into the kitchen where his mom was cooking.

"I'm so glad you came down today," she said.

"You could have called anytime, you know. It wouldn't bother me. You're lucky you have Donna to do that stuff for you."

She nodded, smiling into the pot she was stirring. "I am lucky. So what about you? Seeing anyone?"

"No," he said. He hadn't meant for it to come out angry, but it definitely did.

His mother raised her eyebrows. "Was that directed at me?"

"No," he said again, more softly. "Sorry. I started seeing someone, and it didn't work out. I guess I'm still a little mad."

"How come it didn't work?" she asked, moving to the cutting board to start making a salad.

"It never had a chance to start. He's in the closet. He decided he's not going to be able to come out, so he ended it." Charlie shook his head. "The thing is, I would have been willing to give it more time. I thought he'd be ready eventually, and I was going to wait and see for a while."

"For a while? What does that mean?"

"I don't know." He shrugged. "A few months?"

"And after a few months, after you'd fallen in love, if he didn't change his mind? What then?"

Charlie nodded. "I get your point. I think I'm angry more at myself than with him. I let him get under my skin."

"Well, that's good," she said.

"Huh?"

"It's important to let people make an impression on you. I worry about you sometimes, Charlie. You want everything to be so easy and perfect. You want to avoid conflict and pain so badly that you won't allow yourself to get attached to anyone."

"Gee, Mom, I really only came here for the food, but thanks for the bonus psychoanalysis," Charlie said. "It's not my fault I grew up with everyone loving me and doing everything for me. Maybe if you'd had me first, I'd be a fireman and have a wife and three kids by now."

His mom looked sharply at him. "Don't make fun of your brothers."

"I'm not," he said. "I love my brothers and my sister. Their lives seem great. Well, except Tess. Being a nurse sounds terrible to me, but she seems to like it. I'm just saying, that's not who I am. Just because you want me to find someone and settle down doesn't mean that's what I want for myself. Okay?" His mind flashed to those domestic scenes he'd conjured up the week before, but he quickly dismissed them. They weren't real. They were ads for something everyone said you were supposed to desire.

His mother shrugged and said, "Okay. There's a platter of cold cuts in the fridge. Can you put them out with those rolls over there on the counter?"

"Sure," Charlie said. He hesitated for a second but walked over and gave her a quick side hug. "Love you, Mom."

"I know," she said. She kissed him on the cheek and shooed him away.

Charlie spent the rest of the day in the eye of his family's storm. He slept over, and Donna dropped him at the train station the following morning.

"Thanks for coming, kid," she said.

"Thanks for taking care of my mom, Donna."

She slapped him on the shoulder—hard—and said, "Always."

Normally he felt mostly relief once he got on the train back to the city. He loved his family, but it took a lot of social energy to deal with them all at once, and he was usually exhausted by the end. This time, he felt sad. He was pretty much alone in the city. He had some friends, but they all had their own lives. He thought about what his life would be like if he moved back to New Jersey and got a job teaching down there, near his family. He could have dinner at his siblings' homes, watch his nieces and nephews grow up. Maybe Bill knew a gay cop he could set him up with. That could be kind of hot. He indulged in that fantasy the whole way home, finally shaking himself out of it as they pulled into Penn Station. When he got off the train and back into the rush of New York life, he remembered what he liked about the life he actually had. He didn't want what his siblings had. Part of him probably wanted to want it, but that was as far as it went.

By Monday morning Charlie was feeling a lot better about everything. He was ready to move on. He got to work in a pretty good mood, but when he opened his school e-mail he saw something that put him slightly on edge. There was a note from Deirdre McNaughton asking for a meeting with him. He couldn't imagine what could be so urgent. Fiona was doing beautifully in school, and anyway, they already had a conference scheduled for November. The only thing he could think of was that she'd somehow found out about Ethan and him, but why she'd need to speak to him about it was beyond him. He wrote back to her, saying she could come by during his planning period at one, while the kids were in art class.

She arrived promptly at one o'clock, looking as stylish and put together as always. She also looked nervous. He stood up to shake her hand. "What can I do for you, Ms. McNaughton? Is everything okay with Fiona?"

"Oh yes," she said. "I didn't come to talk about my daughter. I wanted to talk about Ethan."

"What—uh, what about Mr. Daniels?"

She sat back and smirked at him. "He doesn't strike me as the type who'd insist on you calling him that."

He closed his eyes momentarily and then said, "I'm not sure I want to continue this conversation," he said.

She reached forward suddenly and put her hand on his wrist. "I'm sorry. It was hanging there, and it's a character flaw of mine that I can't pass up an obvious joke. Even when it's inappropriate, like now. I only came because I wanted you to know something."

"Oh? What's that?"

"Ethan and I stayed married about three years past our logical expiration date. Partly it was for Fiona, but mostly it was him. Any time I'd start to edge toward talk of separating, he'd shut down the conversation. He'd try to be exactly what he thought I wanted. I cannot overstate how fearful he is of change. When I decided to move here with Fiona, he flipped his shit. He was so angry, but again, I knew it was his fear. Him following us here was probably the hardest thing he'd ever done."

"He did that for Fiona because he loves her. But we're not—I mean, we barely know each other."

"I know how it looks on him," she said gently. "I can see how much he feels like he's giving up. He's hurting."

Charlie shook his head. "He's the one who broke it off with me. What do you expect me to do about it? Am I supposed to go beg him to change his mind? Am I supposed to sit and wait for him to figure his shit out and come back?"

"No, of course not. I'm only asking you not to shut him out when he does. He's trying, even though he doesn't even realize it himself yet. But I know him. I can see it. Where he thinks he is on all this is not where he is in reality. He's so close. Why do you think he finally told me about it?"

Charlie stared at her. "He told you? I assumed you found out somehow and confronted him."

"No. He told me because he was too sad to hold it in. He doesn't want to hide anymore. He just doesn't know it yet."

"Why are you doing this for him?" Charlie asked. "Aren't you mad that he lied to you all those years?"

She gave a little shrug that made her look like a little girl for a second, and she said, "I wish he'd told me, sure. It was a lie of omission. In the end I don't think it would have changed anything for us. We weren't right for each other, that's all. I'm doing it because he's still part of my family, and he's always going to be, because of Fiona. I'd like him to be happy, and I want him to set a good example for her going forward."

Charlie nodded and said, "I'll think about what you told me."

"That's all I ask," she replied and then stood up. "Thank you." She turned to go but stopped and turned back around. "By the way, I should tell you that Fiona adores you. If nothing else, I take that recommendation very seriously."

"I do too," Charlie said.

He'd told her he'd think about it, and he did. He also thought about the last conversation he'd had with Ethan. Ethan had told him that it wasn't the same for him. Charlie had assumed he meant because of his job and the fact that his coming out would be a public matter. An ECHO News on-air personality who came out would get a lot of heat from the queer community, there was no doubt. On further reflection, though, Charlie thought there might be something buried a little deeper. Ethan had mentioned people's assumptions—people choosing not to believe in the way he identified. He was sure they'd assume he'd been lying for his whole life and that he'd used his wife as cover rather than actually having loved her. That would be a pretty painful thing, he supposed. The worst part, in Charlie's opinion, would be the fear that she would believe it, and that when she was old enough, their daughter would too. The fact that he'd told Deirdre the truth might mean something. That he'd done it and it had turned out fine, apparently, could only help.

Charlie decided he could wait and see what happened, but he wasn't about to put his life on hold either. It felt like forever since he'd gotten laid, but the idea of going online and finding someone to hook up with seemed unappealing in a way it rarely had before. He even briefly considered taking Josh up on his offer, but squashed the idea quickly. Josh wanted to fall in love, while Charlie just wanted his dick sucked. He wasn't going to do that to his best friend.

He put it off all week, but on Friday he'd reached his breaking point. He'd have to get past his newfound distaste for the process. He went straight home after work and fixed himself a drink while he perused his options. He swiped past a bunch of guys—apparently he was also pickier than he used to be—and was beginning to get discouraged when he saw one of the most beautiful faces he'd ever seen on a man. He had brown skin and shiny black hair and his name was Girish. He lived only about ten blocks away. Charlie immediately messaged him, as he couldn't imagine him staying available for long. They had a quick discussion about what they were looking for that night, and he agreed to come over.

Charlie had another drink while he waited. He felt nervous the same way he always did when he was about to meet someone to hook up with. You could only tell so much from a picture and a short text conversation, and sometimes they weren't what he'd hoped for. Also, sometimes they were assholes. Just because they didn't want any strings didn't mean they couldn't be friendly. Charlie felt the same way, but he managed to display normal human decency.

He was fixing another drink when the doorbell buzzed. He went to the intercom and said, "Hi, Girish?"

"Yeah, that's me," he said. "Sorry it took me so long to get here." He had an English accent. This was getting better all the time.

Charlie buzzed him in and opened the door for him. He watched him come up the flight of stairs to his floor. If anything, he was hotter than Charlie had expected. Girish saw him waiting in the doorway and grinned at him.

"Whew," he said when he got to the top. "You're as advertised, then."

"You too," Charlie said. "Come in. You want a drink?"

"I don't drink, but I'd love a glass of water," he said. *Well*, Charlie thought, *at least he has one flaw*. He poured a glass from the pitcher in the fridge and brought it over to the sofa.

"I hope it doesn't bother you that I had one," Charlie said.

"Oh, no. Not at all." He drank half the glass and put it on the coffee table. "So, how do you usually like to do this? Chat a bit first or get right to it?"

"The direct approach—I like it. Honestly? It's been a couple weeks, which is kind of a long time for me. I'd be good with jumping right in."

Girish smiled and moved closer. Charlie closed the gap and began to kiss him. He smelled like lemongrass, which Charlie decided was his brand-new favorite smell. He leaned back against the arm of the couch, pulling Girish on top of him. He was so hard when Girish began to grind against him, but suddenly he lost it. He was pretty sure he could get it back, though. He shoved his hands down the back of Girish's pants. Girish moaned and began to kiss his neck.

Girish reached down to undo Charlie's pants. "I want to suck your cock," he panted. When he got his hands on Charlie's mostly limp dick he said, "Let's see what I can do about that." He slid down to his knees on the floor. Charlie sat up and looked down at him, suddenly flashing on his first night with Ethan. Ethan on the floor in front of him, choking on him and completely undone. His dick started to stiffen up, and Girish smiled at him, but Charlie couldn't keep it going. He couldn't stay in the current moment, but the past started to make him feel bad before long. For some reason he kept thinking of Ethan's ex-wife and what it must have been like for him to come out to her. He must have been desperate. He must have felt totally alone.

Girish pulled off and said, "If you want to keep making out and see if it comes back, that's cool. If it's not happening for you tonight that's okay too. Your call."

Charlie put his dick away and smiled sheepishly. "Yeah, probably not tonight. I can suck you off, though. Don't want your trip over here to be in vain."

Girish gave him a considering look and asked, "It's not nerves or something like that, is it? Something's wrong."

Charlie sat back. "Yeah, kind of. But not with you. Look, I really don't mind."

Girish shook his head and stood up. "I don't think so. You clearly don't feel like doing this." He sighed. "I only went on the app because I was bored anyway. And lonely, I suppose. My boyfriend lives in London, and I won't see him until Christmas break."

"Oh, are you a student?"

"What a lovely thing to say, but no. I'm a visiting professor. I'm going back at the end of the school year, but Wes and I have an understanding in the meantime. That's one reason I was glad you said you don't like to fuck the first time—we have a rule against it."

"That makes sense," Charlie said. "I guess."

Girish shrugged. "I don't know if it does or it doesn't, but I think it helps to have some kind of rules in this sort of thing. Honestly, I can't wait for this to be over. I miss him terribly."

"I'm sorry. That sucks. Unlike me, ha-ha."

"Ha-ha indeed. It's all right, though. Feel like telling me what happened? I told you my sob story. Unless you want me to leave. I'd understand."

"Company might be nice for a little while," Charlie said. "You want something to eat? I don't have much in the house, but there's some chips and salsa."

"For as much as Americans love Mexican food, you'd think they'd be a little more welcoming to Mexican immigrants," Girish said. "Sure, I'd love some chips and salsa. Is it hot?"

"Supposedly," Charlie said, looking at the jar. He poured some into a bowl and brought the bag of chips out. He sat down and picked up the drink he'd started before Girish arrived. "Don't get me started on immigration policy," he said. "Or anything else political, for that matter. I've been watching right-wing news lately. It's a fucking wasteland."

Girish laughed. "Why on earth would you do that to yourself?"

Charlie looked over at him. "I have kind of a crush on Ethan Daniels," he said.

"Ah," he said. "Understandable."

They ended up talking for a long time, and in the process discovering that they were both watching the third season of *Vikings*. Girish was two episodes ahead of Charlie but was willing to rewatch those so they could watch the next one together.

While it felt good to have someone over and to meet a new person, Charlie was more than a little disturbed by his own reaction to the sex. So maybe he'd rather have Ethan here, but that was too bad. He couldn't have Ethan. He should have been over it by now, and he couldn't understand why he wasn't.

"Are you paying attention?" Girish asked. "You have to watch this scene with Floki."

"I don't watch this show for the plot," Charlie said. "I only care about the scenes with Ragnar and Athelstan."

"Of course," Girish said. "Because they're clearly in love. You're a bit of a romantic, aren't you?"

"I don't think so," Charlie said.

"If you weren't, you would have said you like the scenes where the muscle-bound Vikings run around with no shirts."

"But that's all the scenes," Charlie replied.

Girish laughed, and Charlie decided to put Ethan out of his mind.

# Chapter Seven

THE MORNING after he came out to Deirdre felt strangely similar, in some ways, to the morning after he'd gotten drunk and took Charlie home with him. He woke up with an unnamed dread lying heavy in his stomach, and it took him about half a minute to remember where it came from. He felt he'd crossed another line that would be impossible to cross back over, only this time the stakes were much higher. Now Deirdre knew, so any possibility of him being able to go back to the way things used to be had disappeared. There was one big difference between this and that other morning, however. This time he felt lighter than he had the day before. It felt like he'd solved the hardest problem on a test first and the rest of it should seem easy in comparison. The only thing was, he didn't know if he could finish it—or, more correctly, if he should.

Deirdre had started coffee when he got up, seemingly unaffected by having drunk enough gin to knock out a horse. He hadn't even been drinking, and he felt like he'd been hit by a bus.

"Morning," she said brightly. "Want some toast?"

"Okay," he said. He got down cups to fix their coffee. "Deirdre, about what I told you last night. It's not going to change anything. I'm not planning to date any other men. I'm going to give myself a little more time to process it, and then I'm going to find a girlfriend."

Deirdre snorted softly. "Do you know that in *Minecraft* they have a mod where you can find girlfriends and boyfriends out in the wilderness and take them home like pets?"

"I don't even know what you mean by 'mod.'"

"Yes, well, Fiona was telling me about it. She thought it was hilarious, and it is, but also a bit disturbing. That's what you reminded me of just then. You're going to go out and find a girlfriend, like it's a mission. As if it doesn't matter who it is, as long as she's willing and looks suitable."

"That's not what I meant," he said.

The toast popped up, and she set the four slices on the table. As she spread jam on hers she said, "Look, Ethan. I don't care who you go out with. It's truly none of my business. But if you've found someone you like already, you'd be stupid to walk away from it before you know where it's going." She set her toast down and looked at him. "That's all I'm going to say to you about it. Eat your toast."

After Deirdre left he went to pick Fiona up from her sleepover. She talked almost nonstop for the rest of the day about what they did and the things her friends said and what they ate, and Ethan was perfectly happy to let her. He was glad she'd had such a good time, and after a while he tuned her out a bit, listening with half an ear, so he could think about things some more.

At some point midweek, he got a call from his college roommate Thad Winthrop. Thad came from money, but it didn't seem to affect his personality. They'd hit it off and roomed together all through school. They'd kept in touch for a couple years after graduation, but—as these things go—it had eventually been reduced to Christmas cards and the odd e-mail a couple times a year. Thad had interned at various nonprofits during school and had taken a low-level management job in New York with an organization focusing on women's health issues in the developing world. Not that he needed to live on his salary, of course. He had a generous trust fund to pull from. He'd moved up quickly and was now running it. Ethan hadn't heard from him since taking the job at ECHO, despite sending him an e-mail to let him know he was moving, so the call was a surprise.

"Hey, buddy!" Ethan said as he picked up. "Great to hear from you."

"Hi, Ethan. Been a while, huh?" He sounded different than Ethan remembered. It wasn't his voice so much as the way he was speaking to him, as if he wasn't sure who Ethan was anymore.

"It's been forever. What's up?"

"Uh, well, I guess you're living in the city now, right?"

Ethan had always hated the convention of calling New York "The City," as if it were the only one that mattered. He'd been living in a perfectly good city before moving there. Still, he really was happy to talk to Thad, so he swallowed his reflexive irritation and said, "Yeah, for a while now. I didn't want to be too far from my kid."

"I understand. I can't imagine being away from Guthrie."

Ethan bit back a giggle. Thad's son would be around two now, but the last pictures he'd seen were of a chubby, laughing baby being raised in the rarified air of wealthy liberal Manhattan. It was hard to imagine him doing any kind of hard traveling. If he decided someday to go roaming and rambling, it would probably be in an SUV with a high-limit credit card. "But anyway," he managed, "any particular reason why you called? Not that we can't just chat."

"I'm having a party this Friday. Well actually, it's a fund-raiser, but I don't expect you to contribute. I realized I hadn't seen you in forever, and you're right in town, so it seems crazy we haven't at least gotten together for coffee. Maybe I should have invited you out for coffee instead, I don't know."

"Jesus, Thad. Calm down. Why are you acting so weird with me? Is it because of where I work now?"

"Well…," Thad began, sounding guilty as hell, "yeah. It was kind of upsetting if I'm being honest. I never thought you were that way."

Ethan smiled. For Thad, "that way" meant right wing. "I'm really not," he said, "but I'm not sure that makes it any better. Maybe it even makes it worse."

"I guess it probably should make it worse, but somehow I'm still relieved. So do you want to come?"

"What's the fund-raiser for? There are certain things I can't be seen supporting," he replied, wincing at the way that sounded. "You know, Planned Parenthood or whatever."

"It's for the charity Diana's involved with. They build rec centers in inner cities. I don't think that should be a problem for you, right? It's not like they're asking the government to build them."

"Sure," Ethan laughed, "that should be okay. What's the recommended contribution?"

"A thousand," he said, in the way most people would say, "Oh, ten bucks."

"Text me the details. I'll see you Friday."

After work he stopped at a boutique toy shop. He'd always meant to send a gift when the baby was born, but he'd put it off too long and eventually forgotten about it. It didn't take long to find the perfect gift, and the store said they could have it engraved by Friday morning. He hoped they wouldn't think he was making fun of them, even though he *was* a tiny bit late. He sent a check for $5,000, both because he was fairly sure most of the guests would have given more than the recommended, and because he hated the way Thad had sounded on the phone with him at first.

On Friday he went out and picked up the gift during lunch. When the shop worker showed it to him, he started laughing and told her to wrap it up. He couldn't wait to give it to them.

Thad's text had said it was cocktail attire, which was a relief to Ethan. He hated black tie because he felt like an imposter wearing a tuxedo unless he was in a wedding party. He arrived at the house promptly at eight in hopes that guests would still be somewhat sparse. He wanted a chance to give them the gift and say hi to Thad before he was in full-on host mode. To his surprise, Thad answered the door himself and immediately gave him a big hug.

"Here," Ethan said, awkwardly holding the large box out to him. "It's for Guthrie. I meant to send something when he was born, but...."

"Wow, thanks!" Thad said. "You didn't have to do that."

"I wanted to."

"Is it a gift for him or a gift for us that's related to him?"

Ethan grinned. "Sort of both. You can open it if you want to. Actually, I hope you will."

"Come with me," he said. He led Ethan to the kitchen where he found Diana giving instructions to the caterers. She looked up and smiled at him, and then came over to kiss his cheek.

"Ethan, it's so good to see you," she said. "It's been too long."

"Ethan brought a gift for Guthrie, but he said we should open it."

"How sweet of you," she said.

Thad tore off the paper and lifted the lid of the box. It was a tiny guitar with the phrase "This machine kills fascists" engraved on the body, like the one Woody Guthrie had. It was even a reasonable approximation of the lettering. Thad lifted it up with an almost awestruck expression on his face. "This is the most awesome thing anyone has ever bought for him."

"Although maybe a little bit of a dig?" Diana asked, grinning slyly at him.

"Not a dig. I hoped you guys would love it. It did make me laugh, though."

"I don't blame you," she said. "I do have some self-awareness. But I also do love it, so thank you."

"You're welcome."

"Oh!" Diana said, "I don't know if Ethan told you, but someone else you guys went to school with is here tonight."

"Oh? Who?" Ethan asked, glancing at Thad who looked slightly nervous.

Thad cleared his throat. "Becca Jacobs," he said. "We see her occasionally. For a while she was dating someone who worked for my organization."

"I see," Ethan said. "She's here already?"

Thad nodded.

"Well, I guess I'll go and say hi," Ethan said.

What he honestly wanted to do was leave immediately. He took a cocktail from a passing waiter's tray and drank it down as he scanned the room. He spotted her in a corner, talking to a well-known wealthy player in state Democratic politics. It looked like an animated conversation, albeit mostly one-sided. She was probably lecturing him about the failure of magnet schools or complaining about the governor. Ethan snagged another drink and finished it as quickly as the first one, but he still didn't feel ready to speak to her. Maybe he didn't have to. He could have easily gotten in touch with her before now if he'd wanted to. Just because they were in the same room didn't mean they had to interact.

Unfortunately, the man she was speaking at walked away, and she looked around the room, her eyes first sliding past him and then jerking back to his face and going wide. She actually looked scared, which he thought was interesting. If she was going to spread bullshit stories about him, she should have some courage about it, in his opinion. He forced a grin onto his face and started walking across the room toward her, grabbing yet another drink on the way. He watched as she tried to figure some way out of the conversation, and then resigned herself to it.

"Ethan," she almost gasped as he came near. "You look wonderful."

He raised his eyebrows. "Interesting opening gambit," he said. "You look good too. But I didn't come over here to have that conversation. Did you really think I had?" The alcohol was kicking in, and he felt like he could say anything he wanted to her. She knew she'd done something wrong, and he wanted to hear her say it. He didn't care if she apologized—he just wanted her to admit she'd fucked up.

"No," she said in a small voice, "I guess not. You probably want to yell at me."

"I'm not going to yell," he said. "I just wanted to tell you how difficult you made things for me with that stupid fucking story, which was barely even true in the first place. And I'd love to hear what in the world I ever did to you that would make you do something so hateful. Just because you think I'm a hypocrite for doing what I do, doesn't give you the right to try to out me publicly. You know that's not okay."

"Out you?" she said. "That's an interesting way to put it."

"Shut up," he said. "Let's hear it."

"Fine," she said, heaving a sigh. "You're right. The story was all innuendo and supposition because the person who wrote it wanted to make it more interesting than it was. I didn't say any of that stuff. All I said was that you and I had dated, and one time I saw you kiss a guy."

"Oh, that's all?" Ethan said.

"I was drinking," she said. "I know that's not an excuse, but it's the truth. I wasn't watching what I was saying. You had just gotten that horrible fucking job, and maybe on some level I was angry with you about it. I know we hadn't seen each other since graduation, but I thought about you. That was a special relationship for me at a pretty intense time in my life, and when I saw you on ECHO, it was upsetting. I couldn't imagine your views had changed so drastically, but I knew something must have changed because I can't imagine the guy I used to know saying things like that. So you were probably already on my mind when you came up in conversation. The person I was talking to knew we'd gone to the same school and asked if it was at the same time."

"Some guy you were fucking, I suppose."

"What do you care? But yeah. For a little while. Until I read that bullshit in the *Post*."

"And it never occurred to you to correct it?"

"Would it have made things better for you if I'd explained we were rolling on E? Somehow I'm not sure that would have played better with your audience." She raised an eyebrow at him. "I don't get why it should have been such a problem. If you're not doing anything to fuel them, rumors like that usually die pretty quickly. I figured you'd start dating some hot blonde Republican, and people would forget about it. I mean, look at you. Surely you can get dates."

Ethan got himself another drink and started on it rather than answer her.

"Huh," she said. "Well, I'd be surprised if you were gay. I'd hate to think I'd been so thoroughly fooled, though I guess I could chalk it up to being twenty years old." Ethan looked at her and sipped his drink. "On the other hand, I wouldn't be the least bit surprised to hear that you're bi. I mean, not after that night."

"Seriously?" he said. "You think we're at the joke-making stage already?"

"Sorry." She shrugged. "What's the big deal, anyway? Hey, guess what, I'm bi too. Should I announce it to the room?"

"I think you know what the big deal is," he said.

"Ugh. I don't want to hear it. You built that. Look, Ethan, I'm incredibly sorry it happened. I didn't intend for it to go public. And I'm sorry you're insisting on being so stupid about it, but that's your beeswax. I won't say anything to anyone." She glanced down at the nearly empty glass he was holding. "Also not my beeswax, but you might want to think about slowing down a little. How many is that?"

"Fuck you," he said.

She made an angry, frustrated noise at him and walked away. Ethan put his glass down and realized how drunk he actually was. After the third one, he'd felt pretty good, but the fourth one in such a short time was about to put him on his ass. The last thing he wanted to do was embarrass Thad and Diana, but he was not especially confident about his ability to hold it together much longer. He waited until they were both occupied with other people and snuck out the door. He was pretty sure Becca saw him do it.

He weaved down the sidewalk until he heard Thad's voice calling from behind him. "Hey, Ethan. You're leaving?"

Ethan turned around and said, "I'm sorry. Drank too much and don't feel great. We should get coffee soon, though."

"Was it seeing Becca? I'm sorry that happened. I should have warned you ahead of time. I just wanted you to come."

Ethan shook his head, which made him dizzy, and said, "Don't worry about it." At least, that's what he tried to say, but he wasn't quite successful. A cab passed by and Ethan hailed it. He left Thad frowning with concern on the front steps of his townhouse.

"You going to puke in my cab?" the driver asked.

"Nope. I'm good." He hoped so anyway.

"Where to?"

"Lower East Side," Ethan said and gave him Charlie's address.

He fell asleep on the drive down, and the driver knocked on the fiberglass divider to wake him up. Ethan rubbed his eyes and fumbled with his wallet. He ended up giving him a fifty and telling him to keep the change because he didn't want to wait around. Things were changing—he was changing—and he needed to tell Charlie. Nothing felt more important than that. He pressed the buzzer next to the building and leaned his head against the door while he waited.

"Yes?" came the reply in slightly garbled tones.

"I need to talk to you. Can I please come up?" After a moment he remembered to add, "It's Ethan."

There was a long pause, and then Charlie said, "It's not a great time. I have company."

"Oh," Ethan said. Somehow he hadn't considered that possibility. That was dumb—of course he had someone over. Probably some random sex hookup, which Ethan couldn't see any reason to be worried about. He'd probably be leaving soon. Maybe he could wait outside until the guy left and try again. But if he didn't leave, Ethan would feel worse about it. He didn't want to know.

Charlie spoke again in a kinder voice. "Call me tomorrow, okay? I'll meet you somewhere, and we can talk."

"Yeah, okay," Ethan said. "That's probably a better idea. Listen, Charlie. I miss you so much, and I made a huge mistake. I wanted to tell you now because I just realized it tonight, and I didn't want to wait."

"I got maybe half of that," Charlie said. "Are you drunk?"

"I'd say so, yes. Pretty drunk. Just came from a weird party. Rich liberals. Becca was there."

"*Becca*? Jesus Christ. No wonder you drank too much. I'm not letting you wander the streets like that. You'll get robbed. Come up."

"No, it's fine. I don't want to interrupt your evening." He didn't want to meet whoever Charlie had up there.

"Shut up, Ethan. Please come up."

The door buzzed for a long time, and finally Ethan pulled it open and started trudging up the stairs. Charlie's door was right at the top, and he opened it to lean against the door jamb.

"Hi," Charlie said.

"Hey," Ethan replied. "I really am sorry. About tonight but even more about… all that other stuff."

Charlie nodded. Ethan had been afraid he'd still be angry. He'd been pretty mad when he left the bar. Now it was hard to get a read on him, but Ethan would be the first to admit he was not functioning at the top of his mental abilities. It was so good to see him, though. He wanted to reach for him, but he was pretty sure that wouldn't be received well at the moment.

Charlie held the door open for him. The man he saw sitting on the couch was almost impossibly beautiful. He didn't look like a woman, but he was as pretty as one. If this was a real date, Ethan figured he might as well give up. The man was staring right back at him with amusement.

"Ethan, this is Girish. He's my new friend. Girish, Ethan Daniels. He's… well, I don't know what he is yet. To be determined." He gave Ethan a little smile that made his stomach clench. "Have a seat. We're watching *Vikings*."

"I've never seen it," Ethan said.

"Doesn't matter," Girish said. "There's something for everyone in this show."

Charlie sat in the middle of the couch and made room for Ethan to sit next to him. They watched in silence, but after a few minutes Charlie slid his arm under Ethan's and linked their fingers together.

When the episode was over, Girish got up and said, "Well, it's been fun."

Charlie let go of Ethan's hand and stood up to walk him out. "It has been. We should watch the next episode together. I feel like something bad is about to happen, and I need the emotional support."

"Okay. I'll hold off until you message me, but if it's more than a week, I'll assume you've thought better of it." He looked over at Ethan and back at Charlie. "That's some powerful crush if it managed to draw him to your apartment."

Charlie looked down and smiled. "Tell you about it next time."

When he'd gone, Charlie turned and walked back to the sofa. "We shouldn't talk about this tonight," he said. "I want to wait until you're sober."

Ethan leaned forward so his head rested on Charlie's shoulder. "I should have waited until tomorrow to come. I'm sorry I fucked up your date. It was stupid of me not to think of it."

Charlie pushed his fingers through Ethan's hair and kissed the top of his head. "It wasn't a date, and you didn't fuck it up. I did try to have sex with him earlier, but the joke was on me. I couldn't get it up because all I could think about was you. How sad is that?"

"Really?" Ethan asked. He raised his head to smile at him.

"Yes," Charlie sighed. "Listen, I want to hear about all your stuff, but it's late now. You need to sleep it off. If I let you in the bed, will you promise to go to sleep and not try anything else?"

"Promise," Ethan said. "How about in the morning?"

"We'll talk."

Charlie found Ethan some sleep pants and went to brush his teeth while he changed. Ethan crawled into bed and put his head down carefully. No spins, but it was starting to ache. He closed his eyes and was mostly asleep when he felt Charlie getting in next to him. Moments later he felt fingers brushing through his hair, over and over until he was completely under.

Ethan woke in the early morning with a desperate need to piss. Still half-asleep, he stumbled next door to the bathroom and stood there for at least a full minute before his erection subsided enough to let him go. Ethan thought there were a lot of things about human anatomy that made no sense, but that one was near the top of the list. It still hadn't gone away completely by the time he'd finished, but he was way too tired to do anything about it.

He climbed into bed as carefully as possible, but Charlie still stirred and mumbled something unintelligible.

"What?" Ethan whispered.

"Closer," Charlie said, or at least that's what it sounded like.

Ethan slid closer and cautiously draped an arm over Charlie's waist. He thought he might be pushed away, so he stayed very still until Charlie put his hand on Ethan's arm and snuggled back into him. Ethan let out his breath and closed his eyes again. They were in the same position as they'd been in the last time he'd slept in this bed, but everything felt different now. It felt like the beginning of something instead of borrowed time. Another change was that Charlie had asked for closeness. The last time, Ethan had gotten the feeling he was forcing something Charlie was unsure of, but now it seemed like he might actually want it.

# Chapter Eight

THE FIRST thing Charlie became aware of when he woke was that Ethan had more or less wrapped himself around him. The second thing was Ethan's hard dick pressing against his ass. He shifted slightly so he could look back at him. He appeared to still be sleeping. He looked younger when he was asleep. Charlie watched him for a minute or so before he opened his eyes.

"Morning," Ethan said.

Charlie put his head back down on the pillow. "Good morning," he said, and pulled Ethan's hand between his legs. Ethan responded immediately by rubbing Charlie's erection through his pants and rutting up against him from behind. Charlie moaned as Ethan mouthed his neck, then reached under the covers to slip off his sleep pants. Ethan did the same and then wrapped his hand around Charlie's bare shaft. He'd truly intended to have a serious talk with Ethan before anything happened between them, but this felt so good. He probably should have considered more than just Ethan's behavior when he invited him into the bed. Ethan hadn't been the one to start it this time. The feeling of Ethan's cock against him was maddening. Charlie decided that if they were going to try to be together for real, Ethan was going to have to learn to top. The thought sent a ripple of excitement through Charlie, and he pushed back against him.

Ethan hooked their legs together for purchase but seemed to be having trouble getting what he needed. Charlie reached back and grabbed his hip to help him, and he uttered a muffled cry of relief as he bit down on Charlie's shoulder. "I do want to fuck you," he growled. "Soon."

"Yeah… fuck yes," Charlie hissed, and then without warning he was coming, his whole body spasming with it. When he was still, he felt a warm wetness on his lower back. Ethan must have been as excited by the idea as he was.

Ethan's body relaxed, but he stayed where he was, trailing his fingers through the come on Charlie's abdomen. "At some point I guess we should get up," he said.

"I'm covered in come," Charlie said, "so yeah. I need a shower, and I should also change these sheets."

"I have to pick up Fiona at ten," Ethan said. "I'm sorry. Deirdre kept her last night so I could go to that thing, but—"

"I know," Charlie said. "It's okay. I'm not going to begrudge your daughter time with her dad, but we do need to have a real talk before you go."

"Can we stay like this while we do it?"

Charlie smiled and stroked the arm wrapped around him. "Fine by me," he said. "You start. What happened to you after you told me we couldn't see each other anymore?"

"Well… I was sad. More than sad. I felt like there was no solution except for me to keep my head down and do what I had to do to get by, indefinitely. The only thing I could hold on to was the idea that I was doing all of this for Fiona. She's the reason I took a job I never wanted, in a city I never wanted to live in, and the reason I had to give up a chance to be with someone I wanted to be with. And that's a ridiculous amount of shit to blame on a six-year-old child—not that I'd ever tell her, of course. She didn't ask for any of it. Anyway. Then Deirdre called to say she had a sleepover and would I mind giving up my Friday night with her, and I almost had a fucking breakdown right then. I didn't exactly understand at the time why it affected me so strongly, but I figured it out later on. It was because some part of me realized in that moment that she was going to start having her own life, outside of me and her mother, and that eventually she wouldn't have much time for me at all, or need much from me. But by then I would have forfeited my own happiness and be left with nothing."

"Is that when you decided to tell Deirdre about everything?" Charlie asked.

"What?" Ethan said, drawing back slightly.

"Oh, um," Charlie began. He wondered how pissed Ethan was going to be. "She came to see me at school. She scheduled a meeting last Monday."

"Goddamn it," Ethan said.

"Don't be too mad at her," Charlie said quickly. "I know—I understand why you're angry. I'm sure I would be too. It was totally not her right to go to me behind your back, but it came from a good place. She cares about you, Ethan. She only wanted to help. She told me she was sure you were closer than you knew, and asked me not to shut you out when it happened."

"That woman," Ethan said. "She just does whatever the fuck she wants and expects everyone to get on board."

"Maybe that's why you married her—so you wouldn't have to make your own decisions. It seems like the only time you force yourself to do anything the least bit difficult is when you're drunk out of your head."

Ethan was quiet for a minute or so and then let out a harsh sigh. "So as I was about to say," he said in a level but clearly irritated voice, "Deirdre could hear over the phone that I wasn't doing too well, so she came over. She asked my permission to come over, by the way, but not to go blab about me to you."

"Moving on...."

"Right. Well, she came over and I tried to talk, but instead I started crying. I was a mess. Eventually I started talking and dumped all of it on her. Then we watched a movie and ate popcorn. The end."

"Hmm...," Charlie said. It occurred to him that if he'd had an ex over and they'd had an emotional outpouring and sat around under a blanket on the couch for two hours, that might not have been the end of it.

"No," Ethan said. "I know what you're thinking, and it never happened."

"It would be okay if it did."

"But it didn't."

"Okay. That was last weekend," Charlie said. "You didn't do anything for a week."

"I didn't know I was ready yet," Ethan replied. "Much as I hate to admit it, what she said to you was right. I was almost there, but I still couldn't see it."

"She's very insightful," Charlie said.

"Shut up. Then I got invited to this fund-raiser a college friend was hosting. He's this ridiculous trust-fund hippie who named his son Guthrie, for Christ's sake. He's a nice person. So is his wife. They're lovely people."

"But ridiculous."

"Very much so. And I guess it shouldn't have surprised me that they'd be in touch with Becca Jacobs. I mean, of course they would be. Thad knew her in college too—we were roommates, and for a while she was always hanging around, and they were probably in Amnesty International or whatever together. And now she's a big voice on the progressive left, so it's a natural fit. But it was still a shock to see her there. I got so angry just looking at her, but I was afraid of what I might say if I talked to her."

"So you got drunk," Charlie prompted.

"Very drunk, very fast. And then I didn't give a shit what I said to her."

Charlie turned his head to grin at him. "So what did you say?"

"Well, probably a lot of things, but the upshot was that I thought she was an asshole. And then she guessed the truth about me, and I couldn't—I didn't want to lie about it. So I didn't. But then she pissed me off again, and I basically told her to fuck off."

Charlie rolled over to face him. "So what does that mean, in like, practical terms?"

Ethan's face became more guarded, and he said, "I'm not sure. I don't want to sneak around with you. I don't want to care what my doorman thinks or who's taking pictures of us in restaurants. I don't want to hide you from the people who are important to me or lie about myself to them either."

"I'm guessing there's a second part to that statement that starts with 'but.'"

"But…," Ethan said with a grimace. "I don't want to come out publicly. I mean, explicitly. I want to eventually, but not now. Do you think you'd be okay with that?"

"I think so, but won't you get outed anyway if we're together in public and people know about us? I mean, what about that guy Girish from last night? I don't know him, and I certainly can't vouch for him. For all I know that whole scene is already on the Internet."

"God, I hope not. That would be embarrassing. I wouldn't want anyone to see me being so pathetic, but I don't care if they know about you. It's like… well, Anderson Cooper. He never came out until a long time after basically everyone knew he was gay. Then it wasn't even a story when he did."

"Yeah, but that was Anderson Cooper. He wasn't on ECHO News where they say crazy shit about queer people all the time. You're going to be a target from both sides."

"Plus he wore those sexy tiny T-shirts."

Charlie smiled and gave him a quick kiss on the lips. "You're hotter than him. I just hope you know what you're doing. If you wait too long, it'll look like you were forced to come out."

"I just want to get my contract renewed. I'll be in a world of shit if I lose my job and have to pay rent on that apartment." Ethan propped himself up on his elbow and looked down at Charlie. "I have to get going. Do you want to get dinner on Monday?"

"Somewhere expensive?"

"Like I told you before, I make a lot of money doing something kind of terrible. I should at least get to spend it on something that makes me happy."

"And that would be me?"

"Yeah, that's you," Ethan said. "You make me happy, and my kid makes me happy, and right now there's not much else, so there's plenty to go around."

Charlie pushed him over onto his back and climbed on top of him. He lowered himself down into a long kiss that was all soft lips and gentle tongues. When it was over, he didn't trust himself to speak. He got out of bed and into the shower, leaning against the tiles while he let his body calm down. His mind was spinning too, but he was pretty sure he'd have to wait until Ethan was gone to start sorting through it.

When he came back to the bedroom, Ethan had already stripped the bed. "I would have made it, but I didn't want to poke around in your stuff trying to find the clean sheets." He looked so cute standing there in his underwear, holding a ball of dirty linens, that Charlie couldn't quite figure out what he was feeling. It was some unfamiliar and almost unpleasant mix of lust and a rush of affection that felt like it was choking him. "What?" Ethan asked, frowning at him. "What's wrong?"

Charlie shook his head. "Nothing." He walked over and took the dirty sheets from him. "Thanks for doing that. There are towels in the bathroom cabinet if you want to take a shower."

"Are you sure it's nothing? You were looking at me almost like you were pissed off."

"It's nothing bad," Charlie said. "I swear."

"Okay. I believe you. I'll get a shower now." He didn't move right away, but stood where he was, studying Charlie's face for a few seconds. Then he smiled and left the room.

Charlie sat down on the edge of the bare mattress. He thought it was possible that what he was feeling was mostly a reaction to suddenly having Ethan back in his life after losing him just as it was starting. His head hadn't caught up yet. He lowered his head into his hands and groaned quietly. He had no idea what to do with it, whatever the reason might be. He forced himself to get up and find sheets to remake the bed with and then pulled on jeans and a sweater. Ethan came out a few minutes later with a towel around his waist.

"You're killing me with this shit," Charlie said. "Put some damn clothes on."

Ethan grinned. "I want to, but do you think I could borrow something to wear? At least a shirt. Mine from last night is kind of a mess."

Charlie looked him up and down. They were both around six feet, but with different builds. Ethan was a little bit smaller, but it should work pretty well. "Take whatever you need," he said.

He was not in any way prepared for his reaction to seeing Ethan walk out of the bedroom wearing his clothing. He put his hand over his mouth because he wasn't sure he could control what it did.

"Don't laugh," Ethan said. "I know these jeans look stupid on me."

Charlie shook his head, still covering his mouth. "It's just—it's— God, I don't know. You look so good. Really very good."

Ethan walked closer to him with the same concerned look on his face as before. "Thank you," he said. "I'm going to go now, if you're okay?"

"Yes," Charlie said, almost too quickly. "I'm fine. Have a good time with Fiona. I'd tell you to say hi for me, but it's probably too soon for that."

"A little," Ethan said. "I gave Deirdre a pretty hard line about not introducing anyone until she was sure and that she had to tell me first. I don't want to be an asshole about it."

"See you Monday," Charlie said.

Ethan kissed him good-bye and then pulled back slightly to look at him again. Charlie could tell he wanted to ask again, but he didn't. He said good-bye and left.

There was no way he wanted to sit around his apartment by himself for the rest of the day. He threw a load of laundry into a duffel bag and went to the Laundromat on the next block. As soon as he finished, he spent two hours at the gym, which was much more helpful to his state of mind than laundry had been, but once he was done, he still had to face an entire evening by himself. He texted Josh to ask if he wanted to do something, but he texted back to say he was at his sister's house in Long Island. He thought about Janice, but he'd never hung out with her on his own, and it seemed like it could be awkward. She was much better friends with Josh since they lived in the same part of town. Finally, although it felt kind of weird, he texted Girish a single word: Vikings?

He heard back almost immediately. *Tonight?*

He smiled and typed in, *Yes. But really just Vikings so if that makes a difference you can bail.*

Girish wrote back, *No way. Vikings plus the whole story from last night. Deal breaker.*

Charlie said, *Okay. Seven. We can order food.*

He came over, and they ordered way too much sushi for two people. After *Vikings*—in which, as Charlie had suspected, something terrible happened—Girish turned off the television and said, "All right, I was patient. Now I need to hear how Ethan Daniels turned up on your doorstep last night, shitfaced, and cuddled up to you on the couch."

Charlie took a breath and filled him in on everything that had happened with Ethan. When he got to the part about Deirdre coming to see him, he said, "Good Lord! Has she no concept of boundaries?"

"Well, I think she knows about them, but she doesn't seem to care much where he's concerned."

"Doesn't that bother you?" Girish asked.

"Not as yet," Charlie replied, "but that could certainly change."

When he'd gotten to the end, Girish said, "So he thinks he's going to be able to be genuine in his personal life and not have it affect his job? Because it seems highly unlikely to me."

"You think people will call him out on it?"

"Well, possibly. But I was thinking more about the kinds of culture war stories they tend to do on that network. He might have been able to compartmentalize before, but I bet that gets harder now."

"Maybe," Charlie said. "I hope it does. It should, at least, be difficult for him."

"And how do you feel about this development? You obviously have some strong feelings for him if you couldn't even stay hard with me. Not to brag, but it's generally not a problem I've had to deal with."

Charlie smiled. "I can imagine. I feel… good about it. I mean, I'm glad he's doing this even if it didn't mean he wanted to be with me. I hate to see people twisting themselves up over their sexuality. But yeah, I'm happy he wants to be with me."

Girish narrowed his eyes at him. "You say you're happy, but your face doesn't seem to agree."

"I am, but I'm unsettled, or something. Nervous, maybe? Or… kind of all over the place." He hesitated and then said, "Like, this morning he borrowed some of my clothes, and I couldn't handle it, the way he looked in them. He looked fucking amazing, and they looked completely different on him than they do on me. And you'd think I would have wanted him to stay so I could look at him some more, but I also wanted him to go because it was too much." He looked up in dismay. "Oh shit."

Girish was laughing silently at him. "I thought you'd get there eventually."

"It's way too soon for that," Charlie said.

"Too soon to say it. You can't help what you feel. It's all feelings at this stage anyway." He tilted his head to the side and looked at Charlie. "Have you never experienced this before?"

"I don't think so," Charlie said. "I told my college boyfriend I loved him. Maybe I did, but it didn't feel like this. Not that I remember anyway, and I think I would. It's kind of terrible. And also the opposite of that. Ugh, how can it be both?"

"One of life's mysteries," Girish said. "But I should be going." He glanced at his phone. "I just got a message from someone who wants to do hand jobs. He says, 'You fuck my hand, I'll fuck yours.' Should I?"

Charlie shrugged. "I don't know. Did he send a dick pic?"

"What do you think?" Girish asked, holding the phone up for him to see.

"I think you should pass, but that's me. I'd rather get a hand job from myself, most of the time."

"Right. Night, then."

Charlie went to the gym again on Sunday, cleaned his apartment and ended up watching the rest of the season of *Vikings* on his own. He knew he was avoiding his feelings and avoiding thinking about what they might mean, but maybe he didn't need to deal with it yet. And anyway, feelings weren't tangible things. They were ephemeral, and their meanings changed along with what was happening in the real world. If things went well with Ethan, and if they were able to move forward, then the feelings would be positive things. If this brand-new relationship crashed and burned, they'd make him miserable. He was pretty sure that was why the emotions were so unstable at the moment—he simply didn't know how he was supposed to feel.

On Monday morning Ethan walked Fiona into school. Charlie saw him hanging outside the doorway looking in, and he went out into the hallway to say hello. He pulled the door most of the way shut and quickly grabbed and released Ethan's hand.

"I hope you don't mind," Ethan said. "I was here, and I knew I could see you if I wanted to, so it would have been hard not to."

"I don't mind," Charlie said, smiling at him and unable to look away from his eyes. "Kind of hard not to touch you, though."

"Yeah," Ethan said. "It is." He broke eye contact and looked down at his feet. "Anyway, I should go. I just…."

"I know. Me too. I'll see you at your place at seven. I'm going to go for a drink with my friends after work, so—" He shut his mouth when he saw Josh round the corner at the top of the stairs, then stop short in the middle of the hallway. He looked back at Ethan and said, "So I'll walk over there after," he finished weakly.

"Okay. See you then." Ethan held his hand out as if to shake, but when Charlie took it he just held it for a moment and gave it a squeeze. He nodded and said hello as he passed Josh on the way to the stairs.

Charlie was tempted to run into the classroom and hide from him, but he'd have to face him eventually. Josh was not going to be on board with this turn of events, clearly. He stood against the wall and waited as Josh walked over slowly, an exaggerated look of outrage on his face.

"Are you kidding me with this?" he asked. "What are you doing?"

"It's kind of a long story. I can't get into it right now. I promise it's okay, though."

Josh shook his head. "I can't imagine how it could be," he said.

"Well, then you're not using your imagination," Charlie replied. "I'll tell you at the bar. Okay? Try to give me even the slightest amount of credit. Can you do that?"

Josh pursed his lips at him and crossed his arms over his chest. "You aren't the best at relationships, Charlie."

"Go back to your classroom," Charlie said, making a shooing motion with both hands. "I need to go take attendance."

Later on, once again at McShea's—which, Charlie noted, did not improve with familiarity—Josh stared at him from across the table. Janice hadn't come along, so he couldn't even count on her to be the reasonable one.

"When?" Josh asked.

"When what?"

"When did you give in and start fucking him again? I hope you at least made him beg."

Charlie rolled his eyes. "Yeah, that sounds like me. Look, it's not like that. It's different this time." Josh looked up at the ceiling as if to appeal to the heavens for Charlie to get some sense. "He came out to his ex-wife," he added, which caught Josh's attention.

"You should have led with that," he said. "Ooh, I wonder if she'll have a closeted husband character in her next book. Poor thing."

"Yeah, I probably wouldn't use that phrase to describe her," Charlie said, grinning. "And she'd probably smack the shit right out of you if she heard you say that."

"So he came out to her, but that doesn't mean he's going to be okay with his adoring aged public finding out he's boning a dude—and a liberal millennial teacher, no less."

"He doesn't want to come out publicly," Charlie admitted. "Anyway, not before he gets a new contract in place."

"Of course," Josh said. "How is this going to be any different? You know, I actually had some respect for him when he ended it with you. He actually tried to do the right thing, but now he's fucked that up too."

"Will you stop?" Charlie almost yelled at him. The people at the next table turned around to stare. "Cut it out," he said, much more quietly. "I'm not some child. I've been around a little bit, as you might recall. I believe him, Josh, but if it turns out I was wrong about him, I'll have to deal with that when it happens. I know you're trying to be a friend, but you know what? If you care about me, you should let me make a fucking mistake, if that's what this is. I never take chances, but I want to now, and don't you think it's about time I did?"

Josh looked almost shocked, and he didn't answer right away. Finally he said, "I didn't think about it that way. We were just worried about you. Me and Janice."

"Yeah, I know you were. That's a good thing. I get why you would be."

"But I'm still wondering how this is different. If he's not out in public, doesn't that mean you can't be seen with him?"

"He says no. He said he's not going to sneak around. He's going to do whatever the fuck he wants and not address it unless he has to, I guess."

Josh looked skeptical, but he said, "Okay. When are you supposed to see him next?"

Charlie gave an involuntary smile and said, "We're having dinner tonight. I'm walking over to his place to meet him, but not until around seven. We have lots of time."

"I'm coming with you. If you want me to leave you alone about it, you have to introduce me."

"Fuck no," Charlie said. "I'm not doing that."

Josh shrugged and seemed to let it go. He changed the subject, and they had an entertaining conversation for the next couple hours. Charlie was drinking beer, and he drank them slowly so he ended up only having two. He didn't want to be drunk or sleepy tonight. He had plans for Ethan.

When the time came to go, they both stood to put on jackets and scarves, and Charlie gave Josh a hug. "Thanks for looking out for me," he said.

"I will expect nothing less from you if I ever decide to date some closeted Republican celebrity."

Charlie ignored him and followed Josh out to the sidewalk. He said good-bye and started walking toward Ethan's building, expecting Josh to go the other way to his stop. When Josh started walking along next to him, he gave him a confused look and said, "Did you forget your way around the city or something? Where are you going?"

"I told you, I'm coming with you."

"And I told you, no. Go home, Josh. You're not coming."

"Try to stop me," Josh said.

Charlie stopped in the middle of the sidewalk, and Josh stopped a second later. "Please don't do this. It's too weird." Josh shrugged and flashed him an infuriating grin. "Goddamn it," Charlie muttered. He shook his head and kept walking, as fast as he could, but he couldn't shake Josh. Of course, that made sense because Josh was six foot three with a long stride.

When they were a block from Ethan's place, Charlie stopped again and said, "Look, you've made your point, but could you please not be an asshole?"

"I don't care if you think I'm an asshole," Josh said. "If he's really a good guy, he won't mind you introducing him to a friend. So I want to see his reaction when you do."

Charlie sighed, and they crossed the street. He could see Roland, the doorman, under the awning of Ethan's building. He smiled at them as they approached and lifted a hand in greeting.

"I'll call to let Mr. Daniels know you're on your way up," Roland said. "Does he know you brought a friend?" he asked, looking Josh over in a less than subtle way.

"No," Charlie said. "That was unplanned, and he'll be waiting down here while I go up."

"No problem," Roland replied, and looked at Josh who suddenly seemed completely uninterested in Charlie. "I'll keep him company." He opened the door to let Charlie in.

Ethan came to the door in dress pants, shirt and tie.

"Uh-oh," Charlie said. "I'm underdressed, aren't I?"

Ethan smiled and shook his head. "Problems at work. I got home literally ten minutes ago and haven't changed yet. You look fine."

Charlie came in and followed him to the bedroom, sitting on the bed while Ethan got undressed. Charlie watched him openly, admiring his hard, slim body. "Do you swim a lot?" he asked.

"Some. Mostly I run and do pushups and core stuff at home. I hate going to the gym."

"You look good. I like to lift, but if I do it too much I start to bulk up and then I don't feel like myself."

"It's probably more genetics than anything," Ethan said. "I tried to get bigger for a while, but I could never make much of a difference." He gave Charlie an amused half smile. "Any particular reason you're suddenly interested in my workout routine? Is this standard?"

Charlie laughed. "Not necessarily. I did actually want to know, but I'm also putting off telling you something." At Ethan's sudden look of concern, Charlie quickly said, "Nothing terrible. Annoying, more than anything."

"Okay," Ethan said, sitting down next to him on the bed. He'd changed into different pants and a more casual shirt. "Just tell me. I'm sure it'll be fine."

"My friend Josh—I think I might have mentioned him before. He's the art teacher at the school? He saw us in the hallway this morning."

"Sure," Ethan said. "What about him?"

"He's a little… protective. He thinks I'm making a mistake with you. He doesn't trust you. It doesn't matter to me what he thinks about it, and I told him that. But he followed me here. I mean, not in secret. That would be creepy. He walked with me and wouldn't fuck off when I told him to. Annoying, right?" He looked at Ethan helplessly. "I'm sorry."

Ethan laughed. "It doesn't annoy me, but I can see why it would bother you. What's the idea? Is he going to threaten me with violence if I hurt you? Does he want to chaperone the date? I'm a generous guy, but he's going to have to pay for his own meal."

"He wants to meet you," Charlie sighed. "His heart is in the right place. He's just being an ass."

"Was I not going to meet him otherwise?"

"Well, yes, eventually, but I didn't expect him to play the dad role in a bad sitcom."

Ethan was still smiling and didn't look particularly bothered, so Charlie put his arm around his waist and kissed him. "I'd be happy to try to set his mind at ease," Ethan said. "This makes us even for what Deirdre did," he said.

"Absolutely," Charlie said, though in truth he didn't much mind what Deirdre had done. It had bothered Ethan a lot, but Charlie was now mostly grateful for her meddling.

"I admit to being a little nervous. What if he still doesn't approve of me?"

"Well," Charlie said, turning to put his hand on Ethan's chest, "we could always see each other in secret." He pushed Ethan back onto the bed and climbed on top of him. "Away from judging stares." He leaned down for another kiss, but before he could do anything else, Ethan grabbed his wrists.

"I don't want to do that this time," he said. "Last time we were supposed to go out, we ended up fucking and staying in."

"Mm, I remember. I can't say I had any regrets."

Ethan sat up and said, "Maybe not, but I did. Or, I do now. I did it on purpose. I was too chickenshit to go out to a bar with you, so I did my best to discourage you."

"What if I'd insisted on going out?"

Ethan shrugged. "I guess I would have gone. I liked you, so… probably. But I was so relieved, and I feel bad about it now. This time we're going out and spending my blood money on something that counts."

"We're making a donation to the Southern Poverty Law Center?" Charlie asked brightly.

"If you like," Ethan said. "Of course I'd have to launder the donation through you. But I was hoping we could start with some twenty dollar cocktails and move on from there."

"Okay, but you can't get drunk or eat too much because I need you sharp for later on."

Ethan raised an eyebrow. "Should I ask?"

"I thought you already did," Charlie said.

Ethan looked at him blankly at first, but then he said, "Oh! I see." He glanced back at the bed. "Maybe we should go out later."

"Come on," Charlie laughed. "Let's go deal with Josh. Though I'm sure he didn't mind the wait."

On the way down in the elevator, Charlie asked him, "Are you sure this is what you want to do?"

"It's what I need to do."

"For me?"

"No," Ethan said. "Not only."

"Good."

Through the lobby doors Charlie could clearly see Josh flirting with the doorman. He was saying something and making broad gestures with his hands while Roland laughed helplessly. Ethan slowed down and touched his arm to get him to stop walking.

"Look," he said.

"I see it," Charlie replied. "Josh is a huge flirt. And who wouldn't flirt with Roland? He's hot. Especially when he smiles, which is probably why Josh is working so hard to make him laugh."

"Have you flirted with him?" Ethan asked.

"Why? Have you?"

"Not really. His role in my life, other than opening doors for me, has basically been to tell me I should do better and stop worrying so much because everything is okay. I'm paraphrasing, obviously."

"Obviously." He looked over at Ethan. "Enough chitchat. Let's get this over with."

They pushed through the doors, and the two men stopped laughing, but they still had smiles on their faces. "Good evening, Mr. Daniels. Can I get you a cab?"

"Yeah, thanks," Ethan said. He turned and said, "You must be Josh. I think I was supposed to meet you on Back to School Night but I had a… work crisis." He held out his hand, and Josh shook it, looking at him warily.

"Yes, I met your ex-wife that night," Josh said.

"Well, that's always an experience." Ethan stood with his hands in his jacket. "My daughter seems to enjoy your class. She brought me a painting the last time she came over."

"Oh!" Josh's face brightened. "She's hilarious. Everyone loves her."

"That doesn't surprise me."

"So," Charlie said, "is it okay if we have our date now?"

Josh glanced at him quickly and then back at Ethan. "You probably think I'm an asshole for coming here."

Ethan shook his head. "No, but if there's anything you felt like you needed to say or ask, it would be great if you could do it now. We have reservations."

"How can you work for those people?" Josh blurted. "Doesn't it bother you at all?"

"Yes," Ethan said. "It bothers me. I used to pretend it didn't, and that it was okay to be cynical about it, but it does."

"Not enough to quit, though," Josh said.

"No. Not enough for that."

"What if someone asks you outright if you're dating a guy? What are you going to say then?"

"I'll say yes."

Josh nodded. "Okay. Thanks for answering my questions."

"You're welcome."

"The cab is waiting," Charlie said, tugging at Ethan's arm.

"Night, Roland," Ethan called. Roland gave him a wave back but didn't even glance in his direction.

# Chapter Nine

"WHAT WAS your favorite movie as a kid?" Charlie asked as soon as the waiter had taken their drink orders.

"Try to guess."

"Okay," Charlie said. "I know you're thirty-eight because I looked at your bio on the ECHO website." He squinted with mock concentration and then said, "*Return of the Jedi*?"

"I don't like space stuff," Ethan said.

"What?" Charlie asked. He looked incredulous. "You're dismissing the entire Star Wars franchise as 'space stuff'?"

"It's not my thing," Ethan replied with a shrug. "Besides, I kind of hate the whole idea of a movie franchise. It lets people off the hook from coming up with original ideas. Believe me—I know how much people like to see and hear the same stuff over and over again. It's my bread and butter. So I don't begrudge those people a living. I just don't want to subsidize it with my money."

Charlie looked at him with suspicion. "Have you actually seen any of the Star Wars movies? It's not like a superhero movie where they keep retelling the same story with increasingly hotter actors. It's a continuing saga."

Ethan smiled. "Of course I've seen them," he said. "I didn't grow up in a cult. The first three anyway. Obviously not the next three. I was an adult by then." Ethan wasn't quite telling the truth about that—he'd gone to see the first one of the second trilogy (or the first chronologically—whatever) out of curiosity. He'd hated it so much that he'd walked out of the theater halfway through.

"Oh, okay, mister serious grown-up person. I have no idea what your favorite movie was as a kid. *Top Gun*? *Karate Kid*? *Dirty Dancing*?

I could keep throwing out movies from the eighties for quite a while, but I don't have any educated guesses."

"It was sort of a trick question anyway. It didn't come out when I was a kid. I think it came out before I was born, actually, or close to that time. My favorite movie as a kid was the animated version of *The Hobbit*."

Charlie's eyes widened in an exaggerated expression of shock. "You hate space stuff but you love Middle Earth?"

"I wouldn't say that. Although, okay, I did read *The Lord of the Rings* trilogy in high school. And I liked the movies. Anyway, it's completely different."

"Sure it is," Charlie said, laughing.

"Do I get to ask a question now?"

"Fire away."

"Who was your first celebrity crush?"

"Easy. Leo DiCaprio," Charlie said without hesitation.

"Boring," Ethan said. "I was hoping it would be someone more embarrassing. Like, I don't know, Hugh Grant. Or Dane Cook."

Charlie cracked up, and Ethan smiled as he watched him laugh. He'd been more nervous about this dinner out than he would have liked to admit, even to himself, but now that they were there he felt better. It wasn't nearly as big of a deal as he'd built it up to be in his head. It wasn't like he'd never eaten a meal with another man in a restaurant before. After their drinks arrived, Ethan asked Charlie questions about his college experiences until a booming, aggressively friendly voice came from beside their table.

"Daniels!"

Ethan looked up and saw Steve Hannigan, who hosted the show after his. It was called *Between the Lines with Steve Hannigan*, and it was one of the most offensive programs the network ran. Hannigan talked over his guests whether they agreed with him or not, because he liked the sound of his own voice more. He had the air of an aging frat boy, but he took excessive pride in his wardrobe. Ethan liked nice clothes as much as anyone, but Hannigan must have had an entire closet full of bespoke suits and silk shirts, and he recommended his tailor to people every chance he got. When he talked politics, however, he sounded like a true believer. In Ethan's experience, that wasn't necessarily the case at a place like ECHO, although you did have to be careful about what you said. It was a toxic atmosphere and dissent from the network's positions was not tolerated for long. Hannigan was, possibly, the last person in the world he wanted to see.

"Hey, Steve," Ethan said. "Good to see you. Getting dinner?"

"No, just drinks. My girlfriend's waiting for me," he said, pointing to a woman standing at the bar. "She insists on five-star places for dinner. Typical, right? I'd be happy with a good scotch and a burger, but not her. That's what I get for only dating tens. She spends my money, but it's worth it to be inside that quality of pussy." He laughed conspiratorially and said, "Until she starts making noises about a ring, right? Then on to the next lucky lady."

Ethan was actually struck speechless for a second. He'd only spoken to Hannigan in a work context up until then, and he'd come to understand that the man was an asshole. He'd had no clue he was this vile. All he wanted was to get him away from their table, because if he stayed much longer he was going to ask who Charlie was. That was probably why he'd come over in the first place. He said, "Sounds like a plan," in the mildest voice he could manage, and then, "Better get back to her before she finds someone richer than you."

Hannigan laughed in a hearty and entirely phony way and then said, "Who's your friend?"

Ethan took a breath and then said, "This is Charlie Woods. Charlie, Steve Hannigan."

Charlie reached up to shake his hand and said in a sincere voice, "I enjoy your show."

Hannigan looked startled, but almost immediately the smile returned to his face. "Great to meet a fan!" He looked over at the bar and said, "Well, I'd better run. See you tomorrow, Daniels."

"Dear God," Charlie said, after he'd left the area. "That was the worst human being I've ever met."

Ethan bit his lip and nodded. "I'm sorry about that," he said.

"Why? It's not your fault he's an ass."

"I'm sorry I didn't say you were my date. I should have. I will next time."

Charlie smiled at him. "What you said was fine. If you want to introduce me as your date, I won't tell you not to, but you don't have to. I'm sure he figured it out anyway. I was relieved you didn't fumble around and call me your nephew or something."

"Really?" Ethan said, looking at him with worry.

"Sure," Charlie said. "It'll happen when you're ready."

"Can I ask you something?"

"Of course."

"Do you seriously watch his show?" Ethan asked.

Charlie laughed and shook his head. "There's only one right-wing talking head for me."

The rest of the time at the restaurant was nice, but on the ride home Ethan turned moody. He still felt a little off because of the incident with Hannigan. Charlie didn't think it was important, but Ethan was worried about it because the thought of actually doing that— introducing a boyfriend to someone like Hannigan—struck a real fear in him that he was ashamed of. He wasn't afraid of reprisal, but the scorn a guy like that would then direct at him. It made no sense because he hated Hannigan and everything he represented. His opinion should have meant nothing.

They were in the elevator heading up to Ethan's floor before Charlie said anything about it. The mirrored wall reflected the two of them, and Charlie edged close enough to take his hand. "We look good together," he said. "Don't you think?"

"I do," Ethan said.

"I like you more than I've liked anyone in a long time. Maybe more than I've liked anyone, ever." He met Ethan's eyes briefly in the reflection and then glanced away. "So, you know, if you want to pout for a while about the fact that you think you let yourself down, that's fine. I can deal. But also, because I like you, I wish you wouldn't. That road leads nowhere good." He raised his eyes again to lock with Ethan's.

"Are you really okay with the way things are?"

"Yeah, I am," Charlie said. "For now. Not forever."

"Forever?" Ethan asked, raising his eyebrows.

"You know what I meant," Charlie said. His cheeks flushed and he looked away.

"I'm not sure I do," Ethan replied. The elevator doors opened, and they walked down the hall to Ethan's door. As he unlocked it, he asked, "Should we talk before we do anything else?"

"Is there anything you want to say that's going to make me not want you to fuck me?"

"I don't think so," Ethan said.

"Good," Charlie said, sliding the jacket from Ethan's back. "Me neither. So let's go take our clothes off. I want you inside me."

Ethan's cock immediately stiffened. He grabbed Charlie by the hips and pulled him close so he could feel it. "Why do you get to be in charge if I'm the top?"

Charlie smiled at him. "Just because you're doing the fucking doesn't necessarily make you a top. But anyway, it's because you don't know what you're doing. Remember?"

Ethan reached down between Charlie's legs and fondled him through his pants. "I'm learning," he said.

They went into the bedroom and stripped down, watching each other the whole time. Charlie finished first and slid under the covers.

"Going to sleep?" Ethan asked.

"Come here," Charlie said. Ethan tossed the last of his clothing into the hamper and got in next to him. "We're going to take this so slowly. You do whatever you want to me for now."

Ethan kissed him and ran his hands all over his body, then dipped down to kiss his shoulders and chest. They stayed there under the blankets, doing nothing but that for a long time. Ethan usually had the finish line in mind when he had sex. His married sex life had been good, at least for the first several years, but it had begun to follow some familiar routines as their marriage went on. He assumed the same would happen with anyone he stayed with long enough, but at the moment he had no idea what would happen next or how long it would take. He wanted to be in that moment—comfortable, warm, aroused, but not yet desperate—for as long as he could.

At some point he had pulled Charlie on top of him and positioned himself so the length of his cock lay along the crack of Charlie's ass, which elicited a pleased sounding grunt and a smile from him.

Charlie reached back and took hold of it, rubbing it between his spread cheeks.

"Oh God," Ethan said, squeezing his eyes shut. "I can't do this for long."

Charlie laughed but stopped right away. "What should we do, then?" he asked.

Ethan licked his lips. "If you could, uh, get on your hands and knees."

"Sure." He crawled off of Ethan and got into position.

Ethan moved around to kneel behind Charlie and held him by the hips. He felt confident about this part of it. It wasn't like he'd never used his tongue during sex before. He did his best to quell his nerves about the next step as he began to kiss Charlie on his lower back and hips, working his way down to his ass. He was unprepared for his own reaction to the moment when his tongue trailed up the crack and over Charlie's hole. Charlie moaned, and Ethan was suddenly achingly hard. He worked the area with his tongue for a long time and eventually reached around to stroke Charlie's straining dick with his right hand. Charlie was panting and whimpering, grasping at the sheets under his hands, and when Ethan pulled back for a breather, Charlie said, "Put your fingers in me. Please."

"I want to be able to look at you," Ethan said. He got the lube out of the nightstand and pumped some into his hand. "Will you tell me what to do? I want to do it right."

"Okay," Charlie said. He lay on his back and put his knees up. "Let me get used to your hand first."

Ethan began to touch him, first sliding his slick hand along Charlie's cock and rubbing the thumb under the head, then cupping his balls and stroking lightly underneath them with his fingers. His own dick was flushed and hard, and the friction every time it came in contact with Charlie's thigh was enough to make him want to scream. He bit down hard on his lip and began to tease Charlie's hole, circling it and pushing just the slightest bit inside. He looked up at Charlie questioningly and got a nod in return. He slid one finger into him and began to move it around, opening him up. He tried to do it as close as possible to the way Charlie did it to him. He replayed that experience as he worked, and had to pause a few times to squeeze his own cock and get himself under control again. He added another finger, and another. He wasn't going to rush it, but his dick was throbbing. He rubbed it against Charlie's leg and nearly came right then.

"Hey," Charlie said, "I'm ready. But you're going to last about two seconds if you don't calm down."

Ethan gently pulled his fingers free and nodded. He lay down next to Charlie and closed his eyes. He rubbed Charlie's chest and willed himself to get some control. "I'm okay," he said after a minute or so. He didn't want to wait any longer. He grabbed the condom he'd left on the nightstand and ripped it open. His fingers were trembling slightly as he rolled it on, though he wasn't sure if that was more from nerves or excitement.

"How do you want to do this?" Charlie asked.

"You choose," Ethan said.

"All right," Charlie said softly, and turned around to face away from Ethan, lying on his side. "Put your arms around me." He lifted his leg and reached between his legs for Ethan's cock. "Ready?"

Ethan held him tighter and kissed the top of his spine. "Please," he begged. Charlie guided the tip of Ethan's cock into himself, and already it was the most intense feeling Ethan had ever had in that part of his body. He'd planned to go slow, but he couldn't stop himself from thrusting forward, pulling Charlie's body in as he did. Ethan groaned loudly, and he heard a gasp from Charlie. "Shit. I'm sorry. Are you okay?"

Charlie let out a silent laugh, but Ethan felt his body vibrate with it. "Definitely okay." He hooked his leg around the back of Ethan's knee, and they moved together, writhing on the bed like they were one being. Ethan could feel the muscles in Charlie's stomach contracting against his hand with every thrust. The friction and the sensation of being squeezed as he went in and out was unlike anything he'd ever experienced, and he loved being so close to Charlie, but he needed something more.

"I want to roll you over," he whispered into Charlie's ear. "I want to fuck you harder. I want—"

"Yes," Charlie said, "do that. God, please."

Ethan pushed him over and moved with him. His cock slipped out, but he got it back in once Charlie was up onto his knees, vaguely aware that it was the first time he'd done that. He went in all the way, and even though he went slowly that time, it felt very different from this angle. He felt powerful. He started to go harder, but still not as much as he wanted to. He wasn't sure how much he could do without hurting Charlie.

"More," Charlie panted. "Fuck me. Come on, Ethan, pound my ass. Do it!"

"Oh God," Ethan said. "Okay."

He pulled out slowly and shoved back in as hard as he could. It felt like an electrical current ran through his entire body, lighting him up everywhere. He did it again, this time holding Charlie by the hips so he didn't sway forward. "Fuck," he whispered.

"Yeah, fuck. Fuck. Fuck me," Charlie chanted under his breath.

"Say it louder," Ethan said. "Let me hear."

"It's so good," he said louder, though still hoarse and low. "Please. Fuck my ass. Fuck me. Make me come so hard."

Ethan's mouth was completely dry, and he had no idea how he was keeping himself from coming. He kept thrusting, concentrating on nothing but the point of contact, while Charlie's words kept coming. "I want you to come," he said. "Please." He wrapped his arm around Charlie and found his cock, rock hard and dripping precum. He smoothed it along the shaft and held him loosely as he continued to fuck him. His rhythm became irregular, and he felt his balls tightening up. "Please," he said again.

Charlie moaned loudly. Whispering again, he said, "Fuck me, oh, I'm coming, I'm coming, keep fucking me...." He cried out, and Ethan felt Charlie's semen spurt over his fist. That was the end of his control, and he pushed in hard three more times before he exploded. He made a sound he'd never heard himself make before. It came from deep in his throat and sounded almost like a sob. He pulled out and rested against Charlie's body, still making that same noise, though more quietly. It took a few seconds, but he realized he actually was crying.

Charlie must have realized it too because he reached back for him. "Come here," he said.

Ethan wiped his face and moved up next to him. God, that was embarrassing. It must have been some kind of weird physical reaction to coming so hard. "I'm fine," he said. "I'm sorry."

Charlie shook his head and pulled Ethan's head down onto his shoulder. "There's nothing to be sorry for," he said. "That was some of the best sex I've ever had. I kind of wanted to cry too."

"I don't know why that happened. I'm not sad."

"I know." He reached up to stroke Ethan's hair, and they didn't talk for a bit.

"I have some pretty strong feelings happening," Ethan said, breaking the silence of the past few minutes. "For you."

"I kind of figured that out," Charlie said. "I guess I do too."

Ethan hugged him tighter around the chest and said, "Good." Then he sat up and said, "If we don't get up and take a shower now, we're going to fall asleep like this."

"You go first," Charlie mumbled.

"We can go together," Ethan said. "I guess you've never seen my shower, huh?"

"I can probably extrapolate from the rest of this ridiculous apartment."

Ethan's shower was a large, square stall with double shower heads, a large showerhead in the ceiling, and four jets that could blast water at you from the sides. He'd never been in a shower like that before moving here, but now he was pretty sure he'd insist on it in any home he might have in the future. He and Charlie were both acting strangely self-conscious as they soaped each other up. Every time their eyes met they'd smile and then laugh awkwardly. They'd both edged toward saying something serious, but it might have been the intense sex that brought it out, and he promised himself he'd be more careful. He didn't want this getting ruined by saying or doing too much, too soon.

When they were covered in suds, Ethan turned on the side jets and they stood in the middle of the shower stall. His eyes met Charlie's again, but instead of laughing and looking away, he put his arms around him and kissed him. The water pounded against their backs and fell like rain on their heads. When the kiss broke, Charlie looked at him with wide eyes and said, "How do you ever manage to leave this thing?"

"It's easier when I'm in here alone," Ethan replied, "but not by much."

They finally got out and dried off before climbing into bed naked. Charlie's eyes looked heavy as he gave Ethan a slow smile. "Good night, stud," he said.

Ethan smiled back at him and reached out to stroke the side of his face. He watched as Charlie closed his eyes and listened to his breathing change before he turned over and went to sleep himself.

# Chapter Ten

CHARLIE HAD packed a change of clothes in the backpack he normally used to bring work home. He'd had to get up earlier than Ethan to be at work by his required arrival time of seven thirty, but that was a lot later than he normally needed to wake up. It was easy to imagine getting used to the luxury of sleeping in until the almost decadent hour of six thirty and still having time to stop at the Starbucks three blocks down that he passed on his walk to work—not to mention Ethan's shower, which automatically meant at least some of his day would be fucking amazing.

Janice was heading into the school as Charlie turned the corner and started down the block where the school was located. She looked up and waved at him, then waited until he reached the front doors before going in. "Why were you coming from that direction?" she asked. "Isn't your stop the other way?"

"I wanted a latte," he said, holding up his cup.

"Isn't there a Starbucks on the way from your stop, though? I could swear I've gone to that one."

Charlie was sure he must have still been too relaxed from the shower, because he was unable to come up with an answer for her. He stood there looking at her for a good ten seconds, during which time she folded her arms and frowned at him suspiciously. Finally, he turned and pushed through the door of the school. She followed him, and they walked up the stairs together. "I stayed over at someone's place last night," he told her.

"You?"

"Yes," he sighed. "It happens occasionally."

"So this must have been someone you've seen more than once, right?"

"Just go ahead and ask me, Janice," Charlie said as he unlocked the door to his classroom.

"Ethan Daniels?"

Charlie nodded and walked over to his desk to put his bag down. Janice came in after him, and he sat on the edge facing her. "Are you seriously telling me Josh didn't text you about this?"

"He actually called me," she said. "But he only talked about you and news boy for a minute. He spent the rest of the time talking about some guy he met outside of the building."

"Roland," Charlie said. "He's the doorman."

"Oh! He didn't say that. I wonder why. You don't think he's some kind of asshole who doesn't want people to know he wants to go out with a doorman, do you?"

"I don't know," Charlie said, laughing. "I hope not. But I'm sure he'll get over it if that's an issue. Roland is smoking hot. Did they make plans or anything?"

"Nope. Josh is kicking himself pretty hard about it. Apparently he stood there flirting for like twenty minutes and then was like 'well, gotta go, it's been fun talking to you.' And then he just left! Didn't get his number and doesn't even know his last name. I was sympathetic on the phone, but I wanted to howl with laughter. What a dumb shit."

Charlie shook his head. "Well, I might see what I can do to help him out, depending on what he said to you about Ethan."

"He said he might turn out to be okay for you. And that he looked hot in that dark blue shirt."

"Yeah he did," Charlie said.

"Do I get to meet him someday?"

"Maybe Fiona will be in your class in two years," he said, grinning at her.

"You're such an ass," she said. "But speaking of that, you know it's against the rules, right?"

"Yeah," Charlie said unhappily. "You don't think they'd fire me, do you?"

"I doubt it. They'd probably transfer her to the other first grade classroom, unless the mother complains. Does she know about it?

She strikes me as the kind of person who'd be terrifying if she were pissed at you."

"She sort of knows," he said. "I don't know if he's mentioned that we started seeing each other again, but she's on board." Charlie looked at the clock and said, "You better get to your classroom. The kids will be here any minute." She started to walk out, and he added, "You can meet him. I'll work it out."

Midmorning he got a text from Josh that read, *I'm an idiot. Need your help.*

Charlie replied, *So I hear.*

Josh texted back, *Can you get me his number? He's amazing. I think I'm in love.*

Charlie said, *I don't think love is the word you're looking for. And I don't want to ask him for his number, but I'll give him yours when I see him. Okay?*

He didn't see Roland until after work on Wednesday, but in the meantime Josh had sent him multiple texts about how awesome Roland was. (*He's in grad school. He lives in one of those amazing old houses in Harlem. He laughed at all of my jokes.*) Ethan called to ask him if he felt like coming over to his place to watch a movie and order food, which he definitely did. He said he'd try to finish up early and leave right after they'd taped the show, so Charlie wouldn't have to wait around in midtown too long. Roland was on the door when Charlie walked up at around four thirty.

"Aren't you on early?" Charlie asked.

"Yeah, I covered part of Luis's shift because he had to take his dad to the doctor. I can always use the extra money."

"Is Ethan home yet?"

"Not yet, but I have a message for you. He called to say he can't get out as early as he'd hoped, but yesterday he gave me this to give to you if you got here before him." He pulled a small envelope out of his pocket and handed it to Charlie.

Charlie opened it and pulled out a piece of paper, into which a key had been folded. The paper read simply, *Sorry. Might as well wait in comfort.*

"Giving you a key, huh? That's something," Roland said.

"He's not giving it to me. It's just so I can get in."

"Still," Roland said, grinning.

"I guess I'll go up," Charlie said.

"Hey, uh, before you do...." Roland's eyes darted to the side, and he licked his lower lip. "Your friend. Josh? Do you think he might want to hang out with me some time?"

Charlie's face lit up with a smile. "I think he practically wants to marry you and have your babies. Let me give you his number. Text him immediately so he stops pestering me about it, okay?"

"Okay," Roland laughed.

Charlie gave him the number and went inside. It was weird being there without Ethan. He felt like he didn't belong. Once he got into Ethan's apartment, he felt even more uneasy. It looked like a movie set. He set the key down on the little table inside the door and went over to the bar to make a drink. Idly, he wondered how much money Ethan was actually pulling in. He walked around the apartment with his drink, looking at everything. He couldn't imagine Ethan had picked out all of this furniture and the art on the walls. He must have had a decorator. Not that Charlie didn't think he had any style, but he seemed to care so little about the place, and because it didn't seem at all personal. It wasn't that it was cold—in fact, it was done in a comfortable and warm style—but it was too perfect.

He poked his head into the bathroom off the hallway and then into the only other room he hadn't looked at before. When he opened the door he immediately got a big smile on his face. It was obviously a little girl's room, but this one didn't look impersonal at all. The walls were pale pink and there was a nice set of white Pottery Barn furniture, but the comforter was zebra striped and there was a pillow with an orange polka-dotted pillow case sitting on top of it. There was a heap of stuffed animals at the end of the bed, including some well-loved ones. The walls were covered with posters of cute animals, cartoon characters, and Taylor Swift. There were toys—the plastic kind kids actually played with—visible in tubs along the walls and on shelves. By the window there was a lime green bean bag chair with Fiona's name stitched on it in hot pink, and a Junie B. Jones book on the floor next to it. It was kind of a decorator's nightmare, and Charlie had to assume Ethan had let his daughter pick everything out herself.

Ethan got home not too long after that, and they ordered food, started their movie, and ended up having sex on the couch before it was half-over, and then again in the wonderful shower after the movie ended. In the morning he enjoyed the easy walk to work again. Things felt so easy and so right that it made Charlie nervous. Eventually, things would change. That was true in all relationships—and in everything else in life, for that matter—but he could already see it coming in this one.

There was Fiona to consider, for one thing, and her reaction to her daddy dating a man in general and Charlie in particular. It wasn't like she didn't know anyone with a same-sex partner. In her class alone, there were two kids with two moms and one with two dads. Still, it was different when it was your own parent—Charlie knew that from personal experience. When his mom came out, he'd taken it in stride. He'd been a tiny bit younger than Fiona at the time. The reaction came when he was a little older, in middle school. There had definitely been times when he wished his mom wasn't so conspicuously different from his friends' parents, though of course he'd never said such a thing to her. Of course, some of his reaction might have been due to his growing awareness of his own sexuality, as if his mother dating women somehow exposed him to scrutiny. Aside from that whole business, there was also the simple fact of being in a relationship with someone who had a child. There was a lot of pressure and responsibility that went along with that, as well as sacrifices he'd have to make.

The other big shift would come whenever Ethan decided to come out publicly. Charlie wasn't sure exactly what that would bring, but if nothing else Ethan would feel different. Coming out always changed things. It would be for the better, but that didn't necessarily mean it wouldn't take a toll on what they had together.

Over the next two months, the only thing that changed was that they continued to grow closer. Ethan met him for drinks a couple times with Josh and Janice, which had been awkward at first but then okay. Josh's opinion of him had shifted quite a bit, which Charlie suspected had to do with the association with Roland. They started spending several nights a week at each other's apartments. At first Ethan had made a point of trying to keep it something close to even. He'd stay at Charlie's once or twice a week, most weeks, until Charlie finally said, "I think we'd both rather stay at your place, right?" The next day, at Ethan's suggestion, Charlie brought a suitcase with several changes of clothes, a razor and a toothbrush to leave there. After he'd hung up the toothbrush in the holder next to Ethan's, Ethan had come up behind him in the bathroom and kissed his neck. They'd fucked against the marble countertop while staring at each other in the bathroom mirror.

One evening they were sitting in Ethan's living room before leaving for the movie theater. Ethan was reading an article on his tablet, and Charlie was working on a lesson plan when Ethan's phone rang. He looked at it and said, "It's Deirdre. I should probably take this."

"You think?" Charlie said, amused. "She's your daughter's mother. Of course you'll take it."

Ethan smiled and pulled Charlie's foot onto his lap as he answered the phone. "What's up?" he said as he answered the call. "Fine, you? Uh-huh...."

Charlie listened with half an ear as Ethan rubbed his foot. He abandoned his schoolwork and closed his eyes, leaning his head against a throw pillow. They were discussing Thanksgiving and Christmas, negotiating their family obligations. He was thinking about other things—including his own holiday plans—until something in Ethan's voice caught his attention.

"Um, I don't know," Ethan said. He sounded oddly nervous. "No, not yet. I'm not sure if—but—" Charlie could hear the squawking of Deirdre's voice coming from the speaker. He couldn't tell what she was saying, but she was obviously making her point strongly. Ethan glanced over at him with a rueful expression, and Charlie grinned. He loved Deirdre. She was hilarious. He occasionally wondered if he should be bothered that his boyfriend was still so whipped by his ex-wife, but he couldn't bring himself to care. "Yes," Ethan was saying, "You're right. He is." Charlie raised his eyebrows at him and Ethan gave him a quick smile and squeezed his foot. "Of course I do. Okay, I will. I will! Yeah, you too. Bye."

"What was she yelling at you about this time?" Charlie asked.

Ethan snorted. He went to work on Charlie's other foot but didn't look him in the eye. "She wanted to know if I was planning to spend Thanksgiving or Christmas with you."

"Oh," Charlie said. "I guess we've sort of avoided that topic, huh?"

"I can't say it hadn't occurred to me, but I wasn't sure if it was... too soon or something. I mean, for family and all that."

"What does she want to do about the holidays?"

"Her family loves Thanksgiving," Ethan said, smiling affectionately. "They're from Ireland, as you might have guessed. They get a big kick out of it. You should see. They do the whole old-school thing—green-bean casserole with those fried onions, sweet potatoes with marshmallows, cranberry Jell-O mold. It's pretty great, actually. My mom liked to experiment with the side dishes, and never in a million years would she use canned mushroom soup in anything. She's a good cook, but some things probably shouldn't be messed with too much." He seemed to realize he'd gone off on a tangent and shook his head. "Anyway, she wants to take Fiona to her parents' house for that. My parents will be fine with that—the last few years they've gone out to a restaurant for Thanksgiving dinner. I figured I'd take Fiona to visit them on Christmas."

"So you have no plans for Thanksgiving," Charlie said.

"Not really, but don't feel like you have to invite me. I won't feel sad being by myself for the holiday."

"Do you want to come to my mom's house for Thanksgiving? Because I'd love for you to come, but I don't want to rush you if you don't feel ready. It's okay if you're not. If it helps you decide, my family is absolutely proletarian. You'll definitely get your slimy casserole and what not."

"You want me to?" Ethan asked.

"Yeah. But it doesn't have to mean anything new, you know? Like... I'm not trying to say anything with this. It's just that you're in my life, and I want you around for stuff."

Ethan nodded. "Okay. Sure. I'd love to come and meet your family. But...." He grimaced and shook his head. "Never mind."

"But what?"

"Maybe it does mean something to me. Maybe I think it does to you too."

Charlie swallowed hard. Were they having this conversation now? He wasn't sure he wanted to. "Ethan," he started, "can we just—"

"Don't worry," Ethan said, interrupting him. "You don't have to be afraid of what I'm going to say. I'm not going to say it, okay? But I can't act like it's nothing, because to me it's kind of a big deal. You're a big deal to me. I doubt I would have made even the small changes I have if it weren't for you. I'd probably still be denying what's apparently a big part of who I am if I hadn't met you."

His face was serious, and there was no way Charlie could brush off what he'd said. "They're not small changes," he said. "You've changed a lot. Maybe you can't see it, but it's obvious to me. I guess you're right about me, though. I am scared, and it's because it's not nothing. It's been such a long time since I've felt anything remotely like this about anyone. Yeah, it's a big deal. I've never brought anyone home, for Thanksgiving or otherwise, unless you count this one time I was home from college, and I hooked up with this kid from the neighborhood who'd become a weed dealer. We got high in the basement rec room at two in the morning and my sister walked in on me sitting on the couch getting my dick sucked. Jesus, how embarrassing. But it's not like he stayed for supper."

When he stopped talking, he saw Ethan smiling at him. "Was that charming story an effort to distract me from what you said before it?" he asked.

"Maybe," Charlie said. "I don't really like talking about this stuff. Can we stop now?"

"Sure. It's time to leave for the movie anyway."

The following Friday Charlie was at his apartment, which was starting to feel unlived in. Every time he went back there, he wondered if it was a good idea to be spending so much time at Ethan's place. He usually enjoyed the weekends he spent alone or seeing friends, and by Monday it felt normal to be in his own place again. Then he'd see Ethan and not want to go home. He loved being at his place, and having his own things there. Probably this was all normal relationship stuff—he had no way of knowing.

Girish texted him on Saturday morning to ask if he wanted to meet for coffee. He was already at the place when Charlie arrived, and he looked like shit. He was unshaven, and he looked like he'd just rolled out of bed. There was a little teapot on the table and a full cup of tea in front of him, but he didn't seem to have touched it.

Charlie sat down with his drink and said, "I was going to regale you with my minor relationship drama, but you don't look like you want to hear that. What happened?"

"My dad called last night. My mum is sick—breast cancer. Apparently she got the diagnosis some time ago but didn't want to 'bother me' about it."

"Oh God," Charlie said. "That's awful. Is she—I mean, are they going to operate?"

Girish nodded. "She's going into hospital tomorrow. My father said he wanted to honor her wish not to tell me, but he didn't feel right about it. Honestly, can you imagine?" He rubbed his face and growled in frustration. "What if something were to happen and I hadn't even gotten a chance to talk to her first?"

"What are you going to do?"

"I'm going home," he said. "I'll contact the university on Monday, but I've already got a plane ticket for tonight. I don't know if I'll be coming back or not. Depends on how things go, I suppose. My sister will be in town to help, but she's got two little kids, so she shouldn't have to do it on her own."

"Can I help at all?" Charlie asked.

"Actually, yes. I feel a little weird asking you since we've only known each other a short time, but I don't have anyone else here. Do you think you could take care of my cat?"

Charlie smiled. "You have a cat?"

"Yes," Girish said, rolling his eyes. "I call her Gertie. She was always hanging around outside my building looking for food. She was so friendly, rubbing against my ankles and such. I had a cat at home—have a cat, but he's staying with Wes. It made me feel a little better to be taking care of one here. Anyway, she's no bother. If you go by a couple times a week to leave food out and change her water, she'll be fine. Or if it's easier to keep her at yours, obviously that's fine too. I can't bring myself to put her back on the street. She likes to sleep in my bed." The last few words were a little strangled, and Girish had tears standing in his eyes. Charlie was fairly sure they weren't about the cat, but he didn't see any way he could refuse him. The only problem was that he was horribly allergic, but he didn't mind going on allergy medication for a few weeks, or months, or whatever.

"Of course you can't put her back out," Charlie said. "What kind of sociopath does that? I'll take her. Gertie, though? Really?"

"That's her nickname. Her real name is even more embarrassing."

"Well, I'm not going to take her unless you tell me," Charlie said.

"Fine," Girish said, rolling his eyes. "I named her after Lagertha on *Vikings*. Are you happy? Now you know how much of a nerd I am."

"Lagertha's the best. She's the biggest badass of them all."

"Right?" Girish said. "If she were real, she'd be my one exception."

Charlie nodded solemnly. "Totally. If she were real, I'd have a threesome with you guys." They both laughed, but Girish still looked sad. "I'm sorry about your mom," Charlie said. "Damn. I'm going to miss you too. Making a new friend these days is like finding a four leaf clover or something."

Girish smiled and sipped his tea. "It is quite surprising. Particularly since a friend wasn't what either of us was looking for that night. Although, now I've said that, I realize it might not be true. Perhaps that's exactly what I was looking for."

"Not sure what I was looking for," Charlie said, "but it was probably what I needed the most."

Charlie went back with him when they'd finished at the coffee shop and packed the cat and her belongings up to bring to his apartment, stopping on the way for a pack of Claritin.

# Chapter Eleven

ETHAN LOVED his weekends with Fiona, but he couldn't help being glad when Monday came around. Often he'd walk her to the classroom so he could see Charlie for a minute before going to work, but on the first Monday of November he was running late. He'd have to wait until the evening to see him, and hopefully they'd have something to celebrate. After several rounds of negotiations with his agent, ECHO had offered him a five-year contract for a great deal more money than he was currently making. He'd be meeting with his attorney and Vince Martin to sign the contract as soon as they wrapped up the taping of his show.

Before he could get to the good part of the day, however, he had to get through his interview with William Browning, head of the Christian Values League and author of the book *Along Straight Paths: Raising Real Boys in a Godless World.* Ethan was dreading it. The story they were doing was on the recent push by several states to outlaw so-called gay conversion camps. The network's official position on the subject was that it was tantamount to religious discrimination, and that the government had no right to tell parents how to raise their children. Ethan's original plan was to have someone on from a human rights organization, offer a few stupid, simplistic arguments they'd easily be able to refute. He'd probably throw in some debunked statistics as well. He'd then do a noncommittal wrap up ending with a question, such as, "Are these camps truly in the best interest of children, or are they in fact dangerous and abusive? Tweet your opinion to @ethandanielsatecho." He'd felt more or less satisfied with this approach until he got a memo stating that any time this topic was covered, they were to have someone sympathetic to the camps on to argue their side.

Ethan was still angry—not because ECHO took that stance, because that was unsurprising, but because he was sure it was aimed at him specifically. That meant one of his producers had most likely told someone higher up what they were doing. In the end having Browning on had been Abby's idea. She thought if they had on the craziest person they could find, someone who couldn't help sounding insane, no one could fault Ethan for pushing back against their arguments. He'd thought it was a good idea at the time, but now he wondered if she was giving people too much credit.

Charlie knew about the interview. He'd seen Ethan reading the man's book the week before and naturally wanted to know why the hell he'd be doing that. He'd listened to Ethan's explanation of the whole situation, nodded calmly, and gone into a different room. When Ethan followed him to ask if he was angry, Charlie said, "I can't be angry at you for doing your job. I knew you had this job when I started seeing you. I'm having a hard time with it at the moment, but I'll get over it. I just need you to leave me alone right now." That had been the most conflict they'd experienced since settling into their current relationship, but even though it was mild and hadn't lasted long, it worried Ethan quite a bit. He didn't know how many of these things Charlie would be able to get over, or how much it was going to eventually change his opinion of Ethan.

Abby went over his interview questions with him shortly before the show. He didn't particularly need a review, but she seemed to sense that he needed some moral support. When they'd finished, she said, "Are you going to be okay with this, Ethan? You're having a hard time not looking angry when you're speaking."

"I'll be fine once I'm on camera," he said. "You know me."

"Is your relationship going to be okay with it?"

Ethan looked at her sharply and said, "I don't think that's for you to worry about."

"I know you don't think it is, but I worry anyway because I actually care about you. And I know what this job is doing to you. It's not just this kind of stuff either. Last week, talking to that libertarian asshole from Freedom from the Minimum Wage? There was a second there I thought you were about to lose it. And the congressman who wanted to ban all nonbarrier forms of birth control because he believed men are the ones who should be in charge of when conception occurs?"

"I knew what this job entailed when I took it," he said. "I'll worry about my own soul, you worry about yours. You work here too, you know."

"I can leave when it gets to be too much. All I have to do is give two weeks' notice. Are you seriously going to sign on for another five years of this?"

Ethan glared at her until she left his office, shaking her head and muttering under her breath. He steeled himself for what he had to do.

He got through the first part of the show without a problem. That was the segment where he covered a series of current-event stories, putting them into a context and explaining them. He didn't mind so much because he was able to stick pretty closely to simple reporting without much of a spin. The second half was usually dedicated to one topic. He'd do an explanation of the story, accompanied by whatever footage they could dig up, and then one or two interviews or a panel of guests, depending. He had been adamantly opposed to doing a panel format with this story. It would have taken the pressure off of him, but it also would have taken any control he had over the direction of the conversation away from him. He knew his viewers and who they'd choose to side with if it devolved into a shouting match.

He opened the segment with a description of the conversion camps and the various methods they used. He listed the complaints and accusations that had been lodged against such places in the past, and the danger that many psychologists felt they posed to the psyche of young LGBT people. He then explained the counter argument, which stated that homosexuality was the real danger, and that if any of these children committed suicide, it was because they were dealing with a spiritual and emotional disease.

He had a psychologist on as his first guest. She was active in the push to ban these camps and had written several papers for academic journals on their dangers. She was intelligent and well spoken, batting away each of his paper thin premises with ease. He'd saved Browning for last, hoping to end by prompting him to say something ludicrous and hateful so that's what would ring in the ears of the viewers while they watched Steve Hannigan's show. He was ready for this. He could nod studiously while Browning frothed at the mouth and ask him respectful questions.

"Good evening, Mr. Browning," Ethan said as Browning sat down and got settled.

Browning gave him a cold smile that didn't come close to reaching his eyes, leaned forward and said in a low voice, "I normally find this network to be commendable, but I don't know what they were thinking, hiring a deviant like you. Everyone knows about you, and it makes them look like fools, but don't think for a second I don't see what's happening here. I saw what you did in that other interview."

Ethan offered a frosty smile back and said quietly, "I don't need to do anything to you except let you talk. You're a raving lunatic and everyone knows *that*."

Browning wasn't wrong—there had been rumors. Ethan was fairly sure they'd been started by Hannigan, but they probably would have been circulating anyway. True to his promise, he hadn't been reticent about being seen with Charlie in public. They never touched or displayed outright affection, but it hardly mattered. People were going to talk, and Ethan was fine with that. His ratings were still excellent, which was all that ultimately mattered to Vince Martin and the network.

What Ethan hadn't told Charlie was that there was a clause in his new contract that forbid him from "contradicting the network's stated positions in a public forum." This included, among many other things, support for marriage equality and of laws specifically protecting LGBT people from discrimination. His agent had tried hard to get it amended but the network had steadfastly refused.

The interview began politely enough despite the exchange they'd just had. Ethan asked Browning to explain his beliefs about the causes of homosexuality and how he thought it could be prevented with the right parenting methods.

"A boy's relationship with his father is key," Browning said. "A family without a strong male leader puts the son at a much greater risk of developing a sexual disorder."

"Homosexuality is no longer considered to be a disorder by the psychiatric community, yet you and your organization continue to regard it as such. On what grounds do you base your decision?"

Browning humored him with a tolerant chuckle and replied, "That change by the AMA had nothing to do with actual science and everything to do with politics. It's one more symptom of our society's dangerous and short-sighted focus on making everyone *feel good*. Rather than encourage people to change the things that are wrong with them, which leads to ultimate happiness—and of course salvation, which these liberal psychiatrists care little about—they want people to accept such things. It is a disgrace."

Ethan felt the anger building inside of him. He'd been feeling it a lot more often lately, as Abby had noticed, but he was normally able to keep it in check. It wasn't his job to discredit this man, or those he represented. His job was to allow him to present his case and give him room to do so. His job was to provide a veneer of respectability to purveyors of harmful lies and long-debunked pseudoscience. *That* was his job.

Ethan took a breath. "How does this apply to people who already identify as gay or bisexual? If, as you believe, the damage has been done?"

Browning nodded seriously and said, "We believe all people are capable of living a godly life. We no longer believe, as we once did, that most adults can change their orientation once it is set. For those people, we offer counseling and prayer to help them make the right choices—this may involve renouncing homosexual behavior in favor of a loving heterosexual marriage, in the case of so-called 'bisexuals,' or embracing a life filled with the companionship of friends and the church, free from the burden of sexual perversion."

"In other words, celibacy," Ethan said. "That seems like a difficult choice to ask someone to make."

"Indeed," Browning said, "which is why it is so important to begin to heal these people while there is still a chance for them. Transformational ministry is far more effective when it is begun in childhood. There is no such thing as a 'gay child.' That is a disgusting idea. We are all born in the image of God."

Ethan's heart was pounding, and his mouth had gone dry. He felt as if he were short of breath. It didn't feel like anger. He had no trouble recognizing anger. This was something else—it was a fight or flight response. He didn't immediately understand what his body could be reacting to, because there was nothing frightening here. The fat, aging man sitting across from him presented no threat to him. Then he realized it wasn't Browning he was afraid of, but himself. He was planning to sign away the next five years of his life to a job that required him to treat people like this with deference. He doubted he could even last another five minutes.

Browning cleared his throat, and Ethan realized he hadn't spoken in far too long. He locked eyes with the other man and said, "There is an overwhelming consensus among mental health professionals that transformational or reparative therapy in children is damaging and leads to an increased risk of suicide in young adults. It is widely considered to be child abuse. How do you justify the continuation of such dangerous and controversial methods?"

"It is frankly absurd to label it as child abuse. These parents are trying to save their children from a life of emptiness, drug abuse, and disease. Look at the statistics. Furthermore, and most directly to the point, this is a matter of religious freedom. The state has no business interfering in the spiritual decisions a parent makes for a minor child. If a parent fears his child is on a bad path, it is his right to act as he sees fit to help the child change course."

Ethan swallowed hard. He knew this was the moment where he would make his own choice as to what path he would follow. He had been telling himself he didn't need to choose, that he could shelve the various parts of his life in separate boxes and that they didn't have to affect each other—even when they were in direct conflict. He knew now that this was impossible. He would end up losing not only the person he cared about—who he was in love with, though he hadn't previously admitted that even to himself—but he'd lose all respect for himself. Continuing on this way would do nothing but hurt himself and everyone around him.

"It's considered abuse to beat your child with a belt hard enough to raise welts," Ethan said, "yet until relatively recently, that was an acceptable form of discipline, encouraged by many religious leaders. Is that also a matter of religious freedom?"

"Corporal punishment is still a form of discipline I believe in, though if you read my book you will see there are guidelines we must follow so it does not cross the line and cause emotional trauma."

"I did read your book, sir," Ethan said. "One thing I noticed was that all of your scientific sources are at least twenty years old, and in many cases forty or more years."

"As I've said many times, the psychiatric community has fallen prey to liberalism. They are so concerned with political correctness that they no longer serve the very real needs of many troubled people. This is why it is so important to maintain a strong ministry specifically tailored to their needs."

Ethan shook his head. "I can't do this," he muttered, quietly, more to himself than anyone else. "I just can't." He cleared his throat and looked directly at Browning. "Forgive me," he said, "but I believe we're going to have to cut this interview short. I appreciate your time."

Browning, taken aback, said, "I beg your pardon? I was invited on this show for what I was led to believe would be an in-depth discussion."

"I apologize. I've realized what an error in judgment it was to allow you air time."

Abby had come rushing out of the control room. Browning was ushered off the set and the taping was stopped. She ran over to the desk and leaned over it. "Is this actually happening, Ethan? Are you doing this for real?"

Ethan nodded. "You were right, of course. You're a smart woman, and you're good at your job. If I ever get a job in the industry again, you'll always have a place with me."

"They'll never air this. You know that, right?"

"They won't have to," Ethan said. "I see three people in this room who have their phones out already. Besides, I'd be shocked if no one manages to make a copy of the entire broadcast. It'll be on the Internet by the time I leave the building—which I'm doing as soon as I finish taping, by the way. I have reservations at Le Bernardin tonight. Wouldn't want to be late."

She ran her hands through her hair and breathed deeply. "Okay. If we're doing this, let's make it good. Do you know what you want to say?"

"I'll figure it out. I'm a professional."

Ethan faced the camera they used for the end of show wrap-up segment. When he got a green light, he began talking.

"For the past year, I've had the privilege of speaking to the American public on a wide-ranging variety of topics. As a journalist I have always strived for objectivity, and as such I believed it didn't matter what the political bend of my employers might be. I believed I could present the facts and allow the viewer to make up his or her mind about them. Over the course of my tenure here, I have come to realize this is not realistic. The facts and opinions we choose to present and those we do not are designed to offer a particular way of seeing the world, and one with which I often strongly disagree.

"I have wasted this wonderful opportunity I was provided. Because of my desire to remain employed and to be successful in this business, I have allowed myself to be compromised in many ways, both professionally and personally. I have failed as a journalist because I did not insist on intellectual honesty from my guests and have allowed lies to stand unchallenged. I have failed in my personal life as well. I've been in a relationship for the past two months that has made me feel happy and fulfilled for the first time in many years. That relationship has been marginalized by the secrecy I felt compelled to maintain. This man has been far more patient and understanding than I had any right to ask for, but I won't ask that of him any longer."

Ethan paused for a few seconds to find the right word to express the rest of what he wanted to say. He knew if he wasn't clear or if he sounded angry or upset in any way, people would dismiss it.

"It was painful for me to listen to the repugnant things our guest had to say. It may have been more difficult for me, as a bisexual man, but I believe such attitudes are offensive to the vast majority of people in this country. I don't believe we have any business dignifying organizations like his by engaging in debate, and I will no longer participate in that charade."

He smiled now in the friendly way that was his trademark. His smile made people trust him and believe he had their best interests at heart. "I want to thank you all for the support I've received from the viewers. I'm sure some of you will change your opinion of me after this, but I hope you'll respect my honesty if nothing else. Good evening."

He removed his microphone and walked away from the desk. His hands were shaking and he felt weak, but he needed to get outside. He couldn't stay in that building for another second. Abby appeared at his side as if by magic and put her arm around his waist. "You going to make it?" she asked.

Ethan nodded tersely. "You don't smoke, do you?"

"No," she said. "Do you?"

"Not usually," he said, "but I sort of feel like I earned one."

"Go outside," she said. "I'll ask the cameraman, and I'll grab your coat."

It was cold out on the sidewalk, but Ethan was grateful for it. He'd been in an adrenaline haze since the second he'd ended the interview with Browning, and his body was still buzzing with it. The crisp air felt good on his burning face. He knew he should figure out what he was going to do next—as in, the next hour of his life—but he couldn't keep his mind on one thing more than a couple seconds. To his relief, Abby came bustling out the door with his coat and a cigarette and lighter.

"Kenny said you could keep the lighter and to tell you he was impressed, even though you looked like you were nearly pissing yourself. Oh, and he said sorry about the cigarette because it's a menthol, and you probably don't like those."

Ethan took it and shrugged. "Beggars can't be choosers. Anyway, my parents both smoked these. My first cigarette was a Salem 100's out of my mom's purse."

"I bet that's like number three on William Browning's list of causes for homosexuality," Abby said.

Ethan barked a laugh, and Abby giggled. He then started laughing some more, and Abby laughed harder. They both got caught up in the hysteria of the moment and couldn't stop for a long time. When it finally tapered off, Ethan leaned against the building and said, "Shit. What am I going to do now?" He lit the cigarette and took a deep drag. He felt like he'd breathed ice crystals into his lungs and it tasted horrible, but he enjoyed it anyway.

"You'll be fine," she said. "You're a good broadcaster, and you're super handsome and still young. I think I'll hold off on crying sad tears for you."

He looked at her. "You don't think this is going to ruin me? I basically had a breakdown in the middle of a nationally known program."

"No, you didn't. You reached your breaking point, yes, but you didn't break down. You stood up for yourself and for others against a bigoted, ignorant apologist for child abuse. People are going to love this shit. I do sort of wish you'd tacked on a PS and said 'oh by the way, climate change is real, and women should be in control of their own bodies,' but you did fine."

Ethan tossed the cigarette away, once again reminding himself he didn't want to do that anymore. "Thanks for keeping it a hundred, Abby."

"That sounds so wrong coming out of your mouth," she said.

"I know. My doorman says it. I like it. I wish I could use it without sounding like such a lame white guy."

"I'm going in now. You want me to box up your stuff? I could drop it off tomorrow."

"No need to drop it off," Ethan said. "I'll have to go in and deal with Vince. I don't have much in there anyway."

Abby winced. "You want me to come with you?"

"You know, if my dad had been as supportive as you, maybe I'd be straight," Ethan said in a completely serious voice. "But no, that's okay. I'm almost looking forward to it."

"I guess I'll see you tomorrow, then," she said, but she didn't leave. She looked like she was about to walk toward Ethan but stopped herself.

"You can hug me this time if you want," he said.

She hugged him around the waist, and when she pulled back, her eyes were wet. "It's been good working with you." She raised her hand in a little wave and walked back into the building.

Ethan hailed a cab and gave the driver Charlie's address. He'd planned to pick him up later—their reservation wasn't until eight—but he wanted to see him right away. He called Deirdre on the way to tell her what was happening before she heard it somewhere else.

# Chapter Twelve

ETHAN WAS supposed to come get him at seven, so when someone buzzed his door at a few minutes past five, he assumed it was for one of his neighbors, and they'd rung the wrong bell. The cat, who had just made her first brave attempt at jumping onto the sofa with him, darted underneath it. He went to the speaker and called down, "Yes?"

"It's me," Ethan said, unmistakable despite the poor quality of the speaker. "I'm sorry I'm so early. I need to see you."

Charlie buzzed him up. Ethan had sounded odd—not exactly upset, but keyed up at least. He knew this was the day he was supposed to sign the contract, so maybe that was it. Or maybe it had been the interview with that asshole from the Christian Values League. That would get anyone with a conscience riled up, and he knew Ethan had one. He wouldn't bother with so many justifications for his job if he didn't. He'd actually been worried Ethan would be depressed at dinner, which would have been annoying. He'd never been to a restaurant as nice as the one they were going to, and he wanted to enjoy it. He'd let Ethan spend as much of his new contract money as he wanted to, tonight.

"Hey," Charlie said, smiling as he opened the door for him. He leaned in for a kiss and Ethan wrapped his arms around him. "Everything okay?"

"Yes," Ethan said, his voice muffled by Charlie's neck. "No. Both, maybe. I don't know."

Charlie gently pushed him back so he could look at his face. "Are you wearing makeup?"

"Oh yeah," Ethan said. He huffed out a laugh and walked over to sit on the sofa. "I didn't stay long enough to wash it off after we wrapped up the taping. Don't let me forget to do that before we go to dinner."

Charlie frowned. "Weren't you supposed to do your signing after the show?"

"About that," Ethan said. Charlie's eyes widened as he waited to hear whatever this was. "Can I ask you something?"

"Uh, sure. Even though you're kind of leaving me hanging here."

"Would you still like me if I were poor? Or is part of why you're attracted to me that I'm this rich asshole with a big midtown apartment?"

Charlie's mouth fell open. "Are you fucking kidding me? Are you honestly asking me that, Ethan?"

"It's not any part of it? Really?"

Charlie got up and walked to the kitchen. He'd planned on grabbing beers and taking a few seconds to calm down, because he was furious. He took the bottles out of the refrigerator, but the full implication of what Ethan had said hit him suddenly, and he had to put them down and lean against the counter. He felt like crying, but he didn't want to do it in front of Ethan—not just then, anyway. He stood in the kitchen with his eyes closed, breathing deeply and trying to get himself under control, when he heard Ethan approaching from behind.

"It's not you," Ethan said softly. "I didn't mean—I don't think you're shallow. That's not where that was coming from. I didn't even hear it until you got up and then I realized what I'd said."

Charlie didn't feel ready to answer him or even to turn around yet, but he didn't flinch when Ethan touched his back. They stood there, unmoving, for at least a full minute before Charlie relented and turned to face him. "If that's not what you meant, then tell me what you did mean. And tell me what the hell is going on with you right now."

Ethan nodded. "I didn't sign the new contract," he said. "And I'm not going to. I couldn't even if I wanted to, or at least I assume that's the case. I'd be shocked if it weren't."

"Jesus. What happened?"

"I kicked William Browning off the set before the interview was over, apologized for my complicity in advancing ECHO's false narratives, and came out about being bisexual and in a relationship with a man."

Charlie's mouth fell open, and he studied Ethan's face to make sure he wasn't joking. "You... for real? You did that?"

"I sure as shit did. And now I don't know what's going to happen. And I only asked you because that's who I was when you met me, and I don't know what else you could like about me. I look good, I guess. I know that. People tell me. Handsome and rich will get anyone laid. Or even one of those things. But that doesn't mean anyone's going to have real feelings for you. It doesn't mean anyone's going to—to—"

"Love you," Charlie said quietly.

"Right. And that scares me, because I love you."

Charlie reached out and pulled him in by the shoulder until their bodies were flush against each other. "How do you not know?" he asked. "How can you think there's nothing to love about you? I bet you don't really think that. You're just freaking out so you're being dramatic. I love you, dummy. Of course I do. Your financial status doesn't enter into it. Although…."

"The shower," Ethan said. "I know."

"Seriously, I'm so excited about this. It's great. Amazing." Charlie was grinning, trying to look as positive as he could.

"What if I can't get another broadcast job?"

"I don't think that's going to happen, but it's going to be fine. You'll be fine." He put his hand to Ethan's cheek and kissed him. "Oh!" he said, pulling back. "Does Deirdre know?"

"I called her on the way over. I gave her the basics in case she hears something. She wanted to talk my ear off about it and ask me all these questions, but I couldn't deal. I had to hang up on her. I hope she's not too mad." Charlie raised his eyebrows skeptically. "Yeah. I should probably call her back, huh? Do you mind?"

"No," Charlie said, handing him one of the beers he'd taken out. "I'm going to get a shower and change. Then you can wash that shit off your face and borrow one of my shirts. This one's got orangey stuff on the collar."

He left Ethan sitting on the couch and went into the bathroom. He felt dazed. He'd meant what he said about not caring if Ethan had money or not. He liked going out to good restaurants and not worrying about how much he was spending, but it wasn't a big deal. He'd meant it when he said he thought this was great—all of it, including the things they'd said to each other. Still, he felt uneasy.

He hadn't wanted Ethan to know it, but he was worried. Things would be changing, and he wasn't sure where he stood in the bigger picture. Ethan had said he loved him, but the fact was they'd only been together a short time. If something had to give, it would most likely be their relationship.

He'd been standing in the shower for a while, trying to map out all of the possible versions of the future, when the curtain was pulled back. Ethan was standing there, naked, with a nervous look on his face. "Can I come in?" he asked.

"If you want," Charlie said. "It's more of a one-person shower than you're used to, though."

Ethan stepped over the edge of the tub and put his hands on Charlie's arms. "Do you really think this is going to be fine?" he asked. "Because everything is going to be different now. I know you like things to be simple, but I don't see how we can avoid complications." He was looking into Charlie's eyes as if he were searching for something. "I just wanted to make sure you know that."

"Doesn't matter how I like things to be," Charlie said. "They are what they are. I can't keep running away just because something makes me uncomfortable. I want to be with you, so we'll just have to figure out how to make it happen. Right?"

The tension ran out of Ethan's face, and he nodded. "That's what I think," he said. He leaned into Charlie and went in for a slow kiss as the water streamed down over their shoulders. When he broke the kiss, he looked down at the space between their bodies and smiled. He let his fingers slip down Charlie's stomach to the base of his hardening cock.

"We should probably make this a quick one," Charlie said.

"That shouldn't be a problem," Ethan replied.

He sat down on the edge of the tub and pulled Charlie in by the hips. After everything that had just happened, and not seeing him for days before that, the feeling of Ethan's mouth on him was an intense relief. He shut down all of his worries about what might happen and focused on that, moaning and talking more than he usually did. His orgasm came fast and hard, and he pulled Ethan up as soon as he'd finished. He spun him around and pushed him roughly against the wall, kissing him hard and stroking him relentlessly until he came with a gasp.

Ethan slumped back and laughed breathlessly. "Whew," he said. "I feel better."

Charlie laughed too as he rinsed his hand off. "Me too. Now we can enjoy our dinner."

"We'd better enjoy it. It might be the last time I can get a reservation on such short notice at a place like that."

Charlie stepped out and let Ethan finish washing up. He wiped the fogged up mirror and studied himself in the mirror. "What would you say if I decided to shave my beard?" he called out.

"It's your face," Ethan said. "Why? Do you want to?"

"I don't know," Charlie said. "All these changes, maybe I'll make one too. Will you still like me?"

"Shut up," Ethan replied.

When Charlie went into the bedroom, he saw Ethan's suit hanging neatly on a chair, but his shirt had been tossed on the floor in the corner by the dresser, and curled up in a tiny gray and white ball on top of it was Gertie, purring loudly. He squatted down to pet her, and she flipped around to stretch out, then curled up again and buried her face in the fabric. Ethan came out a few minutes later and saw them.

"She's cute," he said. "She jumped into my lap when I was on the phone. You didn't tell me you got a cat."

"She belongs to Girish," Charlie said. "He had to go back to England unexpectedly, so I said I'd take care of her. I'm pretty allergic, though. I hope he's not there too long. If he ends up staying I'm going to have to give her to someone. Did she really jump up on you? She didn't let me touch her for two days."

"All cats love me," Ethan said. "No idea why. What's her name?"

"Gertie. Don't ask."

Charlie finished dressing and went out to the living room. It was around seven, which was the normal time for Ethan's show to air. He switched on ECHO News and found a rerun of their afternoon panel show. He turned it off and opened his laptop. He'd only typed three letters into the search bar when he got a suggested search for "Ethan Daniels gay," which had been the top result for a long time. This was followed by

"Ethan Daniels comes out" and then "Ethan Daniels epic meltdown." He clicked on that search and found a story about the taping that included some audio, but no video. The story gave a rundown of what happened during the taping, but the audio clip was only from the end of the show after the interview was over.

Ethan came out of the bedroom to see him on the computer and said, "Well? Is it out there now?"

"Sort of," Charlie said. "The story is, yeah. No one seems to have the tape of it yet. Just audio of the last part when you were talking to the camera. That was pretty cool, though. I wish I'd been there."

"Maybe it's good there's no video. The cameraman thought I looked terrified, apparently."

"Well, you sounded great." He got up and gave Ethan a kiss. "Ready?"

The host at the restaurant greeted them very politely but with a barely constrained curiosity. That seemed to be the demeanor of a good number of people who noticed them, but no one approached them, and if people were talking about it—which they almost certainly were—they were discreet about it. The waiter came to their table, but before they were able to give their drink orders, he said, "One of the other customers would like to buy your table a round of drinks. Whatever you would like. They don't want me to say who they are, only to wish you luck."

Ethan looked like he was having a hard time forming a response, so Charlie said, "That's so nice. Please thank them for us." He ordered a good scotch for Ethan and a cocktail with gin and grapefruit juice for himself.

"How long do you think it's going to be like this?" Ethan asked when the waiter was gone.

"You work in the media. You should know. People will get bored of this in no time. Maybe a week."

"Unless people decide to make a thing of it," Ethan said unhappily. "What if the Christian right decides they don't want to let it go?"

Charlie shrugged. "That will just make you look better to everyone else. But I doubt they will, and if they do, ECHO won't want to pick it up. Too embarrassing for them."

Ethan nodded and let it go. The meal was amazing—the best one Charlie could ever remember eating. They lingered over it, drinking two bottles of wine and splitting the Peruvian chocolate cake at the end. They hadn't planned to go back to Charlie's place after dinner, but Ethan thought it wouldn't be right to leave the cat alone so soon after she'd had to move. Charlie decided right then he needed to find someone else to take the animal, because he wasn't about to miss out on staying at Ethan's place during the time they had left. It was a hell of a lot nicer.

They managed to brush their teeth before collapsing into bed, but just barely. When they were under the covers, Charlie cuddled up to Ethan and put his arm around him. He felt sleepy and a little drunk, and he knew he'd never say what he wanted to say under any other circumstances.

"I knew I wanted to be with you after the second time we were together. When you came back to the school and apologized to me."

"Yeah?" Ethan asked, his speech morphing into a yawn. "I probably would have known too if I hadn't been so stupid about it."

"I started thinking about stuff I'd never imagined for myself before. Stuff that's probably not even real, but I guess it represented something in my mind, you know what I mean?"

"Not really," Ethan said. "Like what?"

"You're going to laugh at me," Charlie said.

"So? I'll still love you. Tell me anyway."

So Charlie told him about the morning coffee and the apple picking and the ridiculous backyard dinner with the lanterns and all. Ethan didn't laugh. He pulled Charlie's arm around him more tightly and said, "I'll see what I can do."

# Chapter Thirteen

ETHAN WENT into the ECHO offices the next day and immediately headed upstairs to speak with Vince Martin. He was let in right away, and Martin was at his desk when Ethan entered. He sat back and said, "Let's get this over with."

"I'm sorry it happened that way," Ethan said. "It wasn't planned."

"Planned or not, I doubt you're all that sorry. Either way, you're a goddamn idiot. We all knew about you. Everyone did—it's not like you've been discreet about it. No one cared. All you had to do was not *say* it. I can't imagine why it was so important that you would throw away all that money."

"It wasn't just that. It's all of it. I couldn't be your mouthpiece anymore. It was killing me."

Martin scoffed and shook his head. "Like I said—idiot. In case you hadn't already figured this out, you don't need to bother coming in here again. Your contract is up at the end of this month, and you'll receive payment for the remainder. Your belongings have been boxed up and security will walk you out. Nothing personal of course—standard practice."

"Of course," Ethan said. "Well… thank you for the opportunity, Vince."

Martin looked at him blankly, which Ethan couldn't honestly blame him for. He wouldn't have known how to respond to that either. He nodded and walked out to where the guards were waiting with his things and then took a taxi home to his apartment, which was already beginning to feel like it wasn't his.

The full video of the unaired episode was leaked that afternoon. Ethan decided to stay off the Internet entirely, and turned his phone off as well when the buzzing from incoming texts became too much. It had been off for several hours when he decided to check it, and he was surprised to see a voice mail waiting for him from the station manager he'd worked for in Philadelphia, before he'd taken the job at ECHO. It said, "Ethan, it's Tom. I wanted to tell you I saw the video, and I thought it was fucking amazing. Truly great television. I'd like to talk to you if you have a few minutes, so call me back whenever. Congratulations, by the way, whoever the lucky guy is."

Ethan couldn't imagine what Tom Kearny wanted to talk to him about. They'd had a good working relationship, but they certainly hadn't been friends. The only thing he could think of was that maybe they wanted to interview him for a story about what he'd done. That held some appeal, but he knew his agent would be furious. It probably wouldn't be the best idea while he was looking for a job. He called Kearny back anyway, because the last thing he wanted to do was burn more bridges.

"Ethan!" Tom said, sounding genuinely happy to get the call. "Jesus, your phone must be blowing up. Thanks for getting back to me."

"Yeah, no problem, Tom. You know I have nothing but respect for everyone at WPHI. I'm always happy to hear from you. What's up?"

"I was wondering what your plan was, to be honest. I assumed you had something lined up already, but I'm not hearing any chatter about it."

"It wasn't exactly planned ahead of time," Ethan said. "I was supposed to sign a contract for five more years with ECHO after the taping. I guess I was the cable news version of a runaway bride."

Tom laughed. "Yeah, but don't let anyone else get away with calling you that," he said. "Well, listen. In that case, I want to put this out there. You'll probably get better offers than I can give you, but if there was any chance you wanted to come home, we've got a place for you. We can talk numbers later, but it would be better than you were getting before. We'd love to have you. Philly's got your back."

Ethan was fairly sure it wasn't a universally held sentiment, but it was nice to hear anyway. "Wow," he said, "I don't know what to say. You know I never wanted to leave in the first place, but my kid is here. That's the only reason I took that job. I need to see what I can do to stay."

"Absolutely," Kearny said. "I'm not looking for a yes today, but I don't want to hear a no yet either. Sleep on it."

"I will. Thanks for calling."

He and Deirdre had decided to hold off explaining anything to Fiona until Friday so she could have the whole weekend with him in case she wanted to ask him any questions, but on Thursday morning Charlie called him from work in the middle of the morning. Ethan had just come from a meeting with his agent, who was irate that Ethan hadn't given him a heads-up about the impulsive thing he'd done, and he was in a shitty mood. For a split second, he'd been happy to see Charlie's name on the display, but almost immediately understood that he wouldn't be calling at that time to talk unless it was important.

"Hi, what's up?"

"Hey. Um… this is not necessarily bad, so don't freak out," Charlie began.

"Jesus Christ, who starts a sentence like that?" Ethan asked. "I'm terrified."

"Sorry, sorry. I wanted to let you know. A couple of kids were talking to Fiona about you. I heard them ask her if you had a boyfriend. It didn't seem like they were teasing her—one of the kids was Alexandra, who has two dads. Maybe she was trying to find them some friends? I have no idea. I redirected them, and I told the teachers in her other classes to keep an ear out for it."

"Shit," Ethan said. "I knew I shouldn't have put it off. I was trying to figure out the right way to explain the whole thing without telling her who my boyfriend actually is. How did she react? Was she upset?"

"No, it didn't seem like it. Pretty much nonplussed, to be honest. All she said was she didn't know."

"Seriously?"

"Yeah. They didn't intend it as an insult, so she didn't take it as one. You should talk to her, but I don't think you should be so worried about it. Don't act like you're scared to tell her or you'll freak her out."

"That's not at all how it would have gone when I was a kid," Ethan said.

"Me neither. Be happy for her."

"I am. Thanks for letting me know. I know we're supposed to get dinner tonight, but—"

"Call me when you're finished," Charlie said. "I'll come over late."

"Come over whenever you want. I'll leave the key with whoever's at the door."

He called Deirdre and explained the situation, which she seemed to take calmly.

"Come for dinner," she offered. "We can talk to her together. Or you can talk, but I think I should be there so she knows I'm not angry with you about it."

"I'd like to pick her up from school, if that's okay."

Ethan stood outside the school at three with a group of parents and—mostly—nannies who were waiting to pick up their charges. He got quite a few curious looks, but a couple of people smiled at him in what he chose to take as support. The students were let out by grade level, with the first graders being the last through the doors. When Fiona saw him, her face lit up, and she ran to give him a hug.

"Why are you picking me up today, Daddy?" she asked.

"Your mom invited me to have dinner with you guys tonight. Is that okay?"

She nodded happily and took his hand as they walked down the street. Deirdre's apartment was only about eight blocks from the school, though in the opposite direction from his. They walked until Fiona started complaining that she was tired, and then Ethan crouched down and let her climb on so he could carry her on his back the rest of the way. For the first time, he was keenly aware that before long she would be too big for piggyback rides. It made him want to carry her around all the time.

At Deirdre's place, she wanted to show him her American Girl doll and all of the absurdly expensive accoutrements she'd gotten for her. She had Julie, the historical doll from the seventies, along with several changes of clothing, a set of furniture, a bike and a pair of roller skates. Ethan didn't need to be shown most of this stuff, since he was the one who'd chosen to spoil her with it, but he was glad she liked it. After that she showed him what she was doing on *Minecraft*, which in his opinion was impressive for a six-year-old. She tried to show him how to make stuff, but he was hopeless at it, and she had to tell him what to do every time.

When dinner was ready, he and Deirdre made small talk for a few minutes, but before long she started giving him significant looks. He sighed and looked at Fiona, who was busy picking the tiny dried herbs off of the slice of chicken breast on her plate. "Hey, sweetie, can I ask you something?" he said. His heart was pounding, and even though logically he knew he was overreacting, he couldn't get it to calm down.

"What, Daddy?" she asked, still looking at her chicken.

"Do you know what my job is?"

Fiona nodded. "You're on the news," she replied.

"That's right. And when you do the news, it's important you're being as honest as possible because people are counting on you to learn the truth about how things are. But the people I was working for wanted me to help them say things I didn't believe were true. I didn't want to say those things anymore, so I had to stop working for them."

Fiona looked up at him and frowned. "Like what things?"

"Oh… the way they wanted me to talk about people with certain religions or beliefs, or about the way women should be treated in the world, or that people are poor because they're lazy. Stuff like that." He glanced up at Deirdre, and she nodded at him. "Also, the things they believe about men who love other men or women who love other women. You know that happens sometimes, right?"

Fiona looked at him like he was stupid and said, "Yes, Daddy. Gay people. Everyone knows about that."

Ethan pushed down a laugh and said, "Sure. Did you know there are also people who sometimes fall in love with women and sometimes with men?" Fiona shook her head. "Well, there are. And you didn't know this, but I'm a person like that. When I met your mom, I fell in love with her, and I loved her so much I wanted to marry her. And I still love her, even though we don't want to be married anymore. But if I fall in love with someone else, it might be a man. I wanted to tell you that now, because you know I'm a little bit famous, right? People know who I am. So someone might decide to tell you that, and I didn't want someone else to tell you about it before I did. Some people might even say it like it's a bad thing."

"That's not a bad thing, Daddy. Bad is when you do something mean to someone else."

Ethan could see Deirdre out of the corner of his eye, wiping her eyes with her napkin. He had to swallow down a sudden lump in his throat too, but he didn't want Fiona to think she'd upset him. "You're right," he said, his voice a little rough. "That's why I don't want to say mean things about anyone, anymore. But that means I'm going to have to start looking for a new job, so I might have to move to a different apartment, but I'm still going to see you just as much."

"Okay," she said, obviously unconcerned. As far as she knew, that was grown-up stuff her parents would figure out, and he wanted to keep it that way as long as possible.

Deirdre, having gotten herself under control, changed the subject to her next book, which was going to be published at the end of the summer. Ethan asked her several more questions than he was truly interested in the answers to, but he was grateful to be talking about something that wasn't himself. After that, Fiona talked about what she was doing in school and with her various friends. When they'd finished, Deirdre told her to say good night to her father and to go get ready for bed. Ethan helped her clear the table, and she asked if he wanted to stay for coffee.

"I'll stay for a cup, but I should get going pretty soon," he said, looking at his watch.

She started a pot and then leaned against the counter to look at him. "Charlie waiting for you?"

Ethan nodded. "It's fine, I said I'd be late."

"I know this is an unusual situation, with him being her teacher, but whenever you feel ready…."

"Thank you, Dee," he said, using a nickname he hadn't uttered for at least three years. "For everything. I didn't know if we'd ever be able to be friends, but you've been a good one to me in the last couple months. I hope I can be for you too. Are you still seeing that guy? I can't believe I never asked you anything about that. I'm an asshole."

"A bit of one," she said with a smile, "but I know you've been a little caught up. And no. Didn't work out. I'll keep you informed, though."

"I want you to, but you don't have to. I don't know why I even had the reaction I did. I don't know if I was being weirdly possessive or if I was jealous that you had someone and I didn't. You don't have to run things by me. You're the best judge of when to introduce people to her."

Deirdre poured coffee for them, and they sat back down at the kitchen table. "Maybe you really were just worried about our daughter?" she said. "Or mostly anyway. I know how you feel about her."

"Sure, let's go with that," Ethan said, winking at her.

"Don't wink, it makes you look smarmy," she said. "So... I don't want to bring up any sore subjects, but do you have any leads on jobs yet?"

Ethan nodded and laughed. "Sure, I got an offer even. Tom Kearny called to offer me my anchor job back."

"What, are you serious? Are you considering it?"

"Deirdre, you know I can't. I left that job so I could be close to Fiona. Nothing's changed about our situation."

"Yes, okay, but if that weren't a consideration, would you want to take it?"

Ethan could see himself back in his old job. He could even see himself driving to work. He actually wanted it so badly he could taste it, but it seemed impossible. "I don't think I can. It's not only Fiona I'd be leaving now."

"Of course," she said, biting her lip and looking at him from beneath her lashes. "There's something I'd been planning to talk to you about on Friday, but then I decided to put it off because I didn't want to stress you out, what with you looking for work and all."

"But...," Ethan prompted.

"I mentioned my book was coming out end of August," she said, "and my agent wants me to do a book tour. There would be quite a bit of travel involved, and I was going to ask you if Bitsy could stay with you. Live with you, I mean, for the next year."

"Of course she can live with me," Ethan said. "If that's what needs to happen, we'll figure it out. I'll figure something out, I promise." He put his empty cup down and stood up. "I need to get going. I can pick her up for the weekend at school tomorrow if you like. I'm a man of leisure now."

"Thanks, Ethan," she said. She hugged him and said, "Don't dismiss that job entirely. I know some part of you wants to take it. At least talk to Charlie about it."

"I will," he said.

He came home to find Charlie lying on the sofa, working on a lesson plan. He put down his work and held his arms out to Ethan when he walked into the room. Ethan went over and lay down next to him, burying his face in Charlie's chest. The sofa wasn't especially wide, so he was hanging halfway off, but he didn't mind. Charlie was holding him tightly enough that he knew he wouldn't fall.

"Did it go badly?"

"No," Ethan said, not lifting his head. "It went fine. I think I said it right. Fiona was perfect."

"Of course she was," Charlie said. "She's a wonderful kid. So what's wrong?"

"There's something I need to tell you," he said. He hadn't given the Philadelphia job offer any consideration until Deirdre had managed to make it seem like a real thing. He'd walked all the way back to his building so he could have some time to think about it, and he realized that if it were possible, he wanted to do it. In fact, he wanted it so much he could taste it. He just wanted to do the news, and not be a pawn in some overarching narrative he had no control over. He wanted a house instead of an apartment. He wanted to go home.

He told Charlie everything—the phone call from Tom Kearny, the frustrating meeting with his agent, the talk he'd had with Fiona and the subsequent conversation with Deirdre. He talked for what felt like a long time, and he finished by saying, "I won't go if it means I can't have you in my life."

Charlie ran his fingers through Ethan's hair and lightly scratched his scalp. "We've only been together for two months. What if it doesn't work out and you gave up something you want, just to stay close to me?"

"What would you do if you were me?" Ethan asked.

Charlie stayed quiet for a long time before saying, "I'd want to do whatever I could to keep you. Because I do love you. But I'd hope you'd say the same thing to me that I said to you, because you care about me."

Ethan nodded. "It's only two hours," he said quickly. "Less if you take Acela. I'll pay for that. I'll spring for first class seats." He pulled up and grabbed Charlie's hands. "Would you try? Please?"

"Ethan…." He looked sad, and Ethan had to make him stop looking like that.

"Don't. Don't say my name like that. I won't go. I'll find something here. I'll work it out."

Charlie shook his head. "I won't let you." He closed his eyes and sighed. "What I was going to say was that I will. I will try. But I'm afraid it'll be too hard, and we'll be tired and we'll forget why this seemed so important in the first place. That would almost be worse. Wouldn't it?"

"*No*," Ethan said. He sat up. "That's not how it works. You don't know because you're so used to talking yourself out of things. It's sad when things end, sure, but you still had what you had. It's still worth having. And maybe it won't end. That does happen, you know. Sometimes."

"It seems like it doesn't," Charlie said.

"It does. It does, but it's hard. You have to try. And keep trying. And you need to luck into someone you're actually compatible with, which we have no way of knowing yet. And… I don't know, probably lots of other factors too that I don't know about because my marriage didn't work."

"Why didn't it? You never said."

"You really want to go into it now?"

"When else?" Charlie asked. "Isn't this the time?"

Ethan frowned. "Have you eaten anything?" he asked.

"I had some crackers and cheese. Don't change the subject."

"Hang on," Ethan said, springing up from the couch. He went to the freezer and dug out a pint of ice cream he'd bought earlier that day. It had been an impulse purchase with the idea that they might want to eat it after sex, but this seemed like an even more worthy occasion.

"We're eating this whole thing, right?" Charlie asked.

"I'm confused by the premise of your question," Ethan replied. He handed Charlie the ice cream and spoon. "You go first. I'll talk."

"Okay." Charlie dug into the hard frozen ice cream.

"I was twenty-six when we met. She was twenty-three, but she seemed older than me, somehow. She always knew exactly who she was and what she wanted. When she made a decision, she went for it. And, when she made a decision for me, she made that happen too." He looked up at Charlie again. He didn't want him to think badly of Deirdre. "It wasn't all her," he said. "I let her. I was so… lost. What I wanted was someone to help me figure myself out, but it doesn't work like that. I thought she had, for a while, but what she'd really done was figure out who she wanted me to be and turned me into that. She didn't know that's what she'd done. By the time we both understood what happened, things were too fucked up to fix. I resented her for doing that to me, and she had no respect for me because I'd allowed it. Probably on some level we both knew we weren't being fair, but fair doesn't mean much when you've done that much damage."

When he stopped talking, Charlie had the spoon in his mouth, having just shoved a big chunk of chocolate ice cream in his mouth. He handed the carton and the spoon to Ethan. "You've given a lot of thought to this," he said.

"We tried counseling, which helped me sort some of it out. We stayed married way past the time we should have split, so we had plenty of time to have the same circular arguments a million times. Anyway, that's part of the reason I didn't try to start dating right away after the divorce. I had to know myself better first. I needed to learn how to make some decisions on my own."

"Like working for ECHO?" Charlie asked with a bit of a smirk.

"That would be one of them. Deirdre being so pissed about it was certainly one of the perks. That and the shower. That's it." He ate a bite of ice cream. "It was clearly a bad decision," he admitted, "but that's fine, because I made it myself. Mistakes are okay. Besides, I fixed it. And if I hadn't moved here, I wouldn't have met you, and you're the best decision I've made in a long time."

"Were you disappointed she approved of me?"

Ethan shook his head and smiled. "She helped me with you. I mean, with the things she said to me—obviously she stepped over the line coming to see you. I'm still irritated about that."

"Moving on," Charlie said.

"Right, sorry. She's gotten a lot better about things too. Now she tries to encourage me to do what I want when it coincides with what she thinks I should do, and snaps at me when I do something she thinks is stupid. And that's fine, because at least it's honest." He gave the ice cream back and said, "I don't have anything more to say on the subject. I get why you needed to hear it, but to tell you the truth, I'm pretty sick of thinking and talking about it. I did it for years, you know?"

"Jesus, Ethan," Charlie said, looking with dismay into the container. "You practically finished it."

"There's at least a quarter of it left. You can have the rest."

"Yeah, no shit. Like I was going to give it back." He rubbed Ethan's knee with his foot and said, "Thanks for telling me all that. Do you really want to pay for Acela? You're going to take a pretty big pay cut."

"You know how much cheaper it is to live there. And besides, it's not that much, is it? Like a hundred fifty, two hundred for a round trip, right?"

"Isn't that a lot?"

"We really don't pay teachers enough, do we?" Ethan sighed, shaking his head. "Don't even think about it."


ETHAN GOT in touch with his agent the next day and told him he needed the rest of the month to tie up loose ends, and to work out the details with Tom Kearny. His agent wasn't happy about it, but Ethan refused to argue. He didn't feel like he had to defend his choice.

He spent a lot of time with Charlie and with Fiona over the next few weeks. It wouldn't be nearly so easy to see her once he moved, at least until she came to live with him in the fall. He also made several trips to Philadelphia to look at houses. He had something specific in mind, and he wanted to make sure it was the right one.

They woke up early on Thanksgiving to make the trip to Charlie's mother's house. Ethan had bought two excellent bottles of wine to contribute to the dinner.

"You know that's totally unnecessary," Charlie said as they walked through the garage to where Ethan kept his car. "They don't expect anything."

"I can't go empty-handed. Unless you think they'll think it's weird for me to bring something."

Charlie smiled and put his arm around Ethan. "So you *are* nervous," he said. "You've been pretty good at hiding it up until now."

"It's just that your family is so big. I'm not used to it." He bit his lip and glanced at Charlie "What will you do if they don't like me?"

"Tell them to fuck off, of course," Charlie said. "I told you, we're blue-collar types."

"It's kind of hard to picture you growing up like that."

"Just you wait. Once you meet them, everything about me will begin to make sense."

The house they pulled up in front of was a modest ranch style home with a small yard. There was an Eagles flag hanging next to the door and the doormat had the Flyers logo on it.

"No Phillies gazing ball in the garden?" Ethan asked. He was already charmed.

"Don't mention the Phillies," Charlie warned. "Donna is somehow a Mets fan, and if you bring it up—or baseball in general—my whole family will get into a fight. You might think I'm kidding and I wish I were, but I swear I'm not."

"Awesome," Ethan said. "That sounds like fun."

"Please don't." He put his hand on the storm door handle. "Ready?"

Ethan nodded and put on his most convincing fake smile. Charlie opened the door of the little house and a warm gush of delicious smelling air was released. He was greeted by the sounds of young children playing a loud make-believe game involving toy light sabers—some things never changed—and several adults engaged in an animated conversation in the living room. One of them—a tall, heavily muscled man in his thirties—looked up when they stepped inside. Ethan knew that was Billy.

"Charlie's here," he said, and then they all looked up. There was a man in his fifties, who Ethan assumed was Charlie's dad; he looked a lot like him. There was a woman maybe ten years younger sitting next to him. There was a middle-aged woman with a practical haircut sitting across from them—that would be Donna. He wasn't going to try to sort out the jumble of thirty-something men and women in the room. They were all looking at him with completely unconcealed curiosity.

A short, pretty, slightly plump woman came out of the kitchen wearing an apron and beaming at Charlie. She walked over and stood on her tiptoes to kiss his cheek before turning her full attention on Ethan. She was still smiling, but it was much more guarded.

"Mom, this is Ethan," Charlie said.

"Well, I would hope so," his mother replied.

"Ethan, this is my mom, Linda," he said, rolling his eyes.

"It's great to meet you," he said, reaching out to shake her hand.

"I'd like to give you a hug if it's all right. I don't know if he's told you yet, but my baby obviously loves you, so I'm sure I will too."

"Mom!" Charlie said. "What if I hadn't?"

Ethan hugged her and grinned over her head at Charlie. He still felt a little nervous but also like he'd been anointed, in a way, by Linda's acceptance.

"You sit," she said. "Charlie can get you a drink."

Charlie looked at him and said, "She seems to think I'm a 1950s housewife all of a sudden."

"I don't think housewife is an acceptable term anymore," Ethan deadpanned. "I'd love a drink, though."

Two of Charlie's brothers were standing close enough to hear the exchange, and they both laughed. The one Ethan recognized as Billy extended his hand. "Hey, I'm Bill," he said. "Everyone here is excited to meet you."

Ethan laughed a little weakly and said, "You're all big ECHO News fans?"

There was a loud chorus of good-natured boos, and Billy said, "Charlie's never brought anyone home before. Either you're special, or he was holding out for a celebrity."

"It's both," Charlie called over from the table where he was pouring Diet Coke into two glasses of ice and cheap whiskey. "Here," he said, handing Ethan a drink. "I told you we weren't fancy."

The entire day consisted of a constant stream of food and conversation. Ethan felt a little overwhelmed at times, but mostly he found that he was enjoying himself. It made him feel a little bad for Fiona, growing up like he had with no brothers or sisters, but it wasn't like he hadn't had a good childhood. He noticed it more now, as an adult, with no siblings to help tie the family together. He was thinking about that when Charlie came over to stand next to him.

"You've gone all quiet," he said. "Doing okay?"

"Yep," Ethan replied. "I was wondering if anyone here remembered what year it was that Steve Carlton pitched a shutout and hit a home run in the same game."

"Oh my God, please don't. And if you really don't know, it was 1982. My parents were there. My mom was seven months pregnant with Tess. There's a whole story about her almost peeing her pants because she didn't want to jinx him by getting up."

"You guys talking about Steve Carlton?" Charlie's dad asked, walking over to them. "You know, Linda and I were there in eighty-two when—"

"I just told him about it, Dad. Can you keep it down before Donna hears you?"

Charlie's father grinned in a gleeful way that definitely bordered on maliciousness. "If Donna doesn't want to hear about the Phillies, she should move to Queens," he said, loud enough for the entire room to hear.

Charlie groaned and grabbed Ethan's arm to pull him away as the room erupted with trash talk. He led him down the hallway to the small bedroom they were going to be staying in. It was Charlie's childhood bedroom, but it had no visible remnants of his youth, other than the bed, which Charlie pulled him down on. It was a double, which was going to feel a little cramped after they'd spent so much time in Ethan's king-size bed. Charlie climbed on top of him and braced himself on his arms.

"Did you want to take a nap?" Ethan asked, in between kisses.

"Kind of, actually," Charlie replied. "Can we?"

"Won't your family think we're doing something besides sleeping in here?"

"We can do that too if you want."

They ended up taking off their shoes and curling up together under the comforter. Instead of napping, they talked quietly until one of Charlie's brothers banged on the door and shouted, "Get a room!" and then cracked up laughing.

"See, it's funny because we're already in a room," Charlie said with a long suffering air.

"Yeah, it's not like we're giving each other blow jobs in the basement," Ethan said.

They got up and went to help set the table for dinner, which was exactly the way Ethan had hoped it would be. By the end of the meal, he was stuffed with food and flushed with wine, and Charlie was holding his hand under the table. By the end of the day, Charlie's relatives seemed to be treating him with the same slightly edgy but never mean-spirited humor they inflicted on each other.

When they finally crawled into bed, too tired and full to do anything but fall asleep, Ethan said, "I want to bring Fiona here for Thanksgiving next year, okay?"

Charlie was quiet for a long time, and Ethan thought he'd fallen asleep. Just as Ethan was starting to drift off, Charlie whispered, "I hope so."

# Chapter Fourteen

ETHAN MOVED to Philadelphia two weeks later, but he was at an extended-stay hotel until he could close on his house. Charlie went to stay with him for the first week of his winter vacation, but had to leave for the second week because Fiona was coming to stay for the rest of it. They exchanged Christmas presents early. He gave Ethan a beautiful vintage silk tie, and Ethan gave him a key.

"It doesn't work in the door yet," Ethan said. "I bought a new lock for the front door so I could give you the key to it." Charlie stared into the box, unable to think of what to say. "I know you have more doubts than I do. That's fine. This is just me telling you I think what we have is good, and I want more of it, and I believe we can do this."

"I don't know if we can or not, but I love you, Ethan," Charlie said. He took the key from the box and put it on his key ring. "It is good. I want more too. I already miss you. I hate not having you nearby."

Ethan nodded. "Me too. Are you mad at me for taking this job?"

"No," Charlie sighed. "I told you that you should, remember? I'm just sad about it. I don't know how this is supposed to work. Weekends are for Fiona, which they should be—I'm not saying that's bad—but I can't come down here during the week, and you can't drive to New York."

"It won't be like that forever. Just through the end of the school year, and then we can tell her about us. And Fiona's taking her to Ireland for a month in July, so you and I can have that whole time together. And after that she's coming here. And—"

"Ethan, the school year is another six months, almost. That's twice as much time as you and I have been together."

Ethan kissed him then, and took him to bed, and whispered to him how much he wanted him and how much he loved him, and Charlie had stopped talking about all of their obstacles. They would have to work it out, because he wasn't about to give up something so good. He wouldn't. When he got back to New York, Charlie called Deirdre. He had an idea, but he hadn't wanted to say anything to Ethan in case she shot him down.

"This is a surprise," Deirdre said in lieu of hello when she answered her phone.

"I'd like to speak with you. Can I buy you a coffee?"

"It's too late for coffee, boyo, but we can have a drink. Why don't you come to my apartment?"

When he got there, she had a bottle of wine open on the coffee table and two glasses sitting out. "I have a feeling I know what you want to talk about," she said, pouring the wine. "I've been wondering how you and Ethan think you're going to have any time to see each other if Fiona's always with him on the weekends. Is it something to do with that?"

Charlie picked up his glass and took a sip. "It is," he replied. "I don't want him to lose any time with her. I'd never suggest that."

"I know that," she said. "So what is it that you'd like to suggest?"

"I'd like for you to request a transfer to the other first grade classroom."

Deirdre drank some wine and looked at him thoughtfully. "You want me to do that so Ethan can introduce you as his boyfriend."

"I wouldn't have asked except he told me you already gave the okay to do that."

"I did. I also hate the idea of switching her. She loves you. If you don't mind my asking, what exactly would the school do to you if they found out? I can't imagine it's a fireable offense."

"I don't know," he said. "They could fire me if they wanted to. They probably wouldn't, but I don't know that for sure. I need my job. And I'm sure you don't want to ask her to lie. I don't want that either."

She nodded. "I really like you too, you know. When you have a kid with someone and you get divorced, it can be a scary prospect when you think about who they might get involved with. People are vulnerable after a serious relationship ends, and they can make some awfully poor choices. But you, I can see that you're a good person. And maybe even more importantly, you seem like you've got some sense in your head. I certainly don't want to risk your relationship ending and him meeting someone awful on the rebound." She nodded decisively. "I'll do it. I'll see about getting her moved starting in the new year. But she's not going to be happy about it, I can tell you that, so you and Ethan will need to tell her right away. Perhaps this weekend, before he takes her to his parents for Christmas."

"He doesn't know I'm talking to you about this. I didn't want to get his hopes up in case you said no."

"You passed up a chance to make the ex the bad guy in a situation?" she asked in mock amazement. "You really are a good person."

He called Ethan as soon as he was out the door of her apartment and told him what they'd talked about. "It's the only way I can see it working," he said.

"So we're telling her next weekend?" he asked. He sounded nervous.

"I'll come down on Saturday, and we can do it then. If you want me to leave and not stay over, that's okay. I can imagine you might want to take it slowly."

"Only if she's upset," Ethan said, "which I doubt."

Charlie met them at a diner for lunch. Fiona looked utterly confused when he walked into the restaurant, but then got very excited. She bounced in her seat and pointed, saying in a loud voice, "Daddy, it's Mr. Woods!"

Charlie sat down in the booth next to her, across from Ethan, and told her he'd come to visit because he wanted to talk to her about something important. Ethan went first.

"Remember how I told you that if I met someone new it might turn out to be a man?" he asked. She nodded, her eyes wide in her little face, and she kept glancing at Charlie like she thought she'd figured it out but wasn't quite sure. "So, I have met someone. And he is a man. Is that still okay?"

She turned to look at Charlie and whispered, "Is it you?"

Charlie smiled at her and nodded. "Is that all right with you?"

"Do you love my daddy?" she asked, still whispering.

"Yes, a whole lot," he said.

She looked at Ethan again and nodded. "It's okay."

Charlie stayed over that night, and the next morning, Ethan called to let his parents know he was bringing someone along.

One month later Ethan moved into his house. It was a lovely, well-maintained row house in the city, and the first time Charlie walked inside, he was hit with a sense of déjà vu. Somehow the cream sofa from his domestic fantasy had been transported into Ethan's living room. There was even an exposed brick wall with a large window cut into it.

"I think you mentioned a loft," Ethan said, watching his reaction nervously, "but I wanted a house. There's a pastry shop down the street, though. We can get croissants in the morning."

"Ethan…," Charlie said, shaking his head. He felt scared, suddenly. It was too much.

"Stop," Ethan said. "I wanted to. It made me happy to do it." He moved in close and put his hand on Charlie's back, pulling him in. "If we break up, I'll only have to get a new couch. You don't have to feel responsible for anything. Okay?"

"I love this. It's perfect. How did you do it? It's like you saw into my head."

Ethan shrugged. "It sounded a lot like an ad they used to run for the *New York Times*."

Charlie's mouth dropped open slightly, and he stared at the room for a second before both of them burst into laughter.

Throughout the rest of the school year, they saw each other two to three times a month. Charlie didn't want to intrude on all of Ethan's weekends with Fiona. Sometimes Ethan would come up to New York, and the three of them would do something during the day, and he'd stay at Charlie's overnight. Other times they'd both be in Philadelphia at the same time, but Charlie would hang back at the house while Ethan took her out somewhere. Still other weekends they spent apart. It wasn't ideal, but it wouldn't last forever. One way or another, things would be changing.

During the month that Deirdre had Fiona out of the country, Charlie came to stay for most of it. Josh had agreed to take Lagertha the cat while he was gone. Girish had come back long enough to pack up the rest of his belongings and wrap things up at the university, but he'd decided to stay in London. He didn't feel right leaving while his mother was undergoing treatment, though Charlie suspected that not wanting to leave his boyfriend again had been a factor in his decision. The month at Ethan's house seemed to fly by, yet somehow at the same time, he felt like he'd been there forever. He'd expected to be anxious to leave when the time was up, but it turned out that he didn't feel ready to go.

He started the new school year with almost a sense of dread. He was tired of taking the train on weekends, tired of not being able to see Ethan after work. They skyped and texted, but it only made him miss Ethan more. This was exactly what he'd been afraid of when they first agreed to try this.

September passed quickly with the bustle of new students, but in October time seemed to slow to a crawl. Ethan came up to see him the second weekend of the month when he dropped Fiona off at Deirdre's place. They spent most of the time in bed, ordering in food and watching movies in between a lot of sex. They finally left the apartment on Sunday morning and went out for coffee.

"I'm not feeling great about things," Charlie admitted. "This is as hard as I thought it was going to be. I don't want you to leave. I miss you all the time."

Ethan nodded, looking down into his latte. "I know," he said. "It's hard. I don't know what the solution is, though. I don't want to give up. Do you?"

"Most of the time I don't."

Ethan stayed until late that evening, and they didn't talk about it any more after that. There wasn't much to say about it anyway—either they could handle it or they couldn't.

Charlie came down to visit the last weekend of the month. Deirdre was on her book tour, so Fiona was there and getting ready for Halloween. On Saturday morning Ethan said, "I had an idea," but wouldn't say what it was. They piled into the car and drove west into the quaint Pennsylvania countryside. When Charlie saw the hand-painted signs for an apple festival, he started laughing.

"What's funny?" Fiona piped up from the backseat.

"Nothing," Charlie said. "I'm just happy."

It was a gorgeous, crisply cool day. They ate a lot of cider donuts, picked a bag of apples, and bought a huge pumpkin to carve that night. The sight of Ethan holding the pumpkin under one arm and taking his daughter's hand with the other was enough to make Charlie's breath catch in his throat. He kissed his cheek as they walked to the car, even though they both felt a little shy about showing physical affection around Fiona.

That night, while Ethan was putting Fiona to bed, Charlie went out onto the small deck in back of the house. It had turned chilly, but he thought it might help him clear his head. After a while he heard the door open and close behind him, and Ethan came over to lean against the railing next to him.

"I don't want you to leave," Ethan said.

"I don't want to either," Charlie said.

"Move in with me."

Charlie stared at him and laughed disbelievingly. "I have a job and an apartment. I'm not a waiter or something. I can't just leave."

"You could, though. You could give notice. If you were sure this was what you wanted, you would."

"Today was beautiful, Ethan. It felt like some perfect thing, like a dream, but it didn't feel real. It felt like something you created for me. It can't possibly be like that all the time."

"You think anything could?" Ethan's voice stayed low, but there was anger in it. "Is there some way of living you're still hoping to find that will involve a permanent state of happiness? Some relationship that won't involve conflict or sacrifice? Or do you think you can trade off bliss for a life without pain?"

Charlie shook his head silently. He didn't know what he was looking for, but he didn't want Ethan to be mad at him. "I'm sorry," he said finally. "I don't want to trade anything away. I love you. I'm still here, but I'm not ready for that. You have to give me some more time."

"You can have all the time," Ethan replied. He slid his hand across the railing to hold on to Charlie's. "But I'm going to keep asking until you say yes."

Ethan asked again at Christmas, and Charlie said no, not yet, but he started spending almost every weekend at the house. In the spring he made an appointment to see his principal and told him he wouldn't be back in the fall. He started to look for jobs in the Philadelphia area, but he didn't tell Ethan. He wanted to wait for him to ask again.

On a beautiful evening in June, Ethan picked him up at the train station.

"Should we get dinner out?" Charlie asked. "I was looking at restaurants, and I saw a new one I wanted to try. I'll treat."

"Let's do that tomorrow," he said. "I'd like to eat at home tonight."

They got back to the house as the sky was beginning to darken into dusk. They climbed the steps of the front stoop, and Ethan dug his keys out, but before he opened the door he stopped and turned to Charlie. "I love you so much," he said. "We've been together for over a year and a half. I haven't asked in a while because I wanted to give you whatever space you needed, but it's time. I want you to move here with me. You can take as much time as you want to find a job. Or don't find one. I honestly wouldn't care. I just want you around. I miss you when you're not here, and when you are, I'm constantly dreading the moment you have to leave. I'm afraid if you don't know by now whether you want this or not, it means you don't. I need to know."

"I already gave notice at the school," Charlie said, smiling at him. "I want it. I've always wanted it, even when it scared me to death. I'm ready now."

The tension drained from Ethan's face. He closed his eyes and leaned his head forward onto Charlie's chest. "You gave notice? Jesus Christ. I've been terrified ever since I decided to ask you. I didn't know what I'd do if you said no again. Why didn't you tell me?"

"I was a little bit afraid you'd changed your mind because I waited too long."

"If I weren't so happy, I'd be pissed at you."

Charlie put his arms around him and said, "I understand. Maybe you can take it out on me later."

"Count on it," Ethan said, "but there's something we have to do first."

Ethan opened the door, and they walked through the darkened house to the kitchen. Charlie could see light coming from the backyard—colorful, glowing light—and he heard faint music. He walked through the back door and saw the yard was lit up by paper lanterns strung up over a long picnic table. He couldn't quite make out the faces of everyone sitting at the table, but he clearly heard Deirdre's voice ringing out as she said, "What's the verdict, then?"

Charlie looked at Ethan, who looked extremely pleased with himself, and said, "You're such a liar. No way you were that scared I'd say no if you invited all these people to celebrate."

"I had a few moments of abject fear," Ethan replied.

Charlie called out, "I said yes," to the small crowd and received a cheer in response. He walked down into the yard and saw his whole family was there, along with Josh and Roland, Janice, Deirdre and Fiona, and even Girish, accompanied by a pasty but cute and very English looking ginger-haired man.

"This is Wes," Girish said.

"I can't believe you came all this way," Charlie said, shaking Wes's hand. "What if I'd said no?"

"Ethan sounded pretty confident," Girish said. "Besides, it was a free vacation. I'd never been to Philadelphia. We saw the Liberty Bell and ate a cheesesteak with Whiz today."

"Well, that practically makes you a native," Charlie said.

Charlie sat down and filled his plate with all the food people had brought. Ethan sat next to him and kept his glass filled with wine. Conversation went on all around them like a storm, but he felt still and quiet in the eye. It was the same feeling he always had when he was with family, only this time he wasn't alone in it. This night was something Ethan had created for him, but he finally understood—that didn't mean it wasn't real. They could make good things for each other all the time. He took Ethan's hand under the table and squeezed it. This was only the beginning.

KEELAN ELLIS is a true crime enthusiast, a political junkie, and a comedy fan. Despite a compulsion to sometimes wallow in the depths of humanity's corruption and sadness, she considers herself a romantic at heart. The stories she really connects with are about love that's been twisted into hatred, and she believes that with honesty and forgiveness, love can overcome. Keelan loves good bourbon and classic country music, great television, and well-prepared food, especially shared with like-minded people. She's not a fan of parties and large groups of people, but there's nothing she loves more than a long conversation with friends. Her favorite part of the writing process is the collaborative stage, hashing out plot and characters with smart and talented friends. It's where she truly comes to understand the people she's writing about, and often falls in love with them. With the support and encouragement—as well as some serious editing help—Keelan has found the writing niche she's always searched for. Sometimes she gets blocked, and when that happens, there's only one thing she knows to do. Just like Inigo Montoya, she goes back to the beginning, writing about the characters who inspired her so much in the past.

E-mail: keelanellisauthor@gmail.com
Facebook: www.facebook.com/keelanellisauthor
Tumblr: www.tumblr.com/blog/keelan-ellis
Twitter: @KeelanEllisAuth

I'll Still Be There

Keelan Ellis

Unfinished Business: Book 1

The summer after high school, Eli Dunn and Jess Early explore an abandoned brothel in the rural Florida Panhandle. They've always kept their mutual attraction unspoken, but in an upstairs room at the end of the hall, everything changes. Suddenly, all the longing Eli and Jess have tried so hard to conceal bursts free, and passion like they've never experienced comes to light, along with the ghosts of Clay Bailey and Silas Denton, murdered owners of the brothel. And Clay and Silas have no problem possessing Eli and Jess in order to express their love for each other, without thought for the living.

Deeply disturbed by the experience, Eli and Jess part and try to get on with life as best they can. But after several years, Eli returns to Florida, only to find that Jess has made some questionable choices. These eventually lead him back to the abandoned house and a confrontation with Eli. Old scores are settled and Eli and Jess reunite. But Clay and Silas's ghosts aren't finished yet, for they've always believed in the power of open and honest love.

# www.dreamspinnerpress.com

# KEELAN ELLIS

# Anywhere You Go

Unfinished Business: Book 2
Sequel to *I'll Still Be There*

Jess Early and Eli Dunn, owners of Ruth's Haven Bed and Breakfast, love married life. Every jealousy bump and insecure thought is just another expected growing pain. But with Jess redefining his relationship with his best friend and ex-fiancée Cassie and Eli's friend Travis staying with the guys while going through marital problems of his own, things haven't been feeling quite right between them.

Not to forget, the home's ghostly previous owners, Clay Bailey and Silas Denton, still reside in their former bedroom and delight in making their presence known—including invading Travis's dreams in an attempt to help. They give Travis a vivid glimpse of their adventurous trip to Paris in the early 1960s and some insight about his marriage.

With tensions mounting, Eli's father suffers a heart attack. Now Jess and Eli must remain strong and at the same time confront their evolving feelings. The young couple's struggles become a lesson in the true meanings of love, loyalty and marriage.

# www.dreamspinnerpress.com

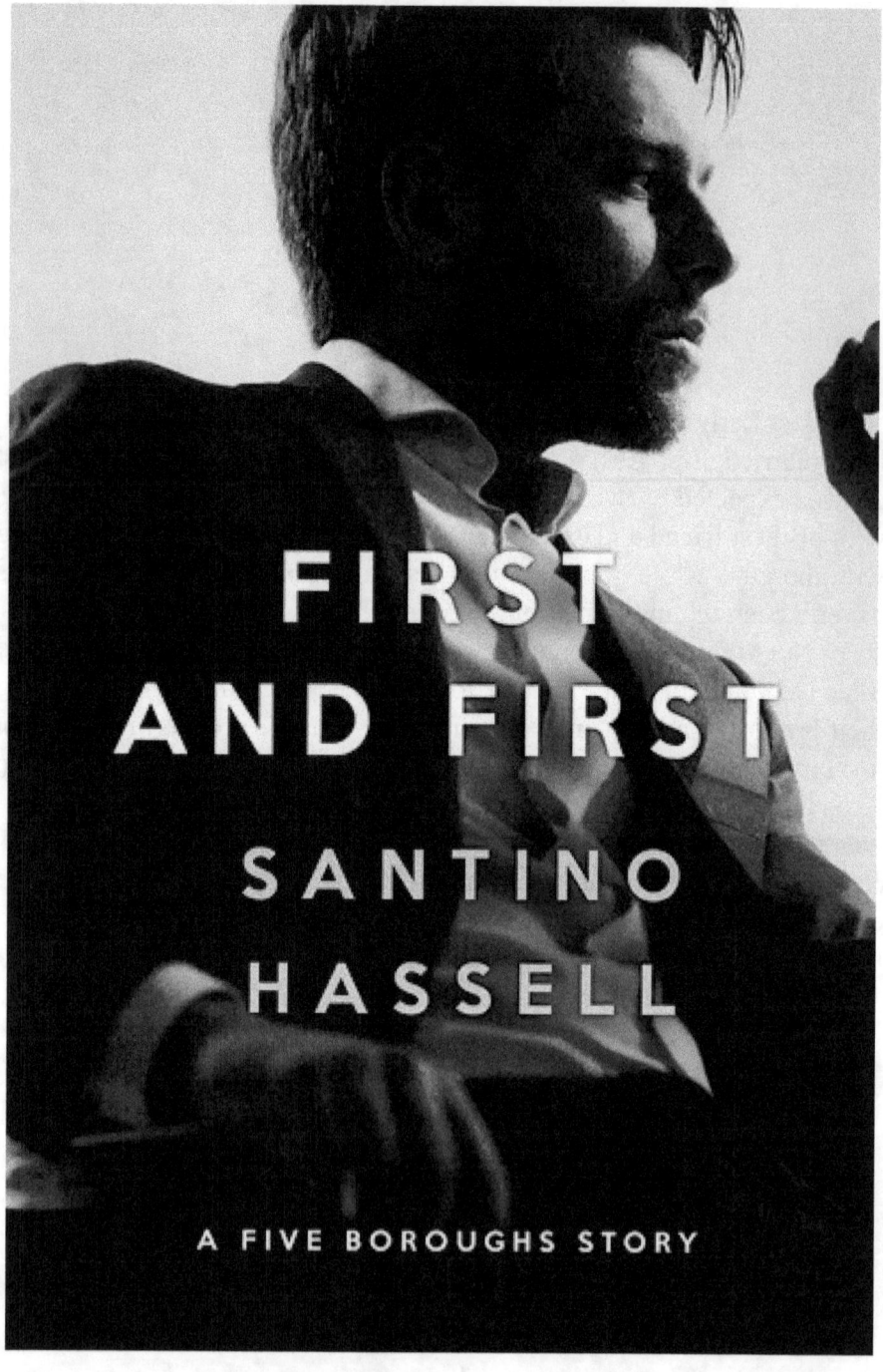

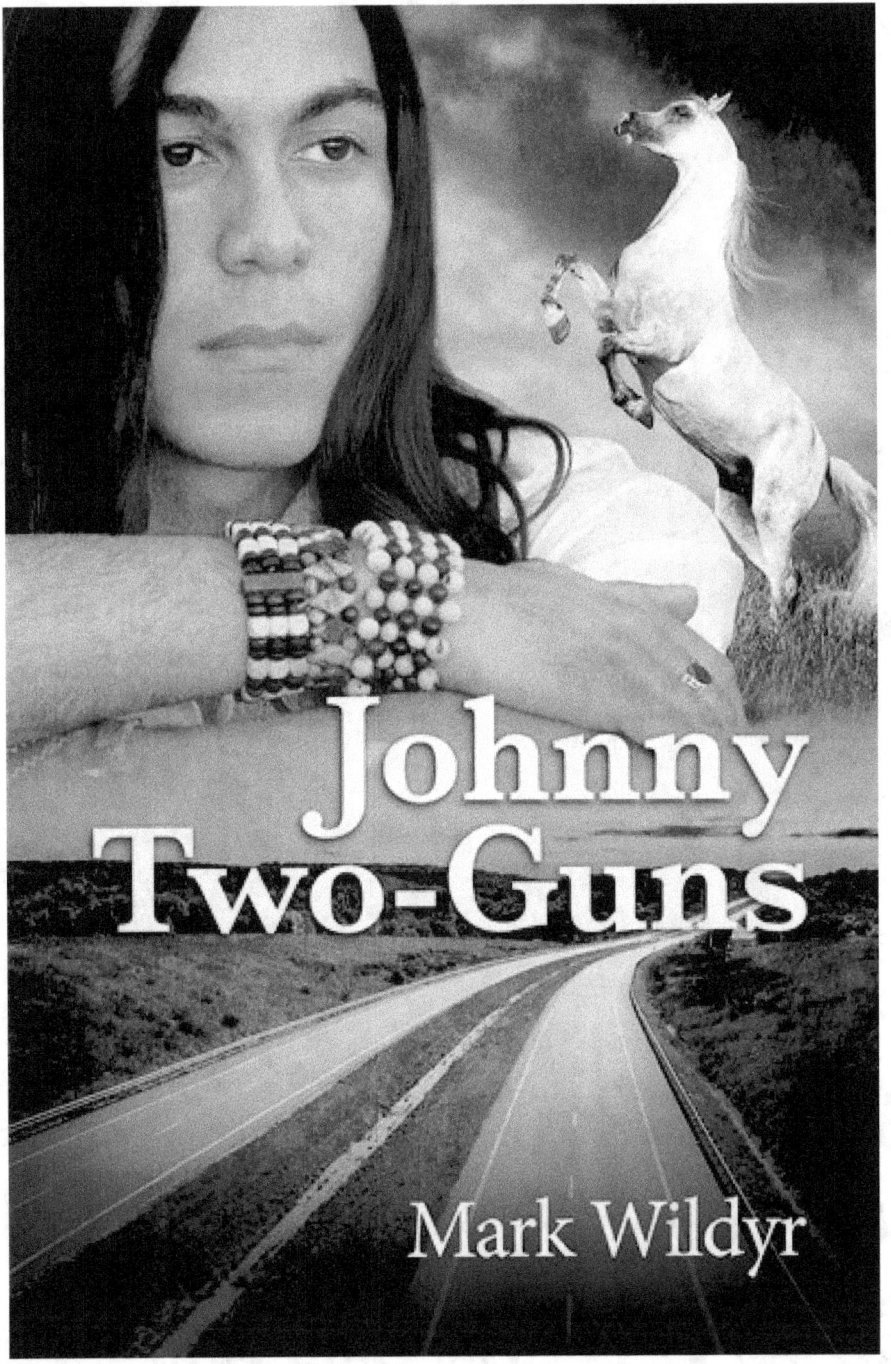

Johnny
Two-Guns

Mark Wildyr

www.dreamspinnerpress.com